TAKEN FOR

a novel by

Charlie De Luca

My Cup of Tea Press

Also by Charlie De Luca;

Rank Outsiders

The Gift Horse

Twelve in the Sixth

Making Allowances

Hoodwinked

Dark Minster

Fall From Grace

Website: www.charliedeluca.co.uk

Ad astra per aspera

Chapter 1

The insistent buzzing continued. Finn McCarthy opened his eyes and was momentarily disoriented. The noise remained like an annoying fly and then he saw the flickering lights from his bedside table and realised his mobile had sprung into life. Who the hell was ringing him at this time? He grabbed his phone, struggled out of bed in his underpants and flicked on the bedroom light which momentarily blinded him.

'McCarthy,' he was still blinking at the obscene brightness. 'It's 2.30 in the bloody morning,' he chuntered without knowing who he was speaking to.

'I know, 'said a familiar voice. 'It's Gabriel Taverner here. Look, I'm sorry to ring so late.'

Finn suddenly felt wide awake as he looked out onto the moonlit roofs of the city of York, his senses instantly alert. It was usually bad news if a member of the local police force rang you during the night, even if it was someone he now counted as a friend. He waited with a sense of dread for the detective to continue.

'The thing is, Finn, my opposite number in traffic has rung me trying to get your number. It's a DI Johnson. One of your lads evaded the police when he was stopped for a breath test coming back from the pub and they gave chase as he tried to evade them. They had to deploy a stinger to stop the silly sod and he assaulted an officer too.'

Finn sighed. 'One of my conditionals, you mean? Which one, is anyone hurt?' he asked as an afterthought.

'No, though it's definitely more by luck than judgement it has to be said. He was reaching speeds of 110 mph out of York and was on the wrong side of the road.' Taverner sounded very disapproving, as though Finn was responsible for the behaviour of his charges.

Finn mentally went through his latest crop of conditionals. As a jockey coach for the British Horseracing Authority, the BHA, he was used to supporting his conditionals with a range of topics, not just riding but diets, finances, making sure they had more than a passing acquaintance with the

4

BHA rules of racing, support with injuries, agents and the press. He was a jockey coach cross social worker, cross counsellor, cross parent on some occasions, but even he had not dealt with someone facing a driving ban for drink driving, someone evading the police, driving like a maniac, who could have killed someone. This was a first. He felt furious at the realisation.

'It's Niall Byrne. He was driving a few people home from a do when he was pulled over. He realised he'd have to give a breath sample and buggered off. The others in the vehicle were trying to talk some sense into him, but he just drove like a mad man. The police are very wary about employing a stinger, but that's what they did, so he must have been seen as a high risk of causing harm to himself or others. He's at York nick feeling very sorry for himself but he's asking for you and has lost his phone in the chaos. Can you come to the station?'

Finn was already ten steps ahead thinking of the likely repercussions. 'Yes, I'm on my way. Listen, what's he looking at in terms of a sentence. He will at least get a driving ban, I presume?'

Taverner sighed as he weighed up the likely charges. 'Looks like he was over the alcohol limit so that's an instant ban but he's also looking at a charge of dangerous driving, an assault on a police officer and attempting to evade justice, so it all adds up. He's likely to get a suspended sentence at the very least.' There was a pause whilst the detective thought through the crimes and calculated the likely sentence. 'Hmm, let's just say he'd be lucky to get a suspended sentence, very lucky.'

'Right, the silly, bloody sod!' Finn realised without Taverner needing to spell it out that if things went badly then he could end up with a prison sentence.

'Promising lad, is he?'

'Absolutely, one of the best.' The words tripped off Finn's tongue automatically, but the thing was Niall was the real deal. How to ruin a career in one easy step, Finn thought savagely. The fact was that he had more talent in his little finger than many of his peers and was well thought of by everyone. He was a natural horseman, a risk taker, someone who rode like he had the devil on his back. In fact, he reminded him a lot of his old mate and six times champion jockey, Nat Wilson. A champion jockey needed to push themselves and their horses to the limit, find the gaps and push on, so they needed to be brave, ruthless and a little bit mad, but they also needed to control these impulses and Niall clearly hadn't been able to. Finn felt anger at the likely wanton destruction of what was destined to be a stellar career. He had forgotten who had first coined the phrase that 'youth was wasted on the young' but it certainly fitted here.

'Ah well, I'll let you get on.'

Finn had almost forgotten about the police officer on the other end of the line, so deep in thought was he.

'Gabriel, thanks for ringing. At least I can try and do some damage limitation so that's something.' He had no idea exactly what he could do, manage the inevitable press fall out, he supposed, just be supportive and give the lad a piece of his mind, he'd certainly do that alright.

'No problem, it's no problem at all.'

Finn pulled on his clothes, stepped out into the clear, cool September night and set off for the police station. York looked so different at this time; all the usual landmarks were partly swathed in darkness which was disorienting. The Minster presided over the city even at night, Clifford's Tower and the castle walls were lit up by the half moon and the stars that twinkled in the bright sky. He arrived at Fulford Road Station in record time as the streets were practically empty at this time. As he approached the concrete, modern building, his emotions veered wildly from irritation, alarm and searing rage at the stupidity of Niall's actions. What on earth had he been thinking? Or maybe that was the problem, he hadn't been thinking at all. The bloody idiot! He intended to tell him that too when he saw him. He wondered whether Seamus Ryan, the trainer Niall was apprenticed to, would stick by him. He had known Seamus's wife, Rosie for years, in fact she had saved his life when he was a conditional from a brute of a trainer, so he knew she would support Niall as she was a soft hearted woman, but Seamus had to be more hard headed and business minded as the registered trainer responsible for him, so the lad might struggle to convince him. He half wondered whether to ring them and tip them off but thought better of it. He'd let them sleep for a while longer before he dropped the bombshell about their conditional's actions.

The police station smelt vaguely of urine mixed with overtones of disinfectant. A dishevelled man sat snoring in a heap, the stench of alcohol and fried foods emanating from him, and two police officers were talking to a distraught woman in a fake fur coat, sporting a bloodied face, her mascara

6

smudged, and her speech slurred. The desk sergeant sat behind a security screen and glanced up every now and again as the officers tried to ascertain how she had come by her injuries.

'Some fucker hit me, didn't they, when I came out The Geisha Club.'

'Who was it? Can you describe them?'

'I dunno, I didn't rightly see, it were dark... the bloody bastard,' she wailed.

The desk sergeant shifted his gaze to Finn and raised an eyebrow. Finn explained why he had come. The officer dragged his attention away from the drunk woman with some difficulty.

'And you are?'

'Finn McCarthy, Niall Byrne's jockey coach. He asked for me apparently.'

A pair of grey eyes appraised him with a flicker of interest.

'A jockey coach, heh? Niall Byrne, you say.' He ran his finger down a list. 'Have a seat and I'll ring round and see if they've finished with yer lad.'

Meanwhile, a female officer was trying to persuade the injured clubber to go to hospital. The young, blonde officer spoke slowly and loudly, as though the complainant was a small child.

'I'll pop you down there now, Kirsty, just to get you checked out.'

An older male officer squatted down beside the woman. 'Come on, love. Yer might need some stitches in that cheek. We don't want to spoil yer beauty, do we?'

The woman finally agreed after rambling incomprehensibly about drinks, her friends and the 'fucker' who'd hit her, swaying alarmingly as she stood up, tottering on six inch heels.

'Alright.' She staggered off, supported by the two officers. The other man snored so loudly he woke himself up, briefly looked about him, then promptly fell asleep again.

After about fifteen minutes, a door opened, beeping as it did so, and Niall walked out. He was wearing a smart coat, trousers and scarf and his eyes were red from crying. He had clearly sobered up and Finn suspected that the full horror of what he had done had now begun to dawn. He was followed by an officer carrying a sheaf of papers and a woman. Niall's shoulders slumped in despair. At the sight of Finn, he began welling up again and his lips trembled. He was 17 but looked like a schoolboy of 14. His Irish

7

accent was even more pronounced in his distress. Finn's eyes were drawn to the woman, who was in her thirties with a cascade of dark curls, intense blue eyes and although she looked tired, there was no mistaking the fact that she was devastatingly attractive. She was deep in conversation with the officer. He caught the words 'recovery vehicle' and 'riding clothes' and she appeared to be arranging for Niall's car to be picked up. She spoke in an Irish accent and thanked the officer profusely, smiling widely at him. Finn found himself smoothing down his hair and wished he had dressed with more care. The police officer disappeared, and the woman looked at Finn expectantly.

'I'm Finn McCarthy, Niall's jockey coach.' He stretched out his hand which the woman shook.

'Oh, I'm Theresa, Niall's sister.' She turned to Niall. 'Look, I'll let you talk to Mr McCarthy and I'll sort out the recovery of your car and get it sent to the garage. I'll get your riding togs, for yer too. I'll drop them off for you tomorrow.' She smiled at Finn and he felt a surge of attraction. 'Can I ask you to drive Niall back?'

'Of course.' Theresa smiled. Niall shook his head sadly.

'Thanks for coming, Mr McCarthy. I didn't know who else to speak to what wi' Theresa needing to sort out the car. The Ryans will be furious. 'His face crumpled. 'Mary, mother of God, I'm a fool, so I am. I've messed up big time...' He shuddered. 'Jesus...' He was weeping openly now. His sister hugged him.

'Now, now, you won't be the first young lad to have made a mistake and you'll not be the last.' Theresa patted the lad's arm. 'I'll speak to mammie, like we said, so try not to worry. Now, I'll just get your car keys, and sort out your stuff.' She had a firm, business like manner and Niall clearly respected her. 'Then I'll be out of your hair, and get yer car sorted. I'm sure you two have a lot to talk about.'

'Thanks, Theresa. It's the stuff in the boot, all me riding gear and that.' Theresa nodded, hugged Niall, and strode off, but not before adding,

'Look after him, Mr McCarthy and try and talk some sense into him, won't yer? And thanks.' She turned to Niall. 'I'll catch up with you tomorrow.' With that she smiled and strode away.

Niall looked like he had the weight of the world on his shoulders. Finn felt a wave of unexpected sympathy for the lad and took his arm.

8

'Come on now lad, nothing is ever as bad as it looks. Let's pop to the 24 hour McDonalds and have a bit to eat and talk it through.'

Niall hung his head in shame. 'I'm in a mess and no mistake.'

Finn nodded. 'You are indeed, but we'll see if we can find a way forward, shall we?'

Niall was silent as they drove. Once settled in the restaurant, as the skeleton staff looked on bored and watchful, he spoke more about his concerns.

'But what about Mr Ryan? He'll kick me out for sure.' He gave a sob. 'What'll I tell me family? I've brought shame on 'em.'

Finn felt all his anger melt away like a snowman in sunshine, despite his earlier intentions.

'Well, it sounds like your sister has got that covered. Don't worry about the Ryans. Leave them to me. What the hell happened?'

Niall explained about the events that evening. Apparently, he had been the designated driver on a night out with three other jockeys and a stable lass, had had more drinks than he should, and panicked when he was asked to pull over by a police car.

'I just didn't think, thought I'd get away and put me foot down. I knew I'd be done for drinking. I stopped then punched the officer and ran back to the car.'

Finn regarded him coolly. He was back to feeling annoyed again.

'And what happened then?'

Niall's face crumpled. 'I drove at speeds of over 100, nearly got into a crash. The others yelled at me to stop but I didn't. The cops put something on the road that popped the tyres...'

Finn shook his head. 'You bloody fool. Why on earth didn't you stop? You knew they'd catch up with you.'

Tears streamed down Niall's face. 'I know, I know, I was just so worried about losing me licence, and now I've made things so much worse...'

Finn sat for a moment looking at the green and orange décor of the restaurant, cheap and cheerful best described it, but thankfully clean. The darkness began to lift. In an hour or two York city would be waking up and the Ryans would be up on the gallops at Walton, the racing town nearby.

9

'I suppose you've been bailed pending charges?'

Niall nodded. 'God, what sort of sentence will I get? I'm bloody ruined.'

'From where I'm sitting, you're bloody lucky to have avoided injury to yourself and others by your foolhardy actions. I suppose you have a solicitor?'

Niall nodded.

'What did he say?'

'Not a lot, to be honest.'

'Well, I was talking to a friend in the police, and he said the worst case scenario is a short prison sentence, the best a suspended one and a certain driving ban.' There was no point sugar coating what Taverner had told him.

Niall gasped and hunched his shoulders as he was wracked by sobs.

'But I'll speak to the Ryans, I can't promise anything mind, but they're decent people and you have done a lot to impress them and me with your riding. It might be hard getting around the driving ban though, but not impossible.'

A flicker of hope lit up Niall's face.

'Who else was in the car with you?'

Niall looked crestfallen. 'There was Jamie Doyle, Lottie and Clare from the yard and Tom.'

Finn knew Jamie, he was one of his conditionals, as was Lottie, and Clare was a stable lass who worked with the Ryans. He didn't know Tom though.

'Tom?'

'Kennedy.'

Finn took this in. Tom was a sensible professional jockey, and he could well imagine his thoughts about Niall's driving. He pictured the scene; the passengers must have been terrified.

'And what did they do when you were driving?'

'Ah, I feel real bad because they were screaming at me to stop. I think I scared the life out of 'em. They spoke to the police briefly but will need to speak to them again.' He had the good grace to look shame faced.

10

'If yer would talk to the guvnor, I promise I'll never do anything stupid. I'll not touch a drop again...'

Finn surveyed his conditional and experienced that strange mixture of annoyance and pity. He looked completely tortured and wretched.

'Look, you're not alone and you're not the first person to do something stupid. You have Theresa to support you, as well.' For a second a strange expression flitted across the lad's face. Then he composed himself and nodded.

'She doesn't know about racing though. And riding's what I want to do more than anything else in the world, you have to believe me.' He looked up, his thickly lashed eyes brimming with tears. 'You've got to help me, there's only you that can, people listen to you...'

Finn did believe him and vowed then and there to try and do as much as he could to make sure that the lad would be able to continue in his chosen career.

Hours later, he drove home having soothed Rosie and Seamus and spoken to his boss at the BHA. He needed to write up his report. It was early morning and he found himself tired but too wired to sleep. As he entered the large, shiny foyer, the concierge, a man called Joseph Mumby, looked up. He was in his fifties and was polite and professional but also rather nosy. He also liked to bet on the horses and was always hoping for a good tip, as he assumed that Finn had lots of insider knowledge about which horses and stables were in form.

'Ah, Mr McCarthy. I have a message for you, several in fact.' He fished out a handwritten note he had written for him. 'A Mr Trentham has been trying to get hold of you. He says it's urgent.' He grinned. 'That wouldn't be **the** Jeremy Trentham, would it.'

'Oh, yes, it is.' Finn fished his phone out of his pocket which he had muted whilst driving to the station and forgotten to unmute. He'd had at least six missed calls all from Trentham's mobile. Jeremy was one of the leading trainers in the area, in the country, in fact. He wondered briefly what was so important. It couldn't be anything to do with the conditional, Kyle Devlin, who was doing very nicely and was well on his way to riding out his claim. Conditionals, apprentice national hunt jockeys, could ride at much higher weights than their flat counterparts, and needed to ride 75 winners by the time they were 26 in order to become a professional and were given a maximum weight allowance of 10 pounds to 3 pounds, depending on the amount of winners they had ridden. Kyle was well established and would certainly ride out his claim early this season unless disaster struck. He had no idea why on earth Jeremy Trentham would need to speak to him so urgently.

He felt bone tired, but curiosity nibbled at his consciousness all the same.

'Did he say what it was about?'

Joseph frowned. 'I think he said something about a painting. Anyway, if you get any tips or inside info then don't forget to pass them my way, Finn.' He tapped the side of his nose.

Finn nodded, keen to impart some knowledge. He didn't bet much himself and had little interest in the world of gambling, to him racing was all about the horses, the riding and the humans involved with them. Still, Joseph was a decent man and always worked hard, so where was the harm. It was the least he could do for such a decent chap, not that it was anything he couldn't find out himself.

'In the Pink is the yard's star, always worth an each way bet, of course. I have heard he's been working well on the gallops. Make sure it's each way though, mind.'

He was rewarded by a huge grin from Joseph, who scribbled the name down immediately.

'Thanks, Finn.'

Finn nodded and made his way to his flat. Inside, he switched on the kettle and decided a bacon sandwich was in order. It had been a hell of a night. He wondered about Niall and his future, thinking that with a bit of luck, he could help him resurrect his shattered career. On the whole, nothing was insurmountable, and he knew from experience that youngsters needed a lot of support and guidance. He'd read that it took the human brain up to the age of 25 to fully mature and until then some had problems making judgements, so he'd try and support Niall as best he could. There was still hope for him. Then, he glanced at Joseph's note and his brain set about dredging up every type of painting emergency he could possibly envisage but still drew a blank. Whatever it was, it could wait.

Chapter 2

Hattie surveyed the scene. It was one of those late September afternoons when the weather was unseasonably balmy. It was forecast to be much cooler next week as October dawned, so her brother Will and his wife Nuala, in an unaccustomed move, had decided to take advantage of the weather and invited the family to a barbecue at their home in a small village called Hutton Buscel near Scarborough. Secretly Hattie thought that her glamorous sister-in-law couldn't really cook, and certainly didn't look like she ate much with her thin elegance and sophisticated appearance. She reckoned a barbecue, with her dad and Will's penchant for fires and being outdoors would mean that they'd basically take over, making it an easy option for her. Nuala was a marketing manager for an upmarket hotel chain and was glamorous but also good fun and Hattie was very fond of her. She did tend to judge people by their interest in food, which being a dietician, she supposed was inevitable, but she resolved to be more open minded in future. After all, good nutrition was not everything, some people ate to live not lived to eat.

Will and Nuala's small cottage was situated on the High Street, a misnomer if ever there was one for such a small village. The cottage opened out at the back into a courtyard with raised borders, and still had a few flowering shrubs in it. Hattie noticed that today Nuala looked softer, a little less perfect somehow. She was wearing boyfriend jeans and a stripy top. Maybe she was tired of perfection and wanted to relax for a change. Dominic, Harriet's younger brother, just about to go back to Uni, played with Jasper the spaniel on the lawn, intermittently swigging beer from a can. The sun shone and the sky was as blue as the Mediterranean, and you could be forgiven for forgetting that you were in the north of England; they could have been in the south of France or Tuscany, on this fine day.

Her father, Bob, helped light the barbecue and her mother, Philippa, fussed over plates, cutlery and put out the exotic salads she had insisted on making. Suddenly Will clapped, looked around beaming and said,

'Listen, it's great to have you all here. Before the others arrive and it's just us, I just wanted to make an announcement...' His face was pink with pleasure and throwing an arm around Nuala's shoulder he added, 'we're going to have a baby. It's due in April! We're just telling the family for now.'

Philippa grinned. 'Oh darlings, that's marvellous, isn't it Bob?'

Bob was already clapping his son on his back and Dominic sauntered over. 'Cool man,' he said, ' I'm gonna be an uncle.'

Hattie found she was hugging Nuala. 'Are you feeling OK?'

Nuala smiled ruefully. 'Sick as a dog most mornings, but then starving. And knackered too.'

'It'll pass love,' laughed Phillippa,'have you seen the doctor?' And they were off talking about scans and due dates and names. She also insisted that Nuala sat down and rested. Hattie made a mental note to look up details of suitable diets for expectant mothers, as well as things to eat that might ease her sickness. Then a few neighbours arrived bringing wine, and the conversation moved on and Bob and Will began flipping burgers and chicken goujons in earnest.

Hattie wandered round topping up glasses and passed round beer cans. She recognised another couple, a sergeant from Will's team, DS Forster who had come with his wife and young daughter. And Julia, Will's recently divorced neighbour who wore a wide straw hat and flowery dress like someone at one of the Palace garden parties. She'd met her a couple of times before. She had a slightly predatory air and was scanning the guests closely. Maneater thought Hattie and then rephrased it to 'lonely woman'. Circulating with a tray of kebabs, she heard a voice.

'Hello Hattie, how are you?' She swung round to face DI Gabriel Taverner.

'Great. You?' Hattie found herself floundering. She always felt like Taverner disapproved of her and Finn and the way they had often wandered into several of Taverner's police investigations, usually involving racing and jockeys and somehow, she was never quite sure how, ended up finding crucial evidence. It was partly that they were employed by the BHA to investigate possible crimes affecting the integrity of racing and also because with their day jobs, Finn as a jockey coach, her as a dietitian for the Professional Jockeys' Association, the PJA, people talked to them. Of course, the work for the BHA was strictly confidential but as the Detective in the cases, Taverner was privy to this information. Somehow, he made her feel like she was a silly 5th former who stumbled upon vital evidence by a series of rookie blunders. She looked at his Grecian profile and registered afresh how good looking he was.

Will strode over. 'Gabriel, great to see you.' He thrust Julia in between them. 'And this is my fantastic neighbour Julia, who I've told all about you.'

'Don't believe a word,' joked Taverner.

Julia giggled and preened. 'And it was all marvellous, what Will said. I've been dying to meet you...' Her voice was throaty, like a voice over for a chocolate advert, 'go on, spoil yourself with this smooth, rich, milky cho-co-late.'

Suddenly Taverner looked up, saw Hattie and gave a slight facial shrug which told her he knew this was a set up, that Will was trying to pair them off, but was taking it all in good part. Grinning to herself Hattie continued her round with the platter of kebabs. Uncle Sebastian and his wife Jo arrived next. He was Phillippa's brother and Jo was his third wife. Jo had once regaled them with the story of how Sebastian had lied to her about his age, stating that he was just 6 years older than her. He had then revealed his real age by increments, admitting to 3 or 4 years each time until Jo had seen his passport and he'd had to concede he was fourteen years her senior. Luckily for him she'd laughed and married him anyway saying,

' Gi'over you daft 'apporth. As if that matters.'

Hattie always thought that Sebastian looked far younger than his age, fifty-two, with his slim build and full head of hair and today looked relaxed in cream chinos and a cerulean blue shirt which exactly matched his eyes. He ran an art gallery in York and was passionate about his subject.

'Hattie darling, you look just like a Titian painting, that colour makes your hair sing.'

She looked down at her green, faded t shirt and stifled a giggle. She and Will had spent a good deal of their childhood guffawing at Sebastian as he declaimed. Women were not fat, they were positively Rubenesque, quite ordinary girls were described as Pre-Raphaelite beauties. Jo, who was pale with dark hair and quite pretty was a Modigliani goddess. As teenagers she and Will had gone through a phase of leaning out of the family saloon car, pointing at chubby people and yelling,

'Positively Rubenesque!' and collapsing with mirth. It drove her mother mad. But Sebastian was a good uncle and happy to supply free gallery tickets and always gave tasteful, expensive presents. But understated he was not. Jo hugged her and whispered in broad Yorkshire,

'Heck lass, I wouldn't kick him outta bed.' She nodded towards Taverner, who was now standing closely next to Julia and laughing at some witticism or other.

Neither would Julia, thought Hattie. They exchanged gossip and Hattie, seeing her mother beckoning, went to find another plate to pass round. Nuala sat still as directed, sipping water, with a look of pure contentment on her face.

The afternoon wore on though it was now a little cooler. Hattie knocked back some more wine and found herself sitting on the bench in the small kitchen garden, behind the courtyard in a reflective mood. The box hedge shielded her from view, and she felt able to kick off her shoes and draw breath. Hattie thought how far ahead everyone was getting in life. Will, her silly, scatty older brother was now a detective, with his own house, wife and now a baby on the way. Daisy, her best friend, was due to get married in a few months and had asked Hattie to be her chief bridesmaid. Hattie was happy for them, of course she was, but somehow it highlighted the paucity of her own achievements. A shattered promising early career as an athlete had eventually led, by a circuitous route, to her training as a dietician. She enjoyed her job but was still essentially living at home with her parents. There had been a few failed romances, several thrilling horse crime investigations, but she still didn't feel properly grown up. She sighed and took a slug of wine.

And then there was Finn. She missed seeing her friend. It was hard to quantify their relationship, she realised, but they had been thrown together in various situations and she trusted him with her life, even had done on several occasions. And, if she was honest, it'd been a while since their last investigation. Life had settled down to a slow humdrum pace and she found she missed the excitement of either a romance or an investigation on the go. She was just draining her glass when Taverner appeared and dived down to sit next to her, ducking his head.

17

'Phew, I think I've escaped.' He grinned, showing a dimple on one side of his cheek. His dark eyes twinkled.

Hattie raised an eyebrow. 'Blind date not working out?'

He shook his head. 'I'll bloody kill that brother of yours...'

They could hear a voice drifting over the hedge. 'Gabriel, Gab-riel...'

Hattie guffawed and Gabriel made a loud shushing noise.

'Christ Hattie, don't give me away,' he hissed, 'I told Will I was leaving. She'll give up in a minute once he's explained.'

There was a pause and then the danger seemed to be over.' She's very attractive, Julia. Not your type then?'

He shook his head and rummaged in his pocket for something, drawing out an e cigarette and puffing. Billows of smoke appeared.

'Didn't know you smoked?'

'I gave up, but I do vape, just socially and when I've been hounded by divorcees...'

'And that happens often, does it?'

Taverner grinned ruefully. 'Sorry, that sounded crass. She's lovely but not for me. Anyway, I wanted to talk to you. I spoke to Finn last night. '

Hattie's brain whirled into action. 'Really? How was he?'

Taverner took another drag and smoke billowed out across the air. His eyes crinkled up pleasantly and he gave her a searching look. 'Look, I'm sorry. I was never sure. Are you and he an item?'

Hattie shook her head. She was never sure either, but she settled for the safe answer. 'Nah, good friends though...'

'Mmm, well I reckon he might need your help. There's trouble with one of his jockeys, again...'

'Right. Any more you can tell me?'

Taverner looked down. 'No, Finn will fill you in.' He gave her a severe look.

Hattie sighed. 'Oh, don't tell me and Finn not to interfere with police investigations! You were going to, weren't you? Actually, we are authorised in our work for the BHA, as you know, but it's meant to be undercover.' Hattie was starting to get angry now. Who did he think he was, imagining all divorced women were ready to throw themselves at him, being the only one to investigate racing crimes? Sanctimonious sod. Arrogant bastard.

'I know that,' he stammered. 'Listen, the reason I asked about you and Finn was, I was just wondering if you'd like to go out for a drink tomorrow night? I mean, I've been made an acting DCI now as my boss is having an operation. It's only for a short period, but it's a big opportunity. I don't have too many people to celebrate with up here.'

Hattie's face took on the appearance of a stopped watch. Christ. He looked suddenly so vulnerable sitting there. So uncomfortable and really quite sweet. She tried to keep her tone light.

'If I can fight through the divorcees, you mean. OK, yes, I'd like that.' She found she really meant it. 'Congratulations on the job too!'

Taverner smiled. 'Thanks.'

His smile of pleasure and relief made her realise that he wasn't arrogant at all. Maybe just shy and a bit awkward. She'd text Finn later to talk about his conditional. She felt her gloom begin to lift. Maybe things were looking up, after all?

Chapter 3

'So, thanks for your report on Niall Byrne. I suppose he's bound to get a driving ban at the very least. What the hell was he doing evading the police like that? What on earth's got into him? Has he got mental health problems?' Tony asked wearily.

Tony Murphy, Finn's boss from the BHA, frowned and took a sip of his coffee. The pair were meeting up in The Singing Kettle, a café in the racing town of Walton that although popular, was large enough for the pair to sit in a corner and conduct their supervision in private. It was a pleasant venue. The tables were covered with red and white gingham tablecloths, the wooden chairs were painted red and the whole theme was topped off with chunky, red crockery. The cakes, supplied by the owner, Dottie Mitchell, were to die for. Tony had eyed the huge slabs of millionaire's shortbread, chocolate and coffee cake, lemon drizzle and coffee and walnut cake with longing but had managed to resist. So had Finn. He may not be race riding anymore, but he still rode out for his friends, Rosie and Seamus Ryan amongst them, from time to time, so couldn't afford to put on too much weight.

'I don't know, I don't think so. Believe me I've torn a strip off him for buggering off when the police stopped him. The others were pleading with him to stop but he put his foot down and reached speeds of 100 mph, went round a roundabout the wrong way, and assaulted the police officer who arrested him after they'd deployed a stinger!'

Tony snorted and shook his head in disgust. 'Christ almighty! So, he'll be looking at a driving ban and what else, do you know?'

'My police contact says he'll likely get a suspended prison sentence at best and at worst a spell in prison and driving ban regardless.'

'The bloody fool. Were there any signs of risk taking, crazy behaviour or mental health issues beforehand? What do the Ryans think of him?'

'Well, that's it. He is a hardworking young man ordinarily. He's well thought of. He is brave, fearless in the saddle, which is a good thing but maybe he needs to temper his risk taking behaviour elsewhere. He is a good rider and they're prepared to stand by him, Rosie was most clear on that point.'

Tony sniffed. 'Even if they do, how's he going to go about his job without access to a car?'

Finn shook his head. 'I've no idea. It certainly won't be easy.' Jockeys were well known for driving from racecourse to racecourse to ride, it wouldn't be uncommon for them to drive 100,000 miles in a year. Niall could rely on lifts from other jockeys to some extent, but it would certainly hamper his ability to pick up spare rides, not to mention strain friendships too.

Tony made some notes in his spikey, masculine hand. 'Right, well I suppose we can't put old heads on young shoulders, more's the pity. We'll try to do some damage limitation press wise, but it's not going to be easy.'

Tony took his role within the BHA of policing racing very seriously and always tried to avoid more bad press than was necessary, as it could have a huge impact on the perceived fairness and integrity of racing.

'Now, there's a course I want you to go on. It's about mental health, a huge issue at the moment.' He pulled a leaflet out of his pocket and handed it to Finn. 'As you know there's been a couple of suicides lately of young jockeys and lads and it is essential that you get trained in recognising the signs of depression and are able to assess a person's mental wellbeing.'

Tony looked downcast. Finn had heard about the two young jockeys who had finished their apprenticeships but struggled with weight, the endless wasting and highly competitive nature of the sport, who had committed suicide. Unfortunately, there had been some high profile cases recently too, of older jockeys whose careers were waning who had taken their lives, unable to conceive of a future without riding. The psychological pressures of wasting, supplemented by alcohol or drug abuse, coupled with any other personal stresses, could tip even the strongest person over the edge as it had with these men. It was tragic and he knew the sport had to do more to support their jockeys and stable staff. Finn took the papers he was given and scanned the details.

'Fine. I do have some contacts, psychologists, staff in drug and alcohol agencies and so on and of course, Harriet is really good on the nutrition and can help them eat properly without starving. So, I like to think I can point people in the right direction, but you're right, we all need to recognise the signs.'

Tony grinned at the mention of Harriet Lucas's name. 'Of course, I hear she's doing well with her nutrition clinic and meal planning. She certainly helped Nat Wilson when he came back from injury.' He settled his coffee cup down in its saucer and suddenly looked serious. 'Now there's another thing I need to discuss with you. It's rather delicate. You'll be getting a new conditional. His name is Freddie Mercer.'

Finn shrugged. 'Right, OK. I haven't heard of him.' He wondered why on earth Tony was making such a big deal of this. He'd normally just add any additional conditionals onto his list or text him. He scanned his memory for any mention of the lad's name but drew a blank.

Tony sighed and lowered his voice. Finn thought he looked wary, almost furtive.

'You do know him, but he's riding under his mother's maiden name since the scandal.' He paused and swallowed hard. 'He was Freddie Teasdale before.'

Finn felt like he'd had cold water poured over him. 'What? Henry Teasdale's son? Is that even allowed? Wasn't Teasdale warned off?'

Tony leaned back in his seat and surveyed Finn. 'Yes, but the lad's not having any contact with him and has promised not to see him in the future. Teasdale's in prison anyway. Believe me, we've hummed and hawed about it at a very senior level at the BHA, but in the end, we agreed that the sins of the father shouldn't affect his son's opportunities when it was clear he wasn't involved. So, we've no option but to take him on, under strict conditions, of course.'

Finn shook his head, incredulously. 'So, let me get this straight. You want me to mentor the son of a trainer who I helped convict of fraud for pulling races and who is warned off and who was instrumental in the murder of my friend, Paddy Owen, and caused untold misery to one of my other lads and countless lads before him?'

Tony had the good grace to blush and opened his mouth to speak before closing it again. 'Yes, but as you know, Dr Christopher Pinkerton was the mastermind behind the fraud and he's the one currently serving a prison sentence for murder. Teasdale was involved in bullying conditionals to pull races. The lad's estranged from his father, and lives with his mother who is in the process of divorcing Henry, so there's no love lost between them. I think we can be reassured that the lad won't have any contact with his father.'

'Hmm.' Finn thought it through. He didn't like it, not one bit. Henry Teasdale had blackmailed conditionals to pull races using sensitive information that Dr Christopher Pinkerton, a local GP in Walton, had acquired about the lads during confidential medical consultations. The pair had then capitalised on this by backing the winner in the dodgy races, which invariably had much longer odds and made them a mint of money. A friend of Finn's, an ex jockey and travelling head lad, Paddy Owen, had been murdered because he had suspicions about what was going on and was about to report them. Paddy had been a good friend and Finn had grieved at the senseless loss of life. Paddy had been pushed down the steps of the Clock Tower Stand in Doncaster Racecourse, which were concrete and very steep. What an awful death. Finn flinched when he imagined Paddy's head hitting the concrete steps repeatedly as he fell. Could he really mentor the son of someone who had been an accomplice in such an act of violence? Then he thought about something else.

'And what about Freddie? Surely, he wouldn't want me to mentor him? After all, I was instrumental in bringing his dad to justice. And which local trainer is going to take him on when they realise who he is?'

Tony smiled. 'Ah, well that's just where you're wrong. Freddie and his mother have washed their hands of Henry and they are keen to distance themselves from him. They consider that he brought great shame on the family, what with the scandal and prison sentence. Freddie greatly admires your riding, so is keen for you to take him on. As for trainers, we have still to sort that out, but one will be found in Walton, I assure you.'

Finn was not so sure. Conditionals and apprentice flat jockeys needed a trainer to take them on, horses to ride and an entrée into the world of horseracing. Everyone locally would soon work out who Freddie was related to. They all knew of his father's actions and took a very dim view of anyone trying to undermine the integrity of racing, as Henry Teasdale had done. But there weren't just the moral arguments, people would be worried about being seen associating with someone whose father had been warned off.

Tony sighed heavily. 'But let's just say the odds on a trainer taking him will be much higher if you agree to mentor him. And his mother literally begged for you to coach him, she has the greatest respect for you.'

And that was the crux of the matter, if he took him on, then it would give Freddie the veneer of respectability. Finn was highly suspicious of people flattering him. Besides he hadn't even met Penny Teasdale, only Henry. He wondered what had become of her after Henry was warned off.

'Whatever happened to Penny, Teasdale's wife? She was an artist, wasn't she?'

'Still is, but she also works to make ends meet.' Tony looked rather grave. 'I think she has had to do cleaning too. They have both suffered because of Henry's actions and the inquiry was clear that they were not involved, so we can't not give the lad a licence.' He sipped his coffee and gave Finn a penetrating look. 'He's been eventing at a decent level, so he can ride. So, you'll do it?'

Finn shrugged. Tony clearly thought being a cleaner was a huge indignity but at least it was good, honest work. It was a tough one but then as Tony had said, Freddie hadn't been involved in the fraud and he certainly owed Tony Murphy. He hadn't forgotten how he had offered him the jockey coaching job when he had retired from racing and was at a very low ebb. Besides, he would keep a very good eye on the lad, and he had to be fair to Freddie and if he could ride then that was a real bonus. He took a sip of coffee. On balance, he decided that the lad should be given a chance.

'Hmm. I'll do it, but he'll need to know the score about having no contact with his father. And he'll get no special treatment from me.' He suddenly thought of something. 'How will we know if he breaches the agreement?'

Tony tapped the side of his nose. 'Let's just say we have contacts in the prison and probation services, so we'll certainly find out if he tries to break the rules.' Tony tried and failed to suppress a grin. 'Great stuff. I wouldn't expect you to treat him any differently.' He frowned. 'I'll email you the paperwork.' He glanced at his watch and scooped up his papers. 'All we need now is a trainer to take him on. Better dash, I'll be in touch.'

Finn watched him go, his unease growing. Should he have refused to have the lad on his list? He couldn't very well, he reasoned, but it

24

certainly brought back all the horror that Dr Christopher Pinkerton and Henry Teasdale had caused. He needed to talk to someone who knew about the case and who better than Harriet Lucas, who had helped him nail the criminals. They had been thrown together to help Sam Foster when he had run away from Teasdale's, having refused to comply with his instructions to stop horses. Thankfully, Sam had done well and was now riding for a leading trainer, Harry Steadman, in Berkshire, after his guvnor retired following a stroke, but he shuddered to think what could have happened to the lad because of Teasdale's actions. He felt deeply uncomfortable. He knew rationally that he shouldn't blame Freddie for his father's sins, but feelings weren't always based on facts. He pulled out his phone and began to compose a message to Harriet Lucas. Only she would understand the complex emotions the prospect of working with Henry's son had generated.

Are you free to meet up this week? Have a new lad I need to discuss with you. Speak soon.

It was then that he realised that he had several more missed calls from trainer, Jeremy Trentham, and remembered that he'd meant to ring him back. No time like the present, he thought. Jeremy answered, his plummy tones sounding rather distant. It soon became apparent why.

'Ah, Finn. I'm at Uttoxeter and about to saddle up. Listen, I really need to speak to you and Harriet. I have a proposition for you. Meet me tomorrow at ours, say 10 o'clock. Sorry, I need to go.' There was a pause. 'Listen, it's essential I speak with you and it's highly confidential, I really need to impress that on you.'

'Right. OK. Nothing to do with Kyle then?'

'Oh no. He's fine. Look, I can't say any more over the phone. I'll see you tomorrow then.'

Jeremy rang off abruptly. Finn sat for a minute gathering his thoughts, as the café began to fill up for lunch, wondering what on earth was so important for Jeremy to ring him multiple times, and why he needed to see him and Harriet, but refuse to say what it was about over the phone? What could possibly be so confidential? He texted Harriet again explaining that Jeremy wanted to see them both. She texted back saying she could make it but like him she was curious as to what it was about, but he was unable to answer her. He privately wondered if Joseph had misheard Trentham when he said it was about a painting. It had certainly been an odd few days, he realised, what with Niall Byrne's arrest and then finding out he would be mentoring Freddie Mercer. He would imagine that the press would be interested in that story. He thought about Topper McGrew, a racing journalist, and wondered whether it might be better to talk to him before he found out about the story, then he decided against it. It was probably better for the information to seep out organically, there was no sense setting people against the lad before he'd even ridden a race, no sense at all. Then his thoughts turned to Jeremy Trentham and why he was behaving as though he was working for MI5. What the hell was going on? He had been looking forward to the season starting proper and expected now he had mastered most aspects of the job, that it would be plain sailing. Fate has intervened and it seemed that there were going to be plenty of unexpected challenges along the way, once again.

Chapter 4

By now the whole of Walton knew that Niall Byrne had been arrested as the jungle telegraph amongst horsy folk was red hot after the event. Topper McGrew, racing correspondent at the Press Agency had heard early next morning from one of his many racing informants, in this case Lofty Ballard the photographer. In true Topper style he sensed a story and having written his tips for tomorrow, grabbed a coffee and settled down in his isolated corner of the office and began to find out more. This is the life, he thought, revelling in his renewed good fortune, a new job after the horrors of working for the Yorkshire Echo and the terrible havoc wreaked by the new broom editor, Christian 'Tosser' Lamont, who only wanted lurid celebrity gossip and had taken the paper to its knees. He was well out of it and the staff here were all proper journos and he was given respect and freedom. He had even been nominated for a writing award for his piece on the now infamous Joel and Lloyd Fox, but that was another story. And in a stroke of luck his new racing thriller that he was currently writing, had lots of interest. OK, so it was only online initially but the independent publishers were very positive, and Topper already had the outline of another novel brewing and interest in his proposed non-fiction book about racing families provisionally called Bloodlines. Blood and background were important elements to Topper. He was related to Anglo Irish gentry on his mother's side and that gave him a sense of security and pride. His family had old money, none of your nouveau riche rubbish. He'd been to public school and had a hunting, fishing and shooting sort of background which was how he'd got into racing.

Now Niall Byrne. Topper found a photo of the lad on the trainer, Seamus Ryan's website. The lad looked like he had the 'map of Ireland all over his face', as Topper's mother would have said. He noted that he had Finn McCarthy as his jockey coach and made a mental note to ask him about him. He knew Finn well, he was a good chap, but tended to be protective of his charges, not that that was a bad thing. He continued searching for Byrne. Probably started out pony racing in Ireland, thought Topper, many of the

27

Irish jockeys had risen via that route, so he trawled various pony racing websites to find him. Hmm, lots of criminal Byrnes came up when he searched. Paddy Byrne had been jailed for assault, Declan Byrne for race fixing. Could be relatives, thought Topper, but then Byrne was a common enough surname. Interesting though. What the hell was the lad doing trying to evade the police? But then a youngster of 17 could be easily spooked, and probably had a devil may care attitude which may have contributed to his actions. He was only grateful that the police had never caught up with him when he'd been behind the wheel, over the limit on whisky. There by the grace of God and all that. But now the destructive way of life was over for him. He was literally a shadow of himself having lost three stone after following advice from Harriet Lucas, and he was into getting fit. Jogging and Boxercise had toned him, and he felt fantastic. Plenty of life in the old dog yet.

He took a sip of coffee and another thought flashed into his brain, as he followed his nose, like a truffle pig. Christian Gerrard, that was the name he was interested in. A new owner at Trentham's who owned Kinder Scout, a much fancied horse who was entered in a good race coming up at Haydock. Gerrard also owned and was refurbishing a hotel in Walton, The Stagecoach. Topper looked up the details of the place online. 'Your comfort is our business' ran the tag line on the website which boasted several upmarket boutique hotels across the country. Topper's eyes fell on a beaming Gerrard, in his forties, well preserved, fit looking, urbane with shining, neat white teeth. Bloody veneers, thought Topper savagely, Gerrard could signal to the moon with those gnashers and he disliked him on sight. You mate are far too bloody good to be true. Topper resolved to find some dirt on the smug tosser. He was suspicious of people who suddenly appeared to come into money and then proceeded to splash it about on expensive racehorses. Where had the money come from, he asked himself? Maybe he was someone who had worked hard and made sound investments or maybe he was a criminal who wanted to splash his ill-gotten gains around? In his experience, the latter option was more likely than the former. As he searched with practiced ease, looking through ancestry websites he found that Gerrard had been born and brought up in Toxteth in Liverpool, not a very salubrious neighbourhood by the address. Very interesting, bet he keeps that quiet, thought Topper. He'd keep his ear to

28

the ground about the man. Sudden wealth was always a red flag for him. He was about to complete more searches when he was interrupted by a text from his oldest son, Tim.

See you later Dad. Can you pick us up at 7pm? Mum says can me and Giles stay over with you for the weekend?

Topper responded immediately, agreeing. He felt a burst of happiness that he was going to see his sons for longer.

Now that Topper and ex wife Jacqui were divorced, he'd brought a cottage in a village east of York. Perfect for having the boys to stay and for work and visiting the many racecourses in the area. He planned the weekend in his mind's eye, he'd take leave especially to spend precious time with his boys who were having an Exeat from prep school. They'd go to the rugby on Saturday, have a lads' night in, watch a film with a takeaway and then he'd help Tim with his English. Tim was showing promise with his writing and Topper was determined to nurture his talent. And Giles was a good all round sportsman and surprisingly good at art, especially at drawing cartoons and Topper was keen to introduce him to some professional cartoonists, in case he wanted to develop that skill and even turn it into a career. Topper knew he might struggle with the fees at their next school, but he would manage, whatever it took. Anyway, everyone knew Topper was on the up. And it didn't really bother him anymore that he suspected Jacqui had a new relationship, not really, hence the sudden change to extend the boys' stay this weekend. That particular ship had sailed a long time ago and now he had set his sights elsewhere. He reckoned Jane from Boxercise might be interested in him. She was widowed and had a tidy figure and a kind smile. He'd ask her for a coffee after next week's class. See, life in the old dog yet!

Chapter 5

'Oh, hello. Go and find a chair and I'll get some coffee on,' said a pleasant looking woman in her forties with long brown hair held in an Alice band. She waved over towards a gate leg table in the centre of a large morning room. The woman had fine features, a warm smile and the slightly weather beaten skin of a person used to being outdoors. She also had an air of being rather frazzled.

'Jeremy will be with you in a minute. I'll sort out your drinks.'

The walls were covered with photos of racehorses in action or groups of owners standing around a horse in the winning enclosure. Always there was the tall, stately figure of Jeremy Trentham standing nearby smiling.

A liver and white spaniel wagged his tail and sniffed at Harriet expectantly. She patted the dog who immediately lay on its back to invite a belly rub, it was clearly used to being petted. Finn glanced over at the neat rows of Timeform books on the shelves of a recess where a small Davenport desk held a laptop and sheaves of papers.

'It was his father's yard first, 'explained Finn quietly, 'and Jeremy took over when he died.'

'Was that his wife?' Hattie inclined her head over towards the door, from which the sounds of a kettle boiling could be heard.

'Yes, Laura. Sorry, I should have said. Lovely woman and an excellent horsewoman.'

'Yes, she seems a bit stressed though...'

Finn nodded. 'I expect she's helping out, doing the entries and declarations and so on. I think she does a lot of the paperwork although they have a secretary too.'

Hattie knew from her friend Daisy how busy the role of a racehorse trainer was as her father also trained in Walton. It seemed in fact to be, a complete, all encompassing way of life. Up at 5.30am, supervising horses on the gallops, planning campaigns for them, with lots of disappointing runs, injuries, general drudgery, occasionally interspersed with the soaring thrill of the odd win. Well, that was how Daisy saw her father Vince's life, but Hattie knew that Jeremy was a higher ranking sort of trainer out of the twenty or so based in and around Walton. Finn had run through Jeremy's achievements on the way there. He'd trained some Group 1 winners and always had several runners at Cheltenham, sometimes in the festival and even some in the Grand National. He even had a few celebrity owners like the footballer, Tyler Dalton, who owned the yard's star In the Pink, or Pinkie as he was known. The house was a vast, but comfortable stone farmhouse and the yard they'd walked past looked well kept and expensive. It was the sort of house where the furniture was all inherited, passed down through the centuries and probably very valuable. Hattie realised that the smart horsebox and the equine swimming pool she'd glimpsed as they arrived, would not come cheap either. It was a far cry from the chaos and homely untidiness of Vince's yard nearby.

Laura came back carrying a tray holding a coffee pot, some mugs and a large coffee and walnut cake.

'Sorry Finn, we're a bit all over the place, the secretary's on leave and so's the cleaner. Can't think how that happened, so it's all go. Anyway, listen here's Jeremy, so I'd better get on.' She looked up at her husband who was pocketing his mobile phone. 'I'll just leave you to talk…' She eyed the coffee. 'Do you want a spot of brandy in that? It is a rather cold morning…'

They both shook their heads. Hattie suspected that brandy in coffee, so early in the morning was de rigueur for the Trentham family.

'Thanks, darling.' Jeremy poured the coffee and handed the mugs round and offered the cake which both politely refused. The spaniel, who was called Nelson, eyed the cake Jeremy cut for himself with as much concentration as he could muster. Jeremy patted the dog's head absently. He watched his wife leave and got up to close the door firmly behind him.

He looked from one to the other. 'Look Finn, Hattie, it's great you're here. I need your help and I just couldn't think who else to contact…'

Finn nodded. 'Go on…'

Jeremy took a mouthful of his cake and sighed. 'I know I can rely on your discretion, and I know the two of you have had success in the past helping the police with investigations.'

Hattie put her mug down and leaned forward. 'And…'

31

'And so, my dear, I want you to find an owner and a horse. You see I had a bad debt, one of the owners couldn't pay up. When I kicked up a stink, well, the fool took his horses away and gave me a painting in lieu of training fees, do you see?' He pointed at a large oil painting on the nearest wall, showing six racehorses lining up ready to race, three bays, a grey and two chestnuts, all jockeys ready for the off. Even to Hattie's untrained eye it looked old, like the sort of painting in galleries from the eighteenth century. It had a gilt frame and Harriet had to admit that the horses were painted to perfection, every sinew, muscle and fetlock were drawn with absolute accuracy. The nearest horse was a chestnut that had three white socks and a virtually white near foreleg which was very unusual for a thoroughbred.

Hattie looked at Finn. 'Well, I'm not sure we can help...' Her brain was racing through their previous cases, race fixing, betting fraud, a hit and run of a jockey. Nothing like this one. Both of them were also partly employed by the BHA Integrity Unit, although this was secret. And all their work came directly through Tony Murphy.

Jeremy lowered his voice. 'The owner, he's a distant relative of mine, Ross Maclaren.'

Hattie knew the name instantly. 'The author?'

'Yes, yes, that's him, the writer chappie. Bit of a recluse and as eccentric as hell. Good judge of a horse though. Anyway, now he's vanished, taking one of my best horses with him, ' he glanced at Finn. 'Admiral Jervis, an excellent chaser. I was preparing him for Cheltenham. I'm gutted about his loss.'

Finn frowned. 'Well, losing good horses, it happens.' He shrugged. 'But look, if you need to, can't you sell the painting? Just send it to an auction house, job done.'

Jeremy sighed and took another sip of coffee. 'But that's just it, it's more complicated than that.'

Finn stood up to study the painting which was hung in a prominent place behind an oak davenport. 'It's a nice piece, wouldn't mind it on my wall.'

'It's only a Gideon Moss, no less.' Jeremy clearly assumed that they knew the artist's name, but Harriet hadn't heard of him. Finn looked as though he knew the name.

'I think it's quite collectible. Similar pieces fetched several hundred thousand pounds. But this painting includes the colt, Red Navajo the chestnut there at the front with the unusual markings.' Jeremy went up to the painting and pointed out the beautifully painted chestnut with the almost completely white leg and white socks. 'The race is the Sovereign Stakes at Newmarket which Red Navajo won easily.'

Finn stood up to examine the painting. 'Of course, and he went on to win the Derby, the Two Thousand Guineas and everything else for the next two years. Then he went on to become one of the most impressive sires. His progeny all did very well and feature in the back breeding of many of today's winners.' Finn suddenly looked very animated. 'I've read about Red Navajo, am aware of his unusual marking, but I've never seen a painting of him. Wasn't he around at the turn of the century?'

'Absolutely. The painting dates from 1912. There are lots of descriptions of him, about the unusual white leg and the other socks, but Maclaren thinks this is the only painting of him. His great great grandfather had it commissioned apparently.'

Finn's eyebrows shot up. 'Wow. So, it'll be worth a fortune, and it's painted by Gideon Moss too. He is becoming increasingly collectible. So, how much did Maclaren owe you?'

'That's just it. He only owed me fifty grand. But this painting, it must be worth far, far more. So, I can't possibly accept it, it's just not done, not decent. I want you to find him and return it. And get the silly sod to return Admiral while you're at it. I mean, the debt was only small, not worth taking the bloody horse away for.' He frowned. 'The whole argument blew up out of nothing. Ross asked me to wait for the money until he had published his latest book, but I refused. I knew he had writer's block, d'you see, and there was a bit of a standoff and things were said in the heat of the moment, you know how it is. The truth is I lost my temper and Ross was moaning at me for not supporting him, which he thought I should do given that we're related. The next thing I knew he sent a box for his horses and sent the painting a couple of days after, all wrapped in some sort of crate and delivered by some posh firm.' Jeremy shook his head. 'I should have supported him, he was right, so I want you to find him and tell him that. He's writing his book and incommunicado.'

Hattie gasped at his view that fifty thousand was such a small debt. It really did show how successful the yard was.

'I'll pay you the going rate, of course.' Jeremy smiled and Hattie could see he was nervous, anxious that they should take the case.

Finn looked thoughtful. 'Can't you sort it out with the family? You said you were related to Maclaren? Surely, someone will know where he is?'

Jeremy sighed. 'If they do know then they're not telling me. I have heard that he is finishing off his latest book and rumoured to be somewhere remote, but he's not responding to my calls.'

Realisation dawned on Hattie's face. 'So, Maclaren has given it to you and does not know the real value, is that it?'

'That is one explanation, yes. But honestly, I just want the status quo restored, Admiral back and I'll damned well wait for the money. One of my owners, Christian Gerrard runs a gallery and he's offered to buy the painting which is why I know what it's worth. It was such a silly argument and he is kith and kin after all, so I just want the horses back and everything straightened out. I suppose we both lost our tempers, and it really won't do.' Jeremy looked anguished. 'The other thing is that Laura doesn't quite know about the size of the debt, so I'd rather things were left strictly between us. She thought I gave Ross too much leeway as it was.'

Finn and Hattie shared a complicit look. Hattie was just about to launch into an explanation of how they couldn't even consider taking the case on, they had no expertise in finding missing people or horses, so it was out of the question, when Finn spoke.

'We'll do it on one condition.'

'And what is that, my dear chap?'

'That you also take on a new conditional.'

Jeremy considered this. 'Well, I could do with one actually. Kyle Devlin is about to ride out his claim and might well get offers to go elsewhere, a talented lad like him, so I could do with the right sort of person...'

Finn nodded. 'Good. It's Freddie Mercer, Henry Teasdale's son...'

Hattie gazed at the pair open mouthed. What on earth was going on?

'That scoundrel! Isn't he warned off? Absolutely no, there are limits. I can't be associated with any hint of scandal, I do have my reputation to consider, Finn.'

Finn nodded. 'Look, I can see why you'd say that, I felt the same way when my boss spoke to me about the lad. I have agreed to mentor him because he has no contact with his father whatsoever, he and his mother are thoroughly ashamed of him, and they were never involved in any of Henry's shenanigans at all. Teasdale is in prison now. The lad will have to sign up to a strict contract and he'll be treated firmly but fairly. Believe you me if there's any sniff of non-compliance, and the BHA have very good contacts, then he'll be out on his ear.'

Jeremy rubbed his nose. 'Hmm. But can he ride?'

'Oh yes, I have it on good authority that he's a decent horseman. He was a promising eventer and has ridden in three star events but wants to make the switch to racing.'

Jeremy looked impressed. 'Eventing? Well, he should certainly know what's what then. Hmm.' He rubbed his chin. 'You'll definitely take this on if I sign him up?'

Harriet was about to protest but Finn beat her to it.

'Absolutely.'

'Then that's settled.' Jeremy put his hand out to shake Finn's and then Harriet's. 'Laura will be pleased, she was friendly with Penny, Freddie's mother, still is actually.'

Jeremy grinned broadly and went on to discuss the painting, what was known about the artist and his relative. He was clearly in an expansive, celebratory mood. He also told them about a new owner, Christian Gerrard who had several horses with him.

'Kinder Scout is the best, outstanding, I'd say.'

Finn grinned broadly. 'Brilliant.'

Just then there was a knock at the door and Jeremy opened it. The spaniel went up to investigate. A figure burst into the room.

'Hello there, Jeremy. I've just popped in to see how the horses are doing. Is it alright if I go and have a look at them? We can talk later if you're busy.'

The man was tall and slim wearing an olive green Barbour jacket, tweed trousers and boots. He had an air of authority and didn't look the slightest bit sorry to have disturbed them. He was in his forties, well groomed and his eyes roved around the room, taking in everything, including the painting. His eyes lit up at the sight of it. He looked at Finn and Harriet inquiringly.

'Oh, of course, Christian, do go ahead and have a look. Have you met Finn McCarthy and Harriet Lucas? This is Christian Gerrard, an owner. I was just telling Harriet and Finn about you.'

Christian smiled and stretched out his hand. 'Of course, I know Finn McCarthy and I'm delighted to meet you, Harriet.'

Jeremy went on to explain, Finn and Harriet's official roles and outlined which horses Christian owned. He also explained that Christian was behind the building of a large hotel in Walton, a structure that was looming large on the way into the town. It was called The Stagecoach.

Christian smiled. 'I'm a hotelier and have a lot of other investments. I'm an art dealer too. The Stagecoach is going to be a high end establishment for all the people of Walton. It's a great little town you have here, and lots of people coming into the place can stay in the lap of luxury whilst they enjoy the delights of the place. There's going to be a spa, a restaurant and even a wedding barn. 'Your comfort is our business' is our mantra and it really is true. You must come to the opening next week.'

Harriet thought he sounded like a walking advertisement and was instinctively wary. Gerrard had a slight accent, Liverpudlian, she thought, and looked like he had tried too hard with his clothes, guessing he was desperate to fit into the horsey set. His outfit looked rather too new and expensive not like the worn out, faded gear worn by many folk in racing. Finn coughed, he clearly wanted to bring the subject back to more familiar ground.

'OK. So how many horses do you have?'

'Four. They're very good prospects, actually, 'added Jeremy. Kinder Scout is going in a good race at Wetherby next week, so we're hoping for a good run.'

Christian smiled. 'We are indeed. I know, why don't you two come along? I have a box, so both you and Harriet would be welcome to join us. I'm very interested in the work of the Professional Jockeys' Association, Harriet, and I'd be delighted to talk to you Finn, about your work in coaching. I was a great fan of yours when you were riding.'

Finn explained that he was at Wetherby anyway and would be pleased to go and Harriet said she would be there, if she could fit it into her schedule. After some more small talk, they made their excuses to leave.

'We're off now anyway,' added Finn. 'It's been lovely to meet you. We'll be in touch, Jeremy.'

As they said their goodbyes, Harriet's head was in a spin. She was frustrated that she hadn't felt able to voice her concerns about what Finn had agreed to in front of Jeremy. She could kill Finn. What had he just committed them to? She was too angry to speak.

Breaking the stunned silence on the way back to the centre of Walton, Finn said, 'Brunch at the Blacksmith's?'

'Too bloody right,' said Hattie, 'and you're paying. I'm starving and there's a lot to talk about. Why on earth did you agree to us finding this bloody author? You could have asked me first! And what's all this about Freddie Mercer, Teasdale's son?'

Over lunch of smashed avocado on toast for Hattie and a New York bagel with Emmental, prosciutto and gherkins for Finn, he explained himself.

'Sorry, look I needed to get a trainer for Freddie and this gave me the perfect opportunity.'

'But bloody missing people, Finn? We don't know the first place to start!'

Finn shrugged. 'Well, I thought we'd just chase up where Admiral Jervis has gone, then we find Maclaren. Surely it can't be that hard? He's not going to sell a good horse like that, so he must have sent him to another yard.'

Harriet shook her head. 'And are you really sure you want to mentor Teasdale's son after everything that happened? Surely not?'

Finn speared a tomato and waved his fork expansively. 'Look, Tony specifically asked me, the lad wants me to mentor him and why should he suffer just because of what his father did? He wasn't involved and neither was his mother. They're both victims really, and the sins of the father shouldn't be visited on the son. He deserves the opportunity.'

Harriet considered this, the reasoning of which did appeal to her sense of fairness. 'But supposing he's like his father? He's bound to see him. Teasdale could even be running some sort of criminal activity from his prison cell!' She thought about Paddy Owen, Finn's friend who had been killed by the gang and winced. 'Why can't another coach take him on? It's a recipe for disaster, if you want my opinion.'

Finn shook his head. 'Listen, he'll have to sign a contract that he won't have any contact with his father, don't forget Teasdale's warned off. Tony has assured me that they will soon find out if there are any breaches. Freddie was away at school at the time and there's no evidence that his mother knew anything about his activities, so it's only fair to give the lad a chance.'

Harriet sighed. Finn was a decent man and was highly principled, of course, he'd treat the lad fairly, it just felt uncomfortable, that was all.

And what about the painting of Red Navajo? I've never heard of him.'

Finn smiled. 'Well, if you studied form as much as I have, you certainly would have, he's one of the very best stallions historically. Loads of good horses have him in their breeding going back a few generations. He had a really successful stud career after his racing success. I know about his markings of course, but I've never seen a painting of him.' He shook his head in wonderment. 'He's very distinctive. I think Jeremy might well be right and that's the only remaining painting of him, which makes it priceless.'

Harriet got that he was really excited about the horse, but she had grave reservations about their role in finding its owner.

'Mmm. I suppose so. But what do we do about finding Maclaren, I mean where would we even begin with something like that?' Then she had a thought. 'I suppose I could ask Gabriel. You know I had a date with Gabriel Taverner last night?'

Finn grinned. 'No, I bloody well didn't because you never said. And it's Gabriel now, is it?'

'Well, I called him DCI Taverner all evening obviously now he's been promoted, well he's an acting DCI whilst his boss is off.' She rolled her eyes. 'I probably won't mention this to him just yet.'

'So, you seeing the Angel Gabriel again, I take it?'

Hattie could feel herself blushing. In fact, the date had gone well. She found that they had a lot in common and he was surprisingly good company and was good looking too. 'Dunno, might. I'll just see what happens.'

She wondered if she could just forget to tell Taverner. Anyway, this wouldn't be a police investigation, probably, so surely there was no reason for him to know. And, of course, she had no way of knowing how the relationship was going to develop. The signs were good so far, but it didn't do to think too far ahead.

Finn nodded, his expression unreadable. 'For what it's worth I think Taverner's a decent bloke and you could do a lot worse.'

'Thanks, big bro. 'Hattie quipped. She often felt that Finn did look out for her. She found she was touched by his concern and pleased by his approval. She had been worried about telling him for some reason but was relieved that it had been easier than she had expected.

Harriet ate her food with relish and her bad mood started to dissipate.

'God, I was so starving I should have had some of that cake from Jeremy's.' She paused to speak to him. 'What did you make of the new owner, Gerrard?'

'I've heard of him. I'm not sure how he made his money, property I think, before the hotel stuff, but Kinder Scout and Lumiere are two very good hurdlers, so he knows his horse flesh. Will you be at Wetherby?'

Hattie savoured her meal, with 'hmm' sounds of appreciation.

'Yep, I think so. Gerrard seemed alright. A bit try hard, but OK.' Hattie paused. 'I could ask my Uncle Sebastian about the painting. He runs a gallery in York, near the Minster. He's a real expert and valuer.' She smiled. 'I'll be discreet. You know, my dad loves Ross Maclaren's novels. They're about spies, the military, MI5 and stuff.' She paused. 'You wouldn't think he'd be short of a bob or two though, would you? Successful writer like that.'

Finn nodded. 'Think I'd read he had writer's block or something so hasn't had a book published for a few years, so maybe he's spent all the money. Anyway, fancy you having an uncle with an art gallery? Might be useful, I don't think things will get that far, seems like Gerrard has valued the painting already. We'll just make some preliminary inquiries as to Admiral's whereabouts and pass the information on and that will be that.'

Hattie felt a flare of annoyance about Finn behaving in such a high handed manner and wasn't about to let him off that easily. 'Still, you could

39

have asked me first, and it's not exactly a BHA job, is it? What will Tony think?'

Finn studied her. 'I don't think it will be too time consuming. It's something we can do in our own time. Anyway, if it's such a problem then I could always do the job alone, if you're too busy.'

It was a calculated move on Finn's part and one that had the desired effect. Harriet bristled at the very idea.

'What? And leave you to have all the fun? Besides, I'm involved now, so that's that.'

Finn gave her a knowing look and grinned. Too late she realised that she had reacted exactly as he knew she would. 'Anyway, we've got an invite to Christian Gerrard's box and all we have to do is ask a few questions, that's all. Besides it will be fun to trace a famous author.'

'Maybe.' Hattie glanced at her watch. 'Oh God, I'd better go. Got a consultation starting in half an hour. I'll text you about Wetherby then. See you.'

As Hattie strode off, she noticed an extra spring in her step as her mood soared. Finn was right, of course. She found she was intrigued by the story Jeremy had told them, despite her reservations. And she had no intention of letting Finn go it alone, that was never, ever going to happen. He had been right about that too. Sometimes she thought he knew her better than she knew herself. Damn him.

Chapter 6

Tony Murphy was delighted when Finn told him that he had found a trainer for Freddie. Waves of approval emanated over the phone line.

'With Jeremy Trentham too! I thought I would have to pull in some favours, but you've saved me the bother. Wonderful!'

'Well, Jeremy reckons that Kyle Devlin will ride out his claim and then might be swamped with offers as he's a good jockey, and besides they could do with another conditional since Maura decided to go back to Ireland.'

There was a murmur of approval over the phone. 'Well, I'm very grateful, I really am. I'm sure he'll do just fine, he seems like a nice lad and can ride a bit too. I honestly don't think he'll be any bother.'

Finn had already conducted some research on Freddie Mercer and had found that he had done quite well in eventing which he knew was a tough sport as both rider and horse had to master the three stages; dressage, showjumping and cross country. He liked riders who had ridden in different disciplines and thought that the riding skills were highly transferable to racing. He had recently come to the conclusion that riders who did pony racing only, were not anything like as well prepared for the stresses of race riding as those who'd hunted or undertaken Pony Club riding. He certainly had had to spend a lot longer with the pony racers improving their riding techniques and ensuring that they had a secure seat by making them spend ages riding without stirrups, much to their annoyance.

'Well, I'll arrange to meet him and then we'll see,' replied Finn.

'Fabulous. Thanks, Finn. Any worries then just let me know.'

He could hear the smile in Tony's voice and just hoped that he wouldn't live to regret taking Freddie on. He was having a quiet morning completing admin, so he settled down to research Gideon Moss's paintings. He had wondered about confiding in Tony the real reason that Jeremy agreed to take Freddie, but as he expected that the investigation would be relatively easy and straightforward, he had decided against it. Sometimes, it was better to keep one's own counsel and the fewer people who knew that Trentham had a valuable painting at his home the better. Anyone who knew about breeding would be thrilled at the prospect of seeing a rare painting of Red Navajo and recognise it's worth. He wished now he had advised Jeremy to put it somewhere safe, still he supposed there was always someone at the yard, be it stable staff or people paid to maintain the stables, gallops and the like, so probably everything would be fine. After all, the yard had expensive horses to look after, so a painting should be easy. His thoughts slid back to his new conditional. There was something he was concerned about though.

'I wondered about tipping off the media about Freddie but decided not to bother. I'll field any questions if they come my way but don't think I should initiate anything.' Finn knew that Topper McGrew was just the sort of person to work it out and ask questions, but it would be easier to address them once Freddie was more established. After all, he might not make the grade, many conditionals didn't make it as jockeys and became work riders instead. He could almost hear the cogs in Tony's brain working through the various possibilities.

'Hmm. Perhaps you're right. Leave it alone for now. I'll talk to the bigwigs and see what they say.' He paused. 'Well done, though, Finn. Very well done.'

He was not surprised to see that Jeremy had been right about how sought after Gideon Moss's paintings were now. He googled the name and found that if anything, Jeremy had underestimated the demand for the artist. Moss had died at the age of thirty-nine of tuberculosis and many of his paintings, most of which depicted racehorses and scenes of rural life in the eighteenth century, were believed to be in private collections, so the last few that had come on to the market had fetched staggering amounts. The Sotheby sale of 'On the Heath' which depicted a string of horses in training in Newmarket, was not in Finn's opinion, as interesting a topic as Maclaren's painting, although the style and accuracy of the horse physiology was excellent in both, made two million pounds. Moss managed to capture the horses' motion and conformation beautifully. A very rare painting of Red Navajo could fetch far, far more. Maybe they'd get Harriet's uncle to value the painting, he wasn't quite sure he could trust Gerrard. Harriet. He really needed to reinforce the need for secrecy with Harriet and her uncle in the case. His thoughts turned to her revelation about her going on a date with Gabriel Taverner. It was not altogether unsurprising. They had all been thrown together from time to time in the course of their work for the BHA, and Finn had noticed the way the policeman had looked at her. He admired the man and thought that overall, he was a decent chap, yet he couldn't help feeling that everything was changing, and he really hoped this wouldn't affect his friendship with her. Don't be ridiculous, he told himself, but he did wonder if Taverner would discourage the friendship. Harriet was a grown woman and would make her own decisions and anyway, Taverner didn't seem like the controlling type. He dismissed his gloomy thoughts about the state of his own love life, wondered briefly about Niall's older sister, Theresa, then decided he was unlikely to see her again. He forced himself to concentrate on the task in hand and did some research on Maclaren's horse, Admiral Jervis. Surely, Maclaren would have kept such a promising horse and if he could find the new trainer then he was halfway to finding the author himself, after all, the trainer had to know where to send his bills, he reasoned.

Of course, it was never going to be that easy and he found that Admiral Jervis appeared to have been sold recently and was now in training somewhere in the midlands and owned by a company by the look of things. He supposed that this reinforced the belief that Maclaren was short of money. He made a note of the name of the company, RMB Holdings and resolved to ring the trainer's contact number to see if he had any ideas about the previous owner's whereabouts. Then he googled, Ross Maclaren, and found that the author hadn't written a book for about eight years and though there was talk of one, it had never actually materialised. So, that also suggested that his fortunes were dwindling although his six previous novels of espionage and politics were described as excellent reads and had clearly been best sellers. He read an article written just prior to the release of his last book, Coup D'Etat, which had a photo of Maclaren sat at a desk somewhere rather grand with a beautiful stone fireplace in the background. He had a strong, aristocratic face, longish hair and an upright bearing. He was described as notoriously private and although he gave a lot of detail regarding his forthcoming release, there was little information of a personal nature except to say that he enjoyed country pursuits and had been in the

Army in his youth, and the SAS, and hinted that he had possibly worked in espionage. It was those experiences that formed the basis of his writing. The location of the house was also rather vague too. Finn made some notes and then decided to continue with his work, mildly irritated that the solution to finding Ross Maclaren's whereabouts was not going to be as straightforward as he had hoped.

He leafed through his list of new conditionals and arranged to meet Niall Byrne that afternoon and Freddie Mercer later in the week. He noticed he also had three females on his list of conditionals, which he was pleased about as he felt it was high time that women were given equal status in racing, and he looked forward to coaching the future female champion jockey. He had a genuine belief that this would happen before too long.

He drove out to Seamus Ryan's yard which was just on the outskirts of Walton. The urban street scene gave way to a rural landscape and the beauty of an English autumn, the orange and red leaves of the trees, set against a muted grey sky was breathtaking, as he approached the racing town of Walton where twenty or so racehorse trainers plied their trade. Autumn was his favourite season, probably because he associated it with the start of the National Hunt season and all the anticipation that that evoked for him over the years. He had been a successful jockey and still missed the thrill of race riding, but his role as a jockey coach was the best he could manage and at least he didn't have to deal with the endless wasting or risk life and limb on a daily basis. He was old enough to be glad about that. As he drove, he contemplated his young conditional's fate. He hoped that Niall had calmed down and was able to see a way forward after his grave mistake. He would have to take his punishment, whatever form it may be. He knew Rosie and Seamus well and as they rated the lad, they would support him through thick and thin, so he was lucky.

Rosie was delighted to see him and both her and Seamus, who had been filling up hay nets, offered him a cup of tea and a slice of Rosie's lemon drizzle cake. Niall joined them and looked flushed from the cold but otherwise far healthier than when he had last seen him. Rosie kept casting anxious looks at him, her freckled face creased up with concern.

'So, how are things?'

44

Niall smiled. 'Thanks such a lot for helping me, Mr McCarthy, the other night. 'I've talked it through with the guvnor and Mrs Ryan and I'm feeling much more positive.'

Seamus ran his fingers through his greying hair. 'Sure, the lad knows he made a terrible mistake, and it would be an awful shame if that ruined things for him. Haven't we all done things we're not proud of? It was so out of character too, lad's not put a foot wrong since he's been here, so we'll definitely support him.'

Rosie nodded. 'So, we've all talked it through. We have put together some character references for the court case and because we're all supporting him, then there's a good chance of getting a suspended sentence, according to the solicitor, but he'll always have a place here even if the decision goes the wrong way, right enough.'

'But there's to be no drinking or drugs!' added Seamus with a frown.

Niall smiled. 'Course, of course. Nothing will pass me lips, I won't let any of you down. I'm just glad to be given the chance.'

Seamus frowned. 'T'would be such a waste, you've a great pair of hands and a way with the difficult horses. I want to see yer do real well, and not squander yer talents.'

Finn knew that if Niall hadn't had such potential, the situation would be very different. He took out his notepad and pen.

'I do need to check whether you have had any alcohol or drug problems in the past or a history of mental health problems.'

Niall shook his head emphatically. 'You've no need to worry on that score, Mr McCarthy. I just drank a wee bit too much and then panic set in when the police caught up with me.' He shook his head in irritation with himself. 'I'm really glad of the support and I'll not let you down again, yer can be sure of that.'

Finn studied the pale, young man and decided that he was completely sincere.

'I certainly hope so, because not many trainers would stand by you in these circumstances, I can tell you that. You have been lucky enough to be given another opportunity and it's up to you to make the most of it.'

Niall looked suitably contrite. 'I will, I will.'

'Well, best get back to work then,' added Seamus. Niall duly obliged.

Finn waited until Niall had left the room. 'I can't thank you enough for your support. I'll keep a close eye on him too. I know the BHA will consider his licence, but he'll likely be able to keep it until sentencing. Then it could be suspended for a period, but he should still be able to ride for now, so that's something. But if you have any concerns, however small, get back to me and I'll come straight down, I'm here often enough as it is.'

That was certainly true. Finn occasionally rode out for the Ryans, just to keep his hand in, so he was around often enough.

'Whilst I'm here, I suppose I ought to see Lottie. How is she doing?'

Lottie Henderson was another conditional who had been riding for the Ryans for over a year now.

Rosie and Seamus exchanged a look.

'Well, she's another one who needs support. She's been a bit down of late, she's not riding her finishes as well as she can. I'm not sure what's wrong,' added Rosie.

'Probably boyfriend problems if you ask me,' muttered Seamus. 'I've had to tell her off for being on her phone twice already this week. And her riding's gone downhill too.'

Finn took this in. Lottie was a complex girl, rather anxious and private, he knew she was reserved and even prickly at times.

'I've tried to talk to her, but she won't say what's bothering her,' Rosie explained. 'She might talk to you though.'

Finn thought this was highly unlikely, but he knew that Harriet has spoken to her about her diet and riding weight, not that she struggled as she was a petite girl, but she'd had an eating disorder as a youngster. He wondered if that had reared its head again. In times of stress, this was possible.

'Right, I'll catch her on the way out.'

They chatted about the prospects for the season. The Ryans had some good horses and each year they had more winners than previously, so things were looking positive. They had a new mare called Sweet Pea who had done very well point to pointing in Ireland and was ready to go hurdling.

'She's misnamed though,' added Seamus. 'She's really fractious and will nip and kick but we've settled her in the corner stable in the yard where she can see everything that's going on and that seems to have helped. We just warn everyone to be careful around her.'

Finn recognised the name and made a mental note to check the mare out. Their best horse was a bay called Cardinal Sin and Seamus was optimistic about his prospects for the season.

'I'll put Tom Kennedy up for the ride at Wetherby, I need someone more experienced than either Lottie or Niall. It's a good class of race and I don't want any hiccups. Both Niall and Lottie have rides anyway, Lottie's on Clementine and Niall's on Foxtrot Bravo. They ride them at home whereas Cardinal Sin can be a bit tricky, although Lottie does ride him from time to time. Tom's been here riding out a bit and has got to know him. He's in a relationship with Clare, you remember her?'

Finn certainly did. Clare Hudson was a well thought of stable lass, who had disclosed to him and Harriet that she had been seriously sexually assaulted by a jockey Finn previously mentored. The same man had gone on to assault another female jockey and was safely locked up now. Finn was pleased that things were going well for her and that she had recovered enough to start a relationship. He knew Tom Kennedy slightly but had formed the impression that he was a decent jockey and human being, so hopefully he would be able to offer emotional support to Clare too.

'OK.' Finn could understand why Seamus wanted a more experienced jockey on board. Lottie had ridden the gelding in a few earlier races but a step up in class did require a more experienced rider, especially as the gelding could be temperamental but was talented enough to win with the right handling. The trouble was he wasn't sure that Lottie would see it like that. Maybe that was behind her mood change?

'Does she have plenty of rides?'

'Oh yes, she had a fair number. After Wetherby, she has several rides at Uttoxeter.'

Finn wrote this down, said his goodbyes and called in the yard to find Lottie. She was cleaning tack and liberally covering the leather with neatsfoot oil. She was a slight woman with an anxious expression and a self deprecating manner.

'How's it going?'

47

'Well. How about you?'

'Good. I just called to see Seamus. He tells me you have a few rides coming up. How are you feeling about them.'

'OK. I'm riding Clementine and I've some rides at Uttoxeter. Eldorado is one.'

Eldorado, Finn knew, was something of a tricky ride and could run like the wind or refuse to jump anything as the mood took him.

'OK. Are you feeling confident?'

Lottie flushed. 'I suppose.' She didn't look very convinced though.

'Shall I pop down to the gallops and catch up with you for some preparation before then?'

Lottie smiled. 'Yes, that would be good.'

'And how are you feeling about Niall's escapades?' Finn knew she had been one of the conditionals in the car with Niall and would probably have strong views about his behaviour. He noticed that she looked round to make sure he wasn't in the immediate vicinity.

'God, what an idiot! He just wouldn't listen when we told him to stop, the prat. Thank God the police used that stinger.'

'Hmm. Were you scared?'

'A bit, I suppose, but all's well that ends well.'

Finn studied her. 'It was such a strange thing to do though. Is there anything else I should know about the incident?'

For a split second a strange expression flitted over Lottie's face. She paused, and then shook her head.

'No. Like what?'

Finn gave her an appraising look. 'I don't know, but if I'm to help Niall, then I need to know everything about him, warts and all.'

Lottie continued to pour neatsfoot oil onto her cloth and then liberally rubbed it into the leather bridle.

'Nah, apart from him having a colossal ego, of course, there's nothing else.'

Finn paused waiting for her to say more but when she didn't, he pushed on to talk about more neutral matters.

'And have you heard from Maura?'

Finn knew she was close to the Irish conditional, who had decided to continue her riding career at a stable in Ireland because she was so

48

homesick. Perhaps, Lottie was just missing her friend and ally and that accounted for her change in mood.

'Oh, yes, She's grand. Doing well, full of it and pleased to be back home.'

'Well, there's Clare here, of course and I've some new females on my list so I'll introduce you and invite you to a session.' Finn studied her. 'It's still hard for female jockeys, I get it, and I'm here to help. Don't forget that.'

Lottie smiled but her heart didn't seem to be quite in it. He decided to try again.

'Only Rosie said you'd been a bit quiet…?'

Lottie shook her head. 'Can't think why she said that, I'm fine, I really am.'

Finn nodded but he was not entirely convinced. 'Right. OK. I'll make tracks and see you either tomorrow or Wednesday then.'

As he was leaving, he made his way to the corner stable where he spotted the dark bay mare, her neck over the door with her ears flat back whilst trying to bite a staff member, Clare, who was about to enter the stable with a water bucket.

'Do you need a hand?'

Clare turned round and nodded. 'Hi, Finn. It's the new mare, Sweet Pea. She's a bit stroppy. '

In no time Finn picked up the horse's headcollar, which was hung on a hook outside the stable, and buckled it on her in one deft movement, ignoring the mare putting her ears flat back and baring her teeth at him. He grasped the headcollar firmly whilst Clare opened the stable door, and he positioned the horse away from the door to allow Clare to come in with the bucket.

'Get back, you.' Fortunately, the horse stood still but not before flattening her ears back and trying to take a chunk out of Finn's arm. She also lifted her rear leg ominously.

Clare was quick, deposited the water then exited and closed the door. Finn thought about removing the headcollar but decided against it.

'I hear she's pretty talented but she's clearly a bit of a diva. How about leaving her headcollar on? If she catches it on anything it will give as it's leather and it might make life easier.' Headcollars were usually removed whilst horses were in the stable because they could get them caught on

49

door hinges or crevices with serious results, but the more expensive leather ones would break which solved the problem to some degree and it would make Clare's life a bit easier if the headgear was left on so she could grab the horse more easily.

'Good idea. She has real scope though and jumps like a stag, otherwise we wouldn't put up with her antics. She'll kick out too but is calmer when she can see the comings and goings in the yard, which is why she's in the corner stable with a full view of the drive.'

Finn looked the mare over. 'Hmm. Seamus said. She's got pretty good hindquarters too.'

Clare laughed. 'All the better for kicking you with! Still, we'll work her out in time, I'm sure. She's just a bit quirky. She's a bit better with men, she's alright with Niall, to be honest. Still, there's no accounting for taste!'

'Well, that's one way of putting it!'

He studied Clare. She had a healthy bloom and looked so much better than she had just a few months ago. The girl had been well supported by Seamus and Rosie. He was glad that she was on her own and decided it would be a good time to ask her what she thought about Niall's antics, as she had also been in the car on the evening when he was stopped by the police.

'I heard that you were in the car with Niall when he was stopped, along with Lottie. It must have been terrifying.'

Clare tossed her head, her blonde ponytail bobbing up and down as she did so. 'That's certainly one way of looking at it. The moron!'

'Did anything else happen that night, only it seems such a strange thing to do, to go speeding off like that?'

Clare shook her head again. 'No, he's just young and a bit daft.'

Finn paused waiting for her to say more, but she didn't volunteer anything further.

'Ah well. I think the police will need to speak to you both anyway.'

Clare frowned. 'Will they? OK then.'

'And how are you generally, after, you know…?' He couldn't bring himself to actually say what had happened, it was so distressing for the poor girl.

Clare looked away and shrugged. 'Ah, I'm fine. I just need to get on wi' things now. I talk to Rosie and Lottie, so it's all good.'

50

'And I heard about you and Tom. He's a good lad, I hear, so I'm pleased for you, but listen if you did need to speak to someone, I do have some really good contacts.'

Clare gave him a radiant smile. 'Thanks, but I don't need anything, not now. I'm trying to forget all of that. Anyway. I'd best get going. I've water buckets to fill up.'

As Finn drove home, he pondered on how Lottie had reacted. She had said all the right things, but her body language conveyed something completely different. He sometimes felt out of his depth with female conditionals and wondered if he could ask Harriet to have a word with her instead. She was hardly likely to talk to him about boyfriend problems, but she might just talk to a woman. Harriet seemed to have the knack of getting people to relax, especially youngsters. He remembered that she would be at Wetherby and wondered if he could engineer a conversation between the pair. And Clare, well she had seemed OK but more worried about talking to the police than anything else. Maybe it reminded her of her recent experience when she had to be interviewed about being raped. At least she had the support of Rosie and Seamus, and now Tom and he knew from personal experience how much that mattered. His thoughts turned to Niall Byrne. Maybe he was overthinking things and Niall had just acted rashly and that was all there was to it? Certainly, neither Lottie nor Clare had said that anything else was going on. Then his phone beeped, signalling that he had received a message.

Can I buy you lunch to thank you for looking after Niall? How about tomorrow in York? The Shambles Café, 12. Theresa.

Finn felt his spirits lift as he shook off his doubts. It was the start of the National Hunt season, and he was going to see the very attractive Theresa again. Things were certainly looking up.

They met in The Shambles Café in central York the next day. He had been worried about the location thinking it would be crammed with tourists. It was reasonably busy; there were the usual groups of school children clutching clipboards and Americans with cameras, but Christmas was still far enough away for him to be able to walk freely through York without dodging people. The Shambles was one of York's most famous streets. It was a

51

cobbled, narrow road with ancient black and white Tudor houses either side, leaning towards each other as though deep in conversation with a friend. He felt his mood lift. He had dressed smartly but still felt an unexpected frisson of nerves.

The café was chic but not too trendy and had a decent lunch menu, alongside every conceivable type of coffee or tea. Theresa was already there, looking stunning in jeans, a multicoloured jumper and a reefer jacket. Her dark hair hung loose, and her face shone with vitality. They ordered; a lasagne for Finn and a baked potato with roasted vegetables, cheese and ham for Theresa. She gave him a dazzling smile.

'I'm so glad you could make it. I just wanted to thank you for helping Niall that night. He's been a worry to us and sure, he's an eejit, but he has such talent he really does. He's just young, that's all.'

Theresa went on to explain about problems in the family, their father's ill health and subsequent death, which left her mother having to rear her brood single handedly.

'Sure, it took a terrible toll on mammie, so it did. It was after I'd left home and Niall got into a bad crowd, thought himself the man of the house and got into bother. Mammie asked me to take care of him and he lived with me before moving to the Ryans.' She put up her hand as though stopping traffic. 'The Ryans know all about it, I've told them the bare bones so to speak, but if you could just help him through this difficult time, it would mean the world to us.'

Finn nodded, taking in Theresa's fine dark eyes and her charming accent. He was keen to put her at ease.

'Listen, I've already spoken to the Ryans and they want to keep Niall. He's a good rider who shows real promise. And, of course, I will do everything in my power to support him, but he must play his part and keep his nose clean. Obviously, he is facing a suspended prison sentence at best, and it could be worse.' Finn wasn't one to dodge the truth.

Theresa's eyes filled with tears. 'I know. He'll have to face the consequences. He's not a bad lad. Impulsive at times.' She pulled out a handkerchief and wiped her eyes. Finn felt unaccountably angry with Niall at the suffering he was causing his sister.

'Sometimes, being impulsive can be an advantage, certainly in riding where a jockey might need to find a gap and take his chances. My friend, Nat Wilson, who I'm sure you've heard of, would certainly be described as impulsive, that is for sure, and it didn't do him any harm. But Niall needs to learn to channel it.'

Theresa smiled, pleased that he could see her brother's potential. The conversation moved on to careers, Theresa was gratifyingly aware of Finn's success, and she told him about her work as an assistant head teacher at a local comprehensive.

'I love the kids, but not the paperwork and the Ofsted inspections though.'

They spoke about their families, favourite films and hobbies. Finn found himself intrigued by Theresa's charm, loyalty to her brother and delicate, good looks.

The hours slipped by and suddenly Finn glanced at his watch.

'Christ, I'd better get going.' Theresa insisted on paying which Finn felt most uncomfortable about.

'You can pay next time,' she added, smiling. Finn didn't need to be asked twice and a further date was arranged for later in the week. It was raining as Finn left and he walked the length of The Shambles and beyond to the car park barely noticing, as his brain was fizzing with endorphins and the sheer thrill of a further date with a lovely woman.

Chapter 7

On the day of Wetherby Races, a weekday, Finn picked Hattie up from her parents and they drove there, full of anticipation. She had some lieu time which she decided to take. Her job was partly funded by the BHA to account for her working for them from time to time regarding integrity issues, but finding a missing person for someone privately, had to be something she and Finn did in their own time. Today she had dressed in a long teal coloured woollen dress, low brown leather boots and a battered leather jacket which she'd picked up from Vinted. Her auburn hair was in a casual side bun, and she had natural makeup and her usual Glossier perfume.

Hattie had news. 'I spoke to my Uncle Sebastian, just hypothetically. He said that Moss's paintings are very collectable and worth a great deal, especially when I told him about the subject matter. Mind you, it's been valued by Christian Gerrard, so we don't need to bother really, it's just that Uncle Sebastian is a real expert.'

'OK. Well, that's good to know.'

Hattie noticed that Finn looked particularly well today and seemed in very good spirits.

'What's going on with you? You look like the cat that got the cream.'

Finn gave a mock frown. 'Oh, nothing. Did I tell you that I had lunch with Niall's sister, Theresa, the other day? She was worried about her brother and wanted to thank me for helping him. He's had a bad background with his dad dying young, apparently and he got into bad company.'

Harriet knew him well enough to know that he liked Theresa and every time he mentioned her, his face sort of lit up.

'Is she the good looking one you mentioned?'

Finn gave her a sharp look. 'Well, she is very attractive as it happens, but I'd still support Niall as you know, because he's on my caseload, of course.'

Harriet grinned but decided that on balance that was probably true. He really was the most decent, upstanding man, aside from Gabriel, of course.

'Anyway, how are things going with Gabriel?'

Harriet feigned casualness. 'Oh, fine.'

Finn overtook a lorry and then slipped back into the left hand lane. Hattie sat back and relaxed, she enjoyed being driven by him in his silver Audi, he exuded confidence and skill. A bit like he was with horses.

'Anyway, any joy on tracing Ross Maclaren or Admiral Jervis?'

'Hmm. The horse appears to have been sold on, but I'm not convinced by that. I think this whole thing might be more complicated than I thought, actually.'

Harriet was too polite to say, 'I told you so' and to her surprise she was intrigued about the missing author and the painting of Red Navajo and just as keen to find them.

As the journey continued, they chatted about the prospects for the day. Tristan Davies was riding Kinder Scout, Christian Gerrard's horse, in the main race of the meeting. Harriet hoped that Poppy, Tristan's girlfriend would be there as they had met previously and got on like a house on fire, but she was working apparently. The Ryans had brought a lorry load of horses. They had Cardinal Sin who was going to be ridden by Tom Kennedy in the main race. He was an experienced jockey and if anyone could get the best out of the horse, he could. They had also brought a first time hurdler, Foxtrot Bravo who was running in a later race and Clementine, who Lottie was riding in the last. Finn was relishing the thought of seeing his conditionals ride. Hattie's mind drifted off imagining how they might find Maclaren. Perhaps, they'd have to contact his publishers on some pretext or other? She could pretend to be a journalist, except that he probably knew all the literary press. She relished the chance to meet Ross Maclaren himself, though. Her father loved his books and she had picked one up the other day and had started to read it and was surprised that so far, she was totally absorbed in it even though she didn't usually read thrillers.

'Should be a good day. I really want to see if you could have a word with Lottie again.'

Hattie dragged her mind back to the present. 'Sure. Is she struggling with her eating, do you think?'

Finn shrugged. 'No, I don't think so, but there's something on her mind. Rosie said she's been quiet and preoccupied. It could be nothing, but I think she might talk to you.' Finn drove into the racecourse. 'Tell you what Hattie, this fog has really come down in the last half hour.'

Hattie looked doubtfully about her, seeing the more distant cars in the park shrouded in mist.

'Heck, will they cancel the races? I mean this is really bad, we won't be able to see a ruddy thing.'

Finn grinned. 'Nah, as long as the horses can get round safely, it'll go ahead. I don't think they'd cancel so late in the day. All the riders will know to be a bit more careful than usual and not get too close to each other.'

The racecourse had been one of the few in Yorkshire to host just National Hunt races but in 2014 it ran flat races too. It was a welcoming Yorkshire course, a left-handed galloping oval of about a mile and a half. There were six flights of hurdles in one circuit, with a short, steep run in. It was the scene of many of Finn's wins, Harriet knew, so he was in a buoyant mood. As they neared the course, they passed the signs to Wetherby Young Offenders' Institute which was just opposite the racecourse, though she could barely read the signs in the fog. How strange to have two institutions so close to one another but at totally different ends of the spectrum, racing was filled with affluent, moneyed individuals, and the Young Offenders' Institute, which housed deprived, disturbed and probably very frightened young boys. The sign made Harriet think about Niall Byrne, and his future although she knew as he was older, he was likely to go to prison, if the verdict went the wrong way, not a YOI. She wondered what on earth had caused the young conditional to behave so irrationally. Driving off after being stopped was bound to make things a whole lot worse, surely, he must have known that? She pondered on the facts, but it still didn't make any sense to her. Was there more to it? Yet Finn seemed satisfied that there wasn't, so who was she to argue.

At the box, which overlooked the course, Christian was waiting to greet his guests. Jeremy Trentham was also there, as the trainer of several horses on the card. Christian introduced his glamorous blonde wife, Sian, who was about fifteen years his junior, more Finn's age. She was dressed in

56

a tight, knitted grey dress, decorated with tiny pearls and wore high heeled black boots and heavy perfume. Hattie saw her and was glad she'd made an effort with her own appearance.

'So glad you made it on this murky day. Come and have a drink and meet everyone.' Christian exuded urbane charm and confidence, dressed in a tweed jacket in muted colours, waistcoat and brown brogues, every inch the well dressed racegoer. Harriet noticed that he remembered everything about them as he introduced them to various people, and she felt flattered. Everyone in racing always remembered Finn because of his prowess as a jockey, but it was unusual that people remembered her role. It was impossible not to feel welcomed.

'Beautiful auburn hair, darling,' said Sian to Hattie, as she reached out to touch her curls, 'and it's natural, too. Here, have a drink,' she took Hattie's arm, adding quietly. 'Don't mind me. I used to be a hairdresser, before I met Christian and began living the dream. Do help yourself to food.' She handed Hattie a glass of champagne and a plate before rushing off on six inch heels to greet some new arrivals.

Hattie smiled, brain whirling. Living the dream. Presumably, she was referring to her husband's wealthy lifestyle. Finn was talking to a couple and Hattie took a few minutes to scan the room. She spotted a young woman who looked to be in her late teens or twenties. She wore a black dress, fishnet tights, big clumpy boots and lots of punk style makeup, reminding Hattie of the Goths she'd seen when she'd visited Whitby one Halloween with her brothers. She also radiated tension and looked completely out of place. Sensing the girl's unease Hattie made her way over and introduced herself.

The girl rolled her eyes. 'I'm Pandora. You met my stepmother, I see?'

Hattie nodded. 'Yes. Are you looking forward to watching the races?'

Pandora smiled. Hattie noticed that she had two nose rings and also one on her lip and eyebrow and was quite pretty, beneath the extreme black, pink and silver striped makeup, piercings and black fingernails.

'You mean I don't look like the usual racing type? Nah, I'm only here to try to photograph and draw some horses. I'm an art student, see?'

They were interrupted by Christian. 'I see you've met my rebellious daughter. I had to explain who she was as I think the people on the gate were considering turning her away in that get up. Luckily her black coat covered the worst of it.'

Pandora reddened and Hattie felt irritated on her behalf at her father's comments. Sarcastic sod.

'I love the look, it suits you,' she told Pandora. The girl smiled gratefully.

Christian waved the comment aside. 'So, Hattie, I meant what I said about you and Finn coming to The Stagecoach opening. It's had an extensive refurb and opens soon. There's a spa, gym and swimming pool and a new wedding barn in the grounds. If you ever want to avail yourself of the facilities just contact me and I'll do you a very good discount. And we've got a great competition where one lucky winner wins the wedding of their dreams, absolutely free. It might come in handy.' He waggled his eyebrows. 'For you and Finn...'

Harriet blushed when she realised his meaning and tried to laugh it off.

'No, no, we're just good friends and have got to know one another because we work with jockeys. But I do have some friends who are planning a wedding, so I shall send them your way. And I love a good spa, of course.' She'd mention it to Daisy though who she knew was looking for a venue for her wedding to Neil, her showjumper boyfriend. They could at least enter the competition Christian had mentioned. Then Hattie remembered that Christian had said he was an art dealer and wondered what he had made of the Moss painting.

'What were your thoughts on the Gideon Moss painting of Jeremy's? You've seen it, I believe.'

Christian smiled. 'A lovely piece and a rare one, in fact, the only painting of Red Navajo in existence. I would be delighted to show it at my exhibition. It's planned as a part of the opening of The Stagecoach, it's for equine and country art. Jeremy showed me the painting and I gave him some idea of the value. Gideon Moss's paintings are highly collectable now and with the subject matter, well, it will generate huge interest. Listen, you must come to the exhibition, you and Finn and your respective partners, of course. I shall send you some invitations, my dear.' Christian bowed. 'I do hope you enjoy the day but I'm afraid I must mingle.' He dashed off to talk to some newcomers.

Hattie took this in. Christian certainly seemed to think that the painting was valuable, which was interesting. Staff began handing around canapes and Hattie made her way over to where Finn was chatting to Jeremy and a middle aged couple who worked for Christian. The woman, Pam, was explaining what a great boss he was.

'Nothing's too much trouble. But then that's the hotel trade for you, the customer's always right, you have to go that extra mile.' Pam gave a warm smile. 'Isn't that right, Nigel?'

Nigel, a heavy man with a red complexion seemed to agree but stayed quiet. So, thought Hattie, Christian Gerrard is in the hotel trade and is clearly on his second marriage. And has a strained relationship with his daughter. There were several other associates of Gerrard, all well turned out and seemingly expectant of a good day's racing. Some were concerned about the weather though, others less so.

'If it gets any worse, they should cancel. We can barely see the horses,' commented one man.

'Never mind, darling. Nobody really watches the racing anyway,' answered his wife. 'Have another drink.'

There were two races before the main one and the party spent the time in a whirl of betting, drinking, eating and good natured chatter and banter. Finn went off to watch Niall ride Foxtrot Bravo in the second, so Harriet mingled. She caught sight of Jeremy once or twice but there wasn't time to speak to him, as he was dashing about saddling up and making sure the horses were ready. Instead, she watched as Pandora spent her time around the parade ring, photographing horses on her phone and she showed Hattie her sketch book, which had lovely flowing pencil sketches of horses in it. She had kept the fog in the drawings, which gave them a lovely, dreamy quality.

'Those are beautiful. You really have talent there.'

Pandora pouted. 'Dad doesn't think so, he thinks they're too modern. He prefers old fashioned paintings of animals, horses especially.'

Hattie took this in. 'Like Gideon Moss's, you mean?'

The girl flushed. 'Exactly. He even has a few and reckons he's a bit of a Moss expert. He has an encyclopaedic knowledge of who owns what painting. I don't like them, I think they're a bit derivative myself.'

Harriet took this in. Interesting that Christian had some Moss paintings. She supposed that she and Finn were behind the curve on fashion in art. She smiled at the typically dismissive response from a teenager. Derivative, indeed!

'Do you want to be an artist then?'

Pandora shrugged. 'S'pose. Something that earns a lot of money so I can leave home. I don't want to go into the hotel business or swan around all the time on shopping trips like Sian.'

'Don't you get on with your stepmother?'

Pandora snorted. 'No! She's a total bitch.'

Hattie wanted to ask about her mother but was interrupted by Finn telling her and Jeremy that they were off to help prepare the jockey and horse respectively for the next race.

'Gerry King had a fall in the first and has a possible fracture to his wrist, so Tom Kennedy is now riding his mount, Green Marauder, and Niall is riding Cardinal Sin in the big one. I'm just going to give the young chap a pep talk. I'll see you in the stands.' Jeremy smiled before dashing off with Finn. The fog was still swirling over the course and the dampness began to make Hattie's hair frizz. Not being vain, Hattie didn't mind but Sian kept rushing about to get undercover 'to save my hair,' as she told everyone.

Still the fog and mist persisted giving the racecourse a sort of other worldly air. The sound also appeared a little muffled, as if the moisture in the air was dampening down the noise. Hattie was reminded of walking near the coast and encountering a sea fret. Everyone was talking about the weather and speculating whether or not the fixture would be abandoned.

'I think my horse won that one, couldn't quite tell,' joked a punter, grinning after the horses rushed past the winning post.

In fact, it was really the far side of the course that was impossible to see from the stands. The side next to the track was much clearer and although still misty, you could see the horses at the finish quite well. At last, the main race was upon them. Christian and Sian went into the parade ring with Jeremy, Sian held onto her husband's arm and took tiny steps in her unsuitable, skyscraper shoes. The jockeys came out and Tristan went up to

60

take his instructions from Jeremy. Niall was talking to Seamus Ryan in the parade ring.

Finn came to find her, leaning near the rails of the ring.

'Niall seems reasonably confident, so fingers crossed he manages a good performance.'

Finn and Hattie returned to the box balcony where they had a good view, albeit marred by fog. Christian was watching his horse with Jeremy near the course and Sian was nowhere to be seen, probably straightening her hair thought Hattie. The horses reached the start round the other side of the course.

'How the hell will the commentator see well enough to describe the action?'

Finn laughed. 'I think he has a view from a nearer camera, but it's still difficult. Two circuits as well.'

The tannoy whistled into life.

'And they're off, twelve runners round this two and a half mile course for the feature race of the day the Superbet Victory Handicap Chase. And they're all safely over the first ditch with Cardinal Sin and Green Marauder prominent and well ahead of the rest of the field.'

Both strained their eyes trying to spot the horses and follow the action. It made for a strange experience.

'There they are,' cried Hattie as the field swung round the bend to come into the near side of the course. The crowd gave an ironic cheer, thrilled just to see the horses for once.

'Cardinal Sin and Niall Byrne are still in front, several lengths clear with Green Marauder moving up, Houdini is in third and Kinder Scout ridden by Tristan Davies is catching up in fourth ...'

The field raced past the stand, a muted blur of colours, all seeming to move well.

'It's wide open,' said Finn. 'Niall's in a good spot.'

Hattie was always amazed how thrilled Finn was if his charges put in a good performance. He seemed to take their careers very seriously. And she was always aware of how much he missed his race riding days, even

61

several years later. Then the field raced on around the far corner and because of the mist, largely out of sight.

'And the leader Green Marauder meets the water jump first, followed by Cardinal Sin. Oh no! Green Marauder and Cardinal Sin are both down and the rest of the field are having to take evasive action to avoid them...'

Hattie grabbed Finn's arm in alarm. 'Oh God, this bloody fog. Hope they're OK.'

The commentator obviously couldn't see either. 'I'm told that both horses are up and so is Niall Byrne, but Tom Kennedy is still down and being attended to. And Kinder Scout takes it up...'

Finn looked ashen. 'Christ. I hope Niall and Tom are alright. This is the last thing Niall needs, more trouble. Let's go and see what's happening.'

Hattie felt panic and dread gripping her. The images of the next fifteen minutes blocked out all thoughts of the race. They reached the trackside to see Tom Kennedy being carried into an ambulance. Clare, the blonde haired stable girl and his partner, looked deathly pale and went rushing off with him, her expression utterly bleak. Seamus Ryan came out of the crowd towards them.

'Christ, it looks bad, Finn. Tom's not moving at all. The horse fell on him. Rosie's with Cardinal Sin and, he and Niall are alright, so they are, but poor Tom. Clare's gone with him, but honestly, it's awful.' The Irish accent always appeared stronger when emotions were running high, thought Hattie.

Finn nodded. 'Try not to worry, these things always look worse than they are.'

The words, Hattie knew were automatic, but bad falls like this were what every jockey dreaded.

Seamus turned to face Finn. 'Listen, I don't know what happened but from what I saw it looked like young Byrne on Cardy barged into Green Marauder. I couldn't swear to it, but I think there'll be an inquiry.' He shrugged. 'But the eejits won't be able to see anything on the video because of the fog, so it'll be Kennedy's word against Niall's. Those two were so far ahead, no one else would have seen much either.'

And with Kennedy unconscious, any inquiry was not going to get very far, thought Hattie.

Just then they spotted the muddy face of Niall Byrne hobbling along to the weighing room. He held up his hand to silence Finn.

'I dunno what happened, I just went for a gap. I don't think I did anything wrong. I hope Tom's alright. Supposing the stewards want to speak to me?'

Finn smiled ruefully. 'All you can do is tell the truth. Let me know if you need any help.'

As he disappeared to the weighing room, Finn said quietly, 'I mean he's going to be banned soon enough anyway, but if he gets done for careless riding as well…'

Hattie knew that Niall was a very talented young man who Finn had a lot of time for. But he also seemed to be strangely impulsive at times.

'Let's wait and see, shall we? Running in this weather was asking for trouble, as far as I can see. Now shall we have a quiet drink away from the box. I could do with a coffee. I don't know about you…'

Finn nodded and they made their way to the Owners and Trainers bar and Hattie ordered them both a flat white. They were sipping their drinks, when Rosie appeared looking frazzled.

'Oh God, now Lottie's been sick. I'm not sure she should ride but she still wants to. Can you talk to her? She's just about to go into the changing room.'

Finn and Harriet dashed off and came across an ashen faced Lottie just as she was about to get changed.

'Are you OK, Lottie? Rosie said you were sick.' Finn was concerned. 'If you have a bug then maybe you ought not to ride.'

Harriet noticed that the girl looked pale, and her complexion was strangely waxy.

'Do you have a temperature, Lottie?' Harriet pressed her hand against her forehead. 'Hmm. Maybe not, you seem OK.'

Lottie nodded. 'I'm fine. I can still ride, I must have eaten something but now I've been sick, I should be fine.'

Harriet noticed that Lottie was staring at someone, her face pinched. She swallowed hard and looked primed for action, like she might just run off. She appeared full of adrenalin and ready for flight. The girl was gazing at someone as he made his way across to the parade ring, her body rigid with tension. Harriet was surprised to see it was Niall Byrne.

63

'Well, if you're OK, then you're good to go.' Finn touched her arm. 'Good luck. Remember what we talked about.'

They both watched as Lottie went off to get changed.

Finn frowned. 'Listen, do you think Lottie made herself feel sick, is it to do with her eating disorder?' he asked in a low voice.

Harriet shrugged. 'I don't know, I don't think so. She just seemed scared to me. I think she's afraid of Niall.'

Finn shook his head. 'Really? I should think it might be the other way round. Lottie can be quite prickly remember, and she might be miffed because Niall got the ride on Cardinal Sin, and she missed out.'

'Hmm.' Harriet wasn't convinced. She knew fear when she saw it.

Finn looked confused. 'And she's ridden Clementine before in public. Maybe it's just nerves and she's upset after seeing Tom's fall. She is a very sensitive girl.'

Christian approached smiling. 'Shocking fall, that. Still, these things happen. There's no steward's inquiry, so I suppose that's that. Anyway, Kinder Scout and Tristan came through to win. So, you must come back with me to the box and pop open another bottle of champers.'

Finn shook his head. 'I think we'd better go and find the Ryans and Niall and find out how Tom is doing,' replied Finn pointedly.

'Of course, of course. How insensitive of me. I'll let you both get on.'

They found Rosie back at the stables checking Cardinal Sin out. Niall was with them looking contrite.

'I think I must have clipped Green Marauder as Cardy has lost a front shoe. Niall looked down. 'I might have got a bit close, but I was going for a gap and couldn't rightly see...'

Finn nodded. 'Well, there's no inquiry, so that's something. Is there any news on Tom?'

Rosie shook her head. 'Seamus rang. They're waiting to hear how he is. I just hope he'll be OK.'

'I think it looked worse than it probably was,' added Finn. It was the sort of thing everyone said, but no one really believed.

The fog didn't lift for Lottie's race, but they watched as the conditional came in sixth out of a field of eight.

Finn frowned. 'Lottie's heart didn't seem in it today,' was his verdict.

Then Niall rode in the fifth on Foxtrot Bravo and managed a fourth. Finn looked thoughtful.

'Come on let's go, shall we?' They said their goodbyes and Finn drove them home. They were both in a sombre mood and did not speak much on the journey back to Walton. Finn concentrated on driving in the still murky conditions and Hattie tried to work out what the heck was going on with Lottie. And Niall. She was convinced that Lottie was scared of Niall, but why? She was sure she hadn't imagined the look on the girl's face, had she?

'Do you think there's something more to Niall's driving offence? I mean, he can act without thinking, look at his ride on Cardinal Sin today.'

'Hmm. I don't think so. He can be reckless, but you need to take your chances to make it in racing. Nat could easily be described as impulsive, even I could be described like that. Besides, the accident today could have happened to anyone, it was just one of those things. I really think Niall could do very well, he has the killer instinct that you need to win.'

Nat Wilson was the six times champion jockey and a mutual friend. In fact, he was Finn's best friend despite them falling out when Nat ran off with Finn's fiancée, Livvy Jordan. It was a fair assessment though. Nat certainly took his chances and could even be described as reckless, to Harriet's way of thinking, and even Finn too, from time to time.

'I'm probably overthinking things. I didn't get to talk to Lottie today with all the drama, but I'll try again.' She suddenly thought of something. 'I spoke to Christian Gerrard about the Moss painting, and he thinks it's very valuable. Pandora, his daughter, said he's something of an expert on Gideon Moss paintings and even owns a few.'

'Hmm. I'll mention it to Trentham. He might need to add to his home insurance.'

Harriet nodded. 'Well, that house is chock full of antiques.'

'It certainly is. It would be awful if the painting was stolen.' Finn frowned. 'We don't seem to be any further on in finding Admiral Jervis or Ross Maclaren. I've been checking the racing entries and Admiral is not listed to race anytime soon. And of course, he may have sold the horse, but he'd be a damned fool if he has. I've scoured the internet for news of Maclaren and he's rumoured to be holed up writing his latest novel, but I've no idea where.'

'Hmm. I suppose he's married, in which case we could go and see his wife?'

'Saying what? It would have to be quite compelling if she were to give up her husband's whereabouts to total strangers, besides we don't have an address.'

Harriet ran her fingers through her hair. 'I bet we can find one. Jeremy will know. If you can get the address, I'll see what I can do. I might be able to get an in.'

Finn raised his eyebrow and laughed. 'Really? I'll be impressed if you can. Really impressed.'

Harriet found herself relishing the challenge. 'I will. I bet you any money, I can think of an angle.'

Finn raised his eyebrows. 'OK. You're on.'

His scepticism nettled her and made her all the more determined to prove him wrong. It was a strange day and Harriet found herself puzzling over everything that had happened with no real conclusion. She vowed to speak to Lottie at some point. Finn had seemed unconcerned, but then he knew both conditionals better than she did, she supposed. There were also some strange undercurrents that she had picked up between Christian Gerrard and his family, not to mention the fact that Christian owned a few of Gideon Moss's paintings. Then she worried about Niall's presentation and Tom Kennedy's fall, and now she had committed herself to coming up with a plausible reason to visit Ross Maclaren's wife. Her thoughts were interrupted by her phone beeping, indicating that she'd received some messages. They were from Gabriel Taverner suggesting a night out. She felt distracted and pleased and was immediately catapulted into a frenzy of what to wear and how to act, as the tensions of the day melted away, like snow in sunlight.

Chapter 8

Finn brooded on the events at Wetherby and rang Seamus later to see if there was any news about Tom Kennedy. Seamus sounded very stressed,

'Sure, I've just rung. He's been put into an induced coma, and there's possible bruising to his spine. Mary, mother of God, he might be paralysed, Finn.' Seamus sighed heavily. 'Either way, he'll be off for a long time, and he might not gain full mobility. Seems he had a fall a month or so ago and the doctors might have missed a lesion on his spine.'

Finn took this in. 'Christ. How's Niall taken it?'

'Not well as you might imagine.'

'And Clare?'

'She's in a state and has gone back to the hospital. She's keeping us updated but she's dreadfully worried.'

'Of course. I'll pop in later in the week and see how things are going. Do we know when Niall's back in court?'

'The police have bailed him and are still investigating. His solicitor says it might not go to court until January, mind, but at least he can drive and ride until then. And someone was round here shooting his mouth off at him, one of yer lads. Jamie Doyle, he's at Vince Hunt's place.'

Finn had recently been reading about the lad who had just been assigned to him and had arranged to see him later in the week.

'What was his beef with Niall?'

Seamus paused. 'I don't rightly know. He was talking to Lottie and then started yelling at Niall. Maybe he blames him for what happened to Tom? Yer know how word gets round in a small place like Walton. Did Tristan Davies see anything, he was the only one who would have seen what really happened, I reckon.'

Finn considered this. 'I've got to pop to Jeremy's, so I'll ask him. Anyway, I'm off to see Vince Hunt too, so I'll see Jamie and tell him to stop being a pain. No one saw what happened, so from where I'm standing, sadly it's just one of those things, especially if a doctor made a mistake in the past. Maybe he shouldn't have been riding at all?'

'Right enough, Finn.'

They all knew that riding in National Hunt races was one of the most dangerous sports known to man. Falls were inevitable and could happen at any time, at least once every 14 rides according to statisticians who studied such things. Most falls were not serious but if the horse fell onto you, then that was an entirely different matter. Still, it was very unfortunate for Niall, who already had the drink driving incident to contend with. Obviously, that was self inflicted and an error of judgement but the incident with Tom, Finn was not so sure. The lad could have simply been trying too hard to make the most of his chances and redeem himself. Finn arranged to visit later in the week.

Then he rang Freddie Mercer and Jeremy Trentham to arrange a meeting between the pair for later that afternoon. He arrived at the yard and was surprised to see that the lad was accompanied by an older woman. He wondered who she was. He soon found out.

'Penny Mercer, Mr McCarthy and this is my son Freddie.' Penny held out her hand and smiled warmly. She had highlighted blonde, wavy hair, and was wearing jeans and a stripey shirt with the collar turned up. She had an open face and the bluest eyes he had ever seen. Her makeup was discreet and her fingernails manicured and polished.

'Nice to meet you. I don't believe we've ever met,' replied Finn.

'No, I don't think we did, but I remember you from your battles with Nat Wilson on the track.'

Finn had to admit it was surprising but gratifying that people still remembered their friendship and rivalry on the racecourse. He was still best mates with Nat, but their friendship had been decidedly strained after what had happened with Livvy. His best friend running off with his fiancée had been hard to take. Still, it was a long time ago, and he and Nat had made up now. He had had to retire following a bad injury and Nat was still going strong and vying for yet another Championship after narrowly missing out last year. Finn had had some difficult times and he felt that Nat had wandered off into the sunset with the girl, the career and everything else, then Tony Murphy had contacted him and offered him a job and things started to look up for him. Now, he was doing well, he was glad to have both

Livvy and Nat back in his life and with a bit of luck, he might even have a romance himself. Theresa popped unbidden into his mind, as she had on many occasions since he had met her. He was seeing her later and felt a heady mixture of delight tempered with nerves. With some difficulty, he dragged himself back to the present situation.

Jeremy introduced himself and they went into the house. Laura came in with a tea tray and a large coffee and walnut cake. Freddie was a good looking, slight young man, who bore a strong resemblance to his father. Still, he couldn't hold that against him.

He smiled apologetically. 'Sorry, Mum had to come along. I haven't passed my driving test yet, so she has to take me everywhere.'

Penny's gaze roved around the room taking everything in, her eyes resting on the Gabriel Moss painting with particular interest. 'I'm happy to wait in the car if that would help. You see, Freddie's test was cancelled and until then it's down to me to transport him, but I presume he will be able to find lodgings in Walton when he starts?'

Jeremy smiled. 'Of course, we have lots of providers locally, but we also have a small hostel, so you can live there if you like. We'll show you around after we've done the paperwork and let Finn explain about the coaching scheme.'

Penny's eyes returned to the Gideon Moss painting. 'A lovely composition, Gideon Moss if I'm not mistaken. Christian said you had one. It's wonderful.'

'I didn't know you knew Christian, but I suppose you're both interested in art, so I shouldn't be surprised,' added Finn.

Penny inclined her head. 'I do the odd bit of art restoration work for him as well as my own commissions.'

There was another matter that Finn wanted to discuss, and he decided to be blunt. He gave Freddie a direct look.

'You know if you wanted another coach, I'd quite understand after what happened. I'm sorry about Henry, your father, and I'd like to work with you, but I'd understand if you changed your mind.' Finn wanted to be clear about the situation from the outset and felt it would be helpful to go through the sensitive stuff first.

Freddie shook his head. 'Of course, I know all about it, Mum has been very frank and honest. Neither of us see my dad, we are both appalled

69

about what happened and I am just so thrilled to be given the chance to work with you both. Mum is divorcing Dad, but things are not quite finalised. The BHA have been amazing, considering the situation. I love riding, being a jockey is the only thing I've ever wanted to do. I won't let you down, Mr Trentham and I'm thrilled to be working with someone as successful as yourself, Mr McCarthy.'

'Please call me Finn. I'm pleased that you have said you're not having contact with your dad because as you know with him being warned off, you can't afford to slip up. It's a huge ask and you might not want to put yourself through this. Are you prepared to sign a contract to that effect?'

Freddie nodded. 'Absolutely.'

Finn pulled out the contract from his file and passed a pen over to Freddie who signed the relevant parts with a flourish. Jeremy was watching him closely and appeared to be satisfied.

'Of course, if there's any breaches then we will have no option but to terminate your position.'

'Of course. The BHA made that clear to us.'

Penny tucked into a slice of cake and sipped her tea. 'It's brilliant news and we're so pleased that Mr Trentham has agreed to take him on.' She looked around. 'You have such a good reputation.'

Jeremy smiled. 'Do call me Jeremy. We had a conditional who went back to Ireland, so we were short of someone, and Finn told me about your riding and your career in eventing. You have done really well, and it seems to me that the disciplines of dressage, showjumping, and cross country would transfer very well to racing.'

Freddie looked animated and seemed flattered that both men had researched his progress to date. 'I think so too. I do love eventing and was starting to move up to 3 star events but I especially love the cross country bits, I'm not as keen on dressage, so I decided to give race riding a go, especially since I don't think I'm going to grow much more. I always wanted to be a jockey, you see.'

Jeremy seemed pleased. 'I'm sure all that riding experience will really stand you in good stead. What weight are you?'

'About 10 to 10: 4, so that should be fine.'

Finn looked from one to the other. 'Of course, people will soon work out who you are, and memories are long in a small place like Walton,

70

but I'll make sure you're treated fairly. You shouldn't suffer because of the actions of your father. The life of a conditional jockey will be hard work, make no mistake about it. Jeremy runs a tight ship but if you work hard and keep your nose clean then I hope you'll do very well. It will certainly be an excellent opportunity for you. Tristan Davies is his stable jockey and Kyle Devlin is another conditional who should soon be riding out his claim. You'll be able to learn so much from those two.'

Freddie smiled broadly. 'Wow. I'm beyond excited.'

It was hard not to be impressed by the lad's enthusiasm and he did seem really appreciative of the chance he was being given. His easy charm and passion for the sport were infectious. Finn went on to explain about the jockey mentoring programme and the support that was available to conditionals including the role of the PJA.

'I have lots of contacts including a really good dietician, Harriet Lucas, if you need any specialist support and you'll need to attend some sessions on the BHA rules. I will support you with riding, dealing with the press, finances, along with the PJA. Now, that's the paperwork done, so Jeremy will show you round.'

Freddie discussed hours, pay and expenses with Jeremy as Penny drained her cup.

Jeremy rubbed his hands together. 'Right. Are you ready for the guided tour?'

Later when Freddie and his mother had been shown around the place and admired every horse, they appeared more than satisfied and drove off having arranged a start date for Freddie. Jeremy seemed pleased too.

'Splendid, Finn. That went rather well, though I say it myself. He wasn't at all like I expected him to be. Young Freddie seems like a decent enough young fellow. Let's just see if he can make something of himself.'

Finn nodded. He felt slightly worried about Penny and how close she seemed to Freddie. Maybe he was being unfair, and everything would be fine when he'd passed his driving test. He wondered why she hadn't waited outside. Then he remembered what Tony Murphy had said about Penny having to get a job as a cleaner to make ends meet and felt instantly ashamed of himself. Probably, it would be expensive putting the lad through his driving test too, he realised, deciding to cut her some slack.

71

'Yes, I hope so. Listen, did you hear about Tom Kennedy? He's in an induced coma and has spinal injuries, in fact, he had a fall before which could have damaged his spine too. Niall is very upset. Did Tristan notice anything as Kinder Scout was nearest to the two leaders?'

Jeremy scratched his chin. 'Oh, that's awful but no, he hasn't said anything. He was still a little way back, so may have missed the incident in that fog. I will have a word though, in fact he should be around now, if you want to ask him yourself.'

Tristan Davies was a successful jockey who had grown in stature within the sport in recent years and had really established himself as a top jockey. He was a lean, blond haired man whose blue eyes crinkled with pleasure as Finn walked into the yard. Tristan was untacking his ride and another stable lass took over when she saw that Finn wanted to speak to him. After exchanging pleasantries, Finn asked him about the race at Wetherby.

'Great win on Kinder Scout, the other day, though the conditions were dire. What was your take on the fall? Did you see what happened with Green Marauder and Cardinal Sin?'

Tristan shook his head. 'I was behind Houdini and they were both ahead so I had to swerve unexpectedly. I saw it looked nasty as I pulled past, but to be honest with you, I couldn't see what happened between them.' He shrugged. 'I could barely make out Houdini's backside.' He frowned. 'I heard that Tom was in a coma, I hope he recovers, poor sod! How's Niall doing?'

'Well, he's feeling bad, but I suppose that's how it goes in this game.'

Tristan nodded. 'Most of the lads would add some brakes and be more careful in those conditions, but it only takes a bit of inexperience for it all to go wrong. ' He shrugged. 'Still, it could happen to the more experienced riders too. It's just unlucky, I suppose and with what happened with the drink driving, Niall just probably wanted to prove himself.'

Finn nodded and thanked him. Tristan was probably right about Niall. It made sense and Finn felt heartened that others recognised this. It made him feel more sympathetic towards him. The lad would surely come good when he felt that his skills were being recognised. Jockeys were philosophical on the whole and used to dealing with the huge risks that they

72

faced every day. Still, fear ran through them like wildfire when a fellow jockey had a serious fall. They all dreaded the same thing happening to them and it was a stark reminder that none of them were really safe.

They chatted about the forthcoming season and Tristan was hopeful about the prospects for the season including Gerrard's horses.

'It was a blow about Admiral Jervis and all of Maclaren's horses being removed, but especially Admiral. Now he was a really good horse.' He shook his head. 'I'm sure if Jeremy could talk to Maclaren, everything would be resolved, but no one can find him.'

Finn nodded along. He wasn't sure what Jeremy had told him, so made no mention of the fact that he and Hattie had been employed to do just that.

Finn went on to meet Jamie Doyle, a new conditional who had just started at Vince Hunt's place, their last lad having gone to ride in Ireland. Vince was a smaller trainer whose daughter, Daisy, was a close friend of Harriet's. Daisy ran a livery yard and she and her showjumper fiancé, Neil, were down to earth and popular. Vince was in the yard when he arrived.

'Ah Finn. How are you doing? No doubt you have come to see your new lad, Jamie.'

They spoke about Vince's prospects for the season. 'I have Limoncello and Gregorian who should do well. Limoncello is really exciting. I've high hopes for him.'

'How's Jamie shaping up?'

'Not bad. He's too attached to his phone, and I've had to tell him a time or two. He's in the yard.' He looked pointedly at Finn's feet.' The stable was flooded after a leak, so you might need to change your shoes, it's a bit of a quagmire in there.'

Finn opened his boot and pulled out his wellies. 'No problem. Jamie used to ride in point to points in Ireland so he should know his way around a horse, at least.'

The rear stable yard had an inch of water in it and Jamie was brushing it away down the drain. He was a slim, blond young man with a bright smile and a thick Irish accent. Finn explained who he was and his role as Jamie's coach.

'I'm here to advise and support you until you ride out your claim. I can help you with anything really.' He went on to explain the requirements of the mentoring scheme. 'It's a great opportunity for you and I hope you will make the most of everything. It's not an easy life and you'll always hear the truth from me, and I hope you'll always be honest and return the favour.'

Jamie looked serious. 'You can depend upon it, sir'.

Finn looked the young lad up and down. 'I heard you had a bit of an altercation with Niall Byrne the other day. What was that about? Do you know him from home?'

Jamie flushed and looked ill at ease. 'No, I only met him here. I was in the car on the night he was done for drink driving and was just telling 'im off for it, right enough. I don't mind telling you it were frightening.' He shook his head. 'I felt bad for Lottie and Clare who were terrified. And the police have contacted me asking for a statement. I hadn't realised they'd do that. It took me by surprise, I suppose.'

Jamie looked worried. Finn wasn't sure that he was telling the truth and wondered why he would be so worried about a visit from the police. Maybe he was simply trying to impress Lottie by acting all macho and decided that this was quite likely. He thought he'd let it pass.

'Well, I can understand where you're coming from but it's not very sensible to go and shoot your mouth off, is it? Your conduct has to be exemplary, and people will be concerned about employing someone with a temper.' Jamie had the good grace to flush. 'Now I presume you'll be on the gallops at some point, so I'll pop down and see you ride. I can see that you rode a lot in Ireland in point to points, so you can ride a bit?'

'So, I can but there's always more to learn. I'm here to do me best and I won't let you down, you know. It's true I've a bit of a temper, but I'll rein it in, so I will.' The lad grinned, and Finn found himself warming to him.

They arranged to meet later in the week on the communal gallops in Walton and Finn decided to travel home. The concierge, Joseph Mumby, was on duty and looked up. He was keen on racing and always quizzed Finn for information that might give him an edge betting wise.

'Now then Finn, got any more tips for me?'

He was a decent sort of a chap and probably earned a low wage, so what harm would it do to give him the odd tip? He thought for a moment.

'Vince Hunt has just told me that he has a good four year old hurdler, Limoncello, who should do well and should have some decent odds until the handicapper catches up with him, so he might be worth an each way bet.'

Joseph gave him a grin and a wink. 'Thanks, Finn. I'll keep a look out for him.'

Finn settled down, made some calls, one to the hospital regarding Tom Kennedy. He didn't know the man very well as he'd mainly ridden down south before making the move up north, but he felt shaken by the fall and hoped the jockey had improved. Not being able to see what happened, somehow made it all the more mysterious and upsetting. He also wanted to give Niall some good news. However, there was no change in the jockey's condition. Then he showered, ironed a shirt, slapped on some discreet aftershave, and set off to meet Theresa, his anticipation building.

They met in The Golden Fleece on Pavement, one of the oldest pubs in York. Along with many places in the city, it was rumoured to be haunted and dated back to the 16th century. There were said to be at least 15 different ghosts there, including One Eyed Jack who wore a red coat and carried a pistol, but it was also full of atmosphere and one of Finn's favourite haunts. Theresa wafted in leaving behind her a trail of scent, her scarf and hair billowing as she walked. Her fact lit up as soon as she saw him.

'So, how's it going?'

A lot better since you arrived, Finn wanted to say but restrained himself.

They ordered drinks and food and settled down in a quiet corner next to a log fire which was burning nicely. It was now early October, summer had ended and the leaves were turning colour as autumn beckoned. Theresa frowned slightly.

'Now what's me brother been up to now? Something about an accident at Wetherby and a jockey having an awful fall. Does anyone blame Niall?'

Finn explained exactly what had happened that day, the fog which hampered visibility and the unexpected ride for Niall on Cardinal Sin.

75

'Tom Kennedy was down to ride him but then the favourite's jockey was injured so Tom rode him instead, a horse called Green Marauder. Niall got the ride on Cardinal Sin. The race was pretty even and we're not sure what happened, I think Niall was trying to go for a gap and maybe he clipped heels with Tom's mount, no one could see because of the fog. Both horses came down, Niall and Cardinal Sin were fine but Green Marauder fell on Tom and he fractured a vertebra and is in a coma at present.'

Theresa's eyes filled with tears. 'Sure, that's awful. Niall's real cut up and I can see why now.'

Finn took her hand. 'Look, it's probably just one of those things. No one's blaming Niall as such, it could have happened to anyone. I mean, it was a bit foolish to run the races in that weather, so if anyone is responsible it's the racecourse but usually jockeys are more careful...'

Theresa had turned very pale. 'So, you do think it's Niall's fault?'

Finn found himself wanting to reassure her. 'No, it's just racing. We all know the risks when we ride, and National Hunt riding is a very dangerous sport.'

Theresa looked anguished. He was beginning to wish she hadn't brought the subject up now because it might be difficult to elevate the mood.

'But he'll make a full recovery, this Tom?'

'Maybe, he's in good hands. I need to pop and see him.' He noticed Theresa twisting her napkin in her hands, her face pinched with anxiety. At that moment the food arrived which was a welcome interruption. 'Look, I'll find out what's what with Tom and let you both know. Jockeys fall every dozen races or so and we all know that one race could be our last, and those where the horse falls on the rider are much more serious, as you can imagine. No one is blaming Niall if that helps.'

Theresa gave the ghost of a smile. 'I know and thanks for being honest. You must let me know if we can do anything, anything at all. I just worry about Niall, you know, wi' this happening after the drink driving...'

They ate and chatted about themselves, Finn told her about his family, his life, his interests. Theresa seemed calmer and told him about growing up in Ireland, going to a Convent School, a shadow crossed her face when she spoke about being taught by nuns, and how she had finished her degree and decided to teach.

76

'And I haven't looked back. I love the kids and it's all grand.'

They went on to talk about relationships, Theresa had been married once, but it was a big mistake and Finn told her about his engagement to Livvy.

Theresa looked at him intently. 'It must have been very hard for her, when you were riding and putting yourself in harm's way every day.'

'Well, she ran off with Nat Wilson my best friend, who is also a jockey, so she seemed to manage it where he's concerned,' he added drily.

Theresa smiled. 'Are you and Nat still friends?'

Finn smiled. 'Yes, we got over it. In the end you can't stay mad with Nat forever.' He realised it was true. He should know, he had tried and failed. Now he was very glad that Nat was back in his life.

'And now you're in a good place?' Theresa studied him carefully, and he had the impression that his answer was important. She had probably heard about his declining fortunes before he retired and wanted to check he'd recovered.

'Yes. I love my job. It was hard leaving racing as a jockey, but I'm settled now.' Finn realised as soon as he said it, that it was true.

Theresa nodded and seemed pleased. They chatted about music, books and films and appeared to have a lot in common. Finn realised that he was enjoying himself enormously. It was suddenly much later, and they decided to get a taxi. Theresa lived on the way to his, so the plan was to drop her off first, but somehow, they ended up at his flat instead.

'You know, I've really enjoyed myself,' Theresa said, her eyes bright. She didn't seem in a hurry to go home which Finn took as a positive sign.

'Would you like a nightcap?' he asked, unsure whether he'd misread the signals. Finn had been intending to take things slowly which was his usual tactic, but what the hell, where had that got him? On his own and sometimes rather lonely, he realised. Harriet was moving on with Taverner, maybe he should too. He didn't have time to think about why Harriet's burgeoning relationship with the dashing police officer bothered him, as Theresa gave him a slow smile that told him that his instincts were right.

Theresa smiled. 'I'd like that very much.'

Chapter 9

Hattie received a text from Finn as she sat opposite Taverner in The Blacksmiths Arms, having just eaten a sumptuous but simple meal of homemade lasagne and thick, crisp chips. They were on a second date and were still at the getting to know each other stage, but things were going well. While Gabriel went to get the bill she squinted at the message, clear that if it involved the art case, she didn't want Taverner to see it.

I'm free tomorrow if we're still on to meet Mrs M? I have the address in Lincolnshire if you can think of an in. x

Hattie quickly texted him back arranging to meet. She had an embryo of an idea, but it needed work. She was starting to regret being so cavalier. She pocketed her phone quickly, almost guiltily, as if to erase any sign of the text conversation. If she analysed her actions, it was because she had only been out with Taverner a couple of times and didn't want to complicate matters by involving him in unofficial investigations with her friend. Also, she was aware that her friendship with Finn was often misinterpreted, and she didn't want to muddy the waters with Taverner. Besides, she just didn't want to talk about the case with him just yet. All their previous contact had been through the prism of solving a crime and it would just be nice to get to know him without that backdrop somehow, to actually concentrate on Gabriel Taverner, the man not the policeman.

The pair talked through their interests. Hattie spoke about her teenage years competing in the modern pentathlon whilst Taverner told her about his time at Arsenal football academy, until an injury meant that he was released. Harriet gazed at his handsome face, thinking that everything was going well. They had so much in common, early sporting dreams that had been dashed and now much more worthy, sensible careers.

'What else do you like to do?' Taverner asked.

'I ride a bit, like keep fit and I love reading.'

'Who are your favourite authors.'

Harriet didn't know why she said it, but the bloody man was on her mind.

'I like David Nicholls and I'm getting into thrillers. I'm reading a Ross Maclaren at the moment which I'm really enjoying.'

Taverner grinned. 'Ah, I like those. I met him once actually ages ago.'

Harriet tried to disguise her interest. 'How did that come about?'

'He received what he thought was fan mail, but it actually was a letter with some pretty awful death threats to his main character, Robert Banks. His wife was really freaked out as I recall and then she thought someone was watching the house, so we had to visit a few times. They were lovely. We found out who did it, it was a crazed fan who thought Maclaren was actually Banks. They lived in London at the time but moved shortly after. His wife was pregnant, and I remember that she was so pleased it was resolved. The funny thing is that they already had a son called Gabriel, so this was their second child. I remember she wanted to call the baby, Angelica, but Ross thought she'd be called Angel for short, and people would think they had a thing for angels. Ross sent some books to the station by way of a thank you and as no one else was interested in them, I took them home and that's how I became a fan.'

'Wow, that's amazing.' Harriet could feel her heart pounding but tried to maintain her composure, outwardly at least. Now she had a name for Maclaren's son. How many Gabriel Maclarens could there be? She was pretty sure that the author profile said Ross lived in Lincolnshire, so it was a start. She was sure with a bit of research on the internet, she could come up with something.

Taverner went on to tell her about his childhood in Deal in Kent, and how he'd come to Yorkshire to finally meet his birth mother, but so far work had got in the way. Harriet sensed his loneliness and need to find his only living relative and her heart went out to him. She had drunk a couple of glasses of wine, felt relaxed and was enjoying herself immensely. Then she began to feel slightly anxious. It was only the second date and she wondered about the etiquette of such things. Play it cool, she decided, though she realised that she did like him. He was, however, a complex man and there were a lot of layers, but she was going to enjoy unravelling them. He drove her home and they were sitting outside her parents' Victorian villa in his car. She wondered about whether to invite him in for a coffee but as she was still living at home this could be tricky. Her father had been an Inspector and with her brother a serving officer, the conversations tended to drift off onto current trends in policing. At Will's barbeque, the three of them had dissected the policing climate minutely, and she thought it wouldn't be conducive to romance to continue in the same vein. Her father was likely to be awake, he often was until she'd come back from a night out. Anyway, she needn't have worried, as Gabriel clearly had other plans.

'Thanks for a lovely evening but I'd better get off. I've got a briefing first thing tomorrow and need to review the evidence, you know what it's like being in the force.' He smiled. 'Look, maybe you'd like to go to the cinema at the weekend, I think the new Bond film is being shown...' he added.

'Great, I'd like that. I've been dying to see it.'

'Good, I'll text you then. Have a good week.'

With that Taverner leaned forward and kissed her, and she found that she was kissing him back with relish. Hattie climbed out of his car with some reluctance. It'd been a good evening. Taverner was a good conversationist but was complex. He had arranged to meet his mother and the curly haired DS Anna Wildblood, who Hattie had met and liked on sight, was going to accompany him initially. The fact that he was so nervous about it was surprising for someone so successful in other areas of his life. Hattie found it sweet, endearing really and was beginning to feel that there was a lot to Gabriel. Not to mention the fact that he had unwittingly really helped her with her quest to find Ross Maclaren. She needed to get to work as soon as possible. She felt a thrill of anticipation as she touched her lips and remembered the passion in the kiss, a hint of what was to come, as she watched his brake lights fade into the distance as he drove away.

Finn's grey Audi pulled up outside the Lucas's comfortable house dead on midday. Hattie ran out to meet him. Finn had managed to get the Maclaren's last known address from Jeremy. It was in a remote area of Lincolnshire.

Finn was looking at her with an air of anticipation. 'So, did you manage to find out something that might help us when we get there?'

Harriet smiled. 'I did actually.'

'And?'

'I found out that Maclaren has a son called Gabriel and when I went on Facebook, I found he has a mountain bike for sale, so I'm off to trial it. I said I'd be there just after lunch.'

Finn smiled. 'Impressive. Do you know anything about mountain bikes?'

'A bit. My brothers were both into biking, I wasn't but I have boned up on this particular one though, with a bit of help.'

Finn couldn't help but smile. 'And how will you get the son talking about his dad?'

Harriet shrugged. 'I'm sure I can think of something.'

A few hours later, they arrived at a smart looking brick built, substantial farm with outbuildings, a few stables, horses in the paddock and an arena with a set of solid looking showjumps in situ. It was a few miles outside Lincoln in a leafy and charming village. There was a newish Golf parked outside and space for more vehicles.

Finn took in the scene. 'Hmm. We might be in luck. The lad could be on his own.'

Harriet looked at him in amazement. 'How did you work that one out?'

Now it was Finn's time to shine. 'Because I did a bit of googling myself last night and found out that the local Pony Club are having a hunter trial today, and that a certain Angelique Maclaren is riding. Isabel Maclaren is jump judging according to the schedule. Maclaren's first book is dedicated to Gabriel, Angelique and Isabel, so it was an educated guess.' He pointed to a hardstanding, 'that could be where a trailer was parked and now it's missing.'

Harriet felt a bit done. Why hadn't she thought of that? But she had to give credit where credit was due.

'OK. Well done. Are you going to have a look round whilst I talk to Gabriel?'

'Will do.'

Harriet made her way up to the house and knocked. The door was opened by the same dark haired, lanky boy, who had yet to grow into his features, as she had seen on his Facebook profile. She had found out that he was 17, into mountain biking and seemed to want to move on to trial biking from his profile. She was shown into a vast hall with a boot room leading off it. The hallway had an expensively tiled floor with a mahogany table which bore a magnificent display of lilies. The place screamed money so it was hard to imagine that Maclaren could be pleading poverty but then again, she knew that all these things were relative. He might be in a lot of debt.

'Hi, I'm Harriet. You must be Gabriel.'

'That's right. Have you come far?'

'No, not really. Market Rasen way.'

'OK. The bike's outside.'

Gabriel pulled on some wellies and took her outside to the row of stables and unlocked what was clearly a tackroom and food store.

'Do you ride then?' asked Harriet, hoping that the lad might open up.

'Not me. My sister does. She's at a competition. Mum's taken her,' he replied. 'My dad's into horses, he has a few racehorses, but me, I prefer bikes. I'm saving up to get a trial bike, see.'

'Oh great. I know a few jockeys and trainers actually. Where does your dad keep his horses? I might know the yards, that's all.'

The lad frowned. 'Oh, there was some sort of row between Dad and his last trainer. I'm not sure what it was about, so he moved them.'

'Oh right.' She looked at the bike, a blue Boardman MHT with an aluminium body, that he showed her. It had been cleaned and was in good condition.

Gabriel started to get technical. 'It has 10 speed gears with a 32t chain ring and Tektro hydraulic disc brakes. Brilliant for the money and a great all rounder.'

Harriet made appreciative noises. 'Great. Can I have a go?'

Gabriel smiled and wheeled the bike out into the winter sun. 'Sure. You can take it for a spin round the drive if you want. '

Harriet tried to look enthusiastic as she hopped on board and cycled around the vast driveway, desperately trying to think of a way of retrieving the situation. She was beginning to flounder when it came to the technical stuff about bikes, and had really found out very little apart from the fact that in all likelihood Maclaren still owned his horses. She wondered what Finn was doing and if he had better luck. She was just turning the bike and going back toward the house, when she passed a wooden single storey

82

outbuilding that on closer inspection was clearly an office. She slowed down as she passed the window and then stopped as if struggling with the gears. She peered into the window and saw that there were bookcases full of Ross Maclaren's books. Could this be where he usually wrote? She looked around for Finn and fired off a quick text telling him to inspect this outside office building. Then she made her way back to where Gabriel was waiting expectantly.

Gabriel gave her a shy smile. 'Well, what do you think? It's a brilliant bike for someone just getting started,' he added, obviously noticing her poor technique.

'I'm sure. How much did you say?'

'£500. They're £800 new and I've hardly used it actually. I'm moving on to trial bikes and Mum says I need to sell this first...' Gabriel added hopefully.

Harriet smiled sympathetically and inspected the bike again. How could she get him to talk about his father? Then it came to her.

'You know, you look like someone I know, someone famous, I can't just think of who exactly...' she added, staring at him. 'I can't think of his name, but it'll come to me.'

Gabriel flushed. 'Actually, you might know my dad, he's Ross Maclaren he's a famous author.' He shrugged. 'I get this a lot.'

'Wow. Ross Maclaren, THE Ross Maclaren? How amazing! He's your dad? That must be it. My father reads all his stuff so I must have seen him on the book cover, that'll be it. Well, well, well. You do look so alike. Is your dad around?'

Gabriel frowned. 'No, he's away writing. He's got some sort of deadline or other and he's struggling finishing his book.'

'Wow. Where does he write then? Where does the magic happen?'

'He used to write in his office,' he nodded at the single storey shed. 'But he's had writer's block so he's somewhere in the Peak District, I think. He needs complete peace and quiet, he says.'

'Wow, that's so interesting. I suppose somewhere remote would help, though it's a lovely place here, of course.' Harriet continued. 'Well, it's a small world. Fancy your dad being Ross Maclaren.'

Gabriel frowned, a flicker of suspicion flitting over his face. 'So, about the bike, I can maybe do £475 but that's as low as I can go.'

Harriet winced. 'You know, I do like it, but I need a second opinion. Can I ask my boyfriend to come and have a look? He's so much more knowledgeable than I am, and he'll be able to tell me if he thinks it will do for me.' Gabriel looked downcast and Harriet suddenly felt rather ashamed of herself. 'Look, I'll ring you and we'll come back. Sorry.'

Gabriel nodded grimly. 'No, that's quite alright. I'll look forward to hearing from you.'

'Well, see you then. I'll be in touch, bye.'

Harriet turned and walked back to Finn's Audi. Finn was nowhere to be seen. She thought she'd find him examining the family's horses. She was right.

'Any joy?' he asked.

Harriet looked pained. 'Remind me not to do that again. I feel so sorry for the poor lad, he really thought he'd sold his bloody bike. I feel like such a cow.'

'Well, if the cap fits…'

'Oi!' Harriet slapped his arm. 'Anyway, I did find out that Maclaren has taken a cottage in the Peak District.'

Finn nodded and pulled out a scrap of paper. 'There was a brochure from English Cottages in his office on the table. I couldn't see the whole thing, but I made out somewhere called Rock Cottage which was ringed several times in red ink. He could be there. It's in the Peak District, I could only make out the town as beginning with LE, though.'

Harriet felt rather deflated. 'God, we'll never find the place. Anyway, according to Gabriel, his dad has still got all his horses, he's just moved them from his old trainer, he didn't know where to though.'

'OK. Well, that's something then.'

Harriet pulled out her phone and quickly pressed a few keys.

'What are you doing?'

'Barring Gabriel's number in case he rings me back. I told him I'd come back with my boyfriend.'

Finn laughed. 'See what happens when you lie? You need another lie to cover it up. Anyway, all we need to do is go through the listings for Rock Cottages near a town beginning with LE and then we're there. How many holiday cottages are there in the area, do you think?'

Harriet felt despondent. 'Thousands. The Peak District is pretty vast and there are bound to be loads of Rock Cottages.'

It felt like an impossible task.

Finn had arranged to meet Theresa later. He decided to cook for her and was busily preparing a suitable feast. When she arrived, he handed her a glass of champagne.

'What are we celebrating?' she asked.

'Meeting each other, 'he replied.

Theresa laughed. 'I really feel like it was meant to be, don't you?'

Finn smiled. 'I do.'

He found himself anticipating their meetings more and more. He knew he was in danger of falling head over heels for her. He had put a lot of thought into their meal, had laid the table, and even bought some flowers. Theresa looked around and smiled. She was dressed in a fitted dress and heels. She sniffed the air.

'Something smells nice?'

'Salmon en croute, how does that sound?'

A smile played around her lips. 'Delightful. I can think of something even better though, can't you?'

Theresa turned off the oven and led him into the bedroom.

The next day he was awoken by a call from his old friend and ex champion jockey, Nat Wilson. Nat had narrowly missed out on the championship last year but was aiming to win it again.

'I'm just in the area, not racing though, I've a two day ban for careless riding, at Newton Abbott, so I thought I'd take the opportunity to pop in and see you.'

Finn had read something about the incident in the press. It had obviously drawn the attention of the stewards who had meted out their punishment. It was typical of Nat, find a space and go for it, no matter what the consequences might be.

'Great stuff. Will you be staying and is Livvy coming?'

Nat laughed. 'No, she's away modelling in New York. I might stay if you can put up with me.'

'Course, I'd be delighted. I'll let Harriet know.'

Great. I'll be with you about teatime.'

Finn grinned. Nat was always a tonic, and he had a sharp mind too and lots of contacts. He might know about Admiral Jervis as he picked up loads of stuff in the weighing room, much of it gossip, but some of it was grounded in reality. He made a mental note to check out the footage of the incident at Newton Abbott. Nat never changed and suddenly Finn felt very pleased that that was the case.

Chapter 10

Finn spent the morning arranging to see his new conditionals, setting up training and booking himself on courses. He rang the hospital to inquire about Tom Kennedy's progress and was told he had spent a comfortable night and 'was as well as could be expected' which told him precisely nothing. Tom's agent, Mark Parker, was slightly more forthcoming, he'd decided to ring him rather than bother Clare, and told him that the medics were planning to bring him out of his coma in the next day or two. They were cautiously optimistic about his head injury but less sure about damage to his spine, and he still had no movement in his lower body. Mark declared it a 'miserable business' and inquired about that 'idiot' Byrne. He also warned Finn that Tom's family had complained to the BHA about the race meeting being allowed to go ahead despite the terrible fog, but as yet no direct blame seemed to be heading Niall's way. Finn passed on his regards to Tom and his family and assured him that Niall was feeling terrible and that he would be keeping an eye on him. He reminded him that no one knew exactly what had happened because of the poor visibility. Mark had harrumphed and intimated that he did know something, but it transpired that he hadn't even been at Wetherby that day. Finn decided to humour him and asked to be kept in the loop regarding Tom's condition. At least if he was coming out of the coma, he might be able to shed some light on what had happened. Finn rang off, feeling despondent. Tom Kennedy was a decent young man, and he could well understand the family's anger at the situation. He just hoped he would make a full recovery.

Right on cue, Tony Murphy rang him to tell him about the complaint Tom's family had made.

'I'm just letting you know that the Kennedy family have written to the BHA and racecourse complaining about the race meeting continuing in such bad weather which they feel contributed to Tom's accident. We are dealing with it but the press are bound to ask Niall his opinion, and I would like you to advise him not to speak to them directly. We want a co-ordinated response so any media fall out can be managed.'

'I can certainly advise him of that, whether he listens remains to be seen...' Niall had always seemed reasonable to him but then again, his behaviour when the police caught up with him for drink driving was anything but.

'Hmm. Well, I know you will do your best, Finn. But we could do without the bad publicity, and I would hate for him to go shooting his mouth off to absolve himself from any blame. Do you have any idea what happened?'

'Not really. Tom and Niall's mounts were ahead, the nearest rider being Tristan Davies and the visibility was poor. I've spoken to Tristan, and he didn't really see anything, he was too busy trying to keep his own mount upright and in the running.' Then he suddenly remembered something. 'And there was mention of a previous spinal injury, so I wonder if that hadn't been properly dealt with.'

'Thanks, we'll look into it. But this Niall character, he is turning out to be a bit of a liability. Can you keep a really close eye on him? I mean to drive off from the police in the way that he did, it's a strange reaction if you ask me.'

'I know, it is.' The same thing had certainly occurred to Finn on many occasions. There was really no getting away from it when you thought about it. 'But I suppose he was over the limit and he's young and behaved stupidly. I think he was trying to prove himself at Wetherby and the whole thing went a bit wrong. Understandable, in a way. I will see him more frequently and, of course, Rosie and Seamus will certainly let me know if they have any concerns.'

'Do you think he has mental health problems?' asked Tony. The awareness training that Tony had been on had certainly had an influence on him, Finn realised.

'I don't think so, but I can put him in touch with a psychologist if he's feeling stressed with the court case coming up and the incident with Tom. He's bound to be feeling low, at the very least.'

'That is a very good idea and I hope you've booked on to that mental health awareness training too. It's really good and makes you realise just how prevalent these things are, in men particularly.' Tony sighed. 'There's often no warning at all with male suicides, and it's often too late by the time anyone is aware that they had problems.'

88

He assured Tony that he had booked onto the training and that he would speak to Niall. He sounded mollified and rang off impressing on Finn the need to see Niall as soon as possible, still at least no one was directly blaming Niall for Tom's accident, not yet anyway.

He also found himself searching through the 48 hour declarations for Admiral Jervis, to see if he was running anywhere. Then he spent some time idly going through Ross Maclaren's website. The author picture showed the same man he had seen previously and hadn't been updated for some time except to say that his new book was out soon and reminding fans to look out for it, but there was no launch date as yet, so it could be months away. He ordered a couple of the author's older books on Amazon, thinking it might well be worth reading them as it could give him some insight into the author's personality, which in turn might help them track him down.

Finn had made some arrangements for training sessions for the conditionals and drove to the Ryans' yard to see Niall and Lottie. He spotted Seamus in the yard and decided to catch up with him first.

'Now then, Finn. Rosie said you were coming. Is there any news on Tom Kennedy?'

Finn gave him the latest update from Tom's agent and filled him in the complaint from the family. Seamus scratched his head.

'Aye well, I suppose the fog had come down a wee bit worse. Still, Niall is doing alright, so he is, he's a bit down, and he's been struggling with his weight a bit, too many beers in The Blacksmith's if you ask me, but at least no one's blaming him so that's something.'

'And Clare?'

Seamus sighed. 'She's proper quiet, just working away. She's not getting on with Niall though, she seems to blame him for Tom's accident, but it will all blow over. The police came to speak to Clare and Lottie about the incident with Niall and although they had arranged it, they missed it, something about a flat tyre, but no doubt it will all be sorted out. Clare's at the hospital as we speak but Niall's around somewhere if you want a word?'

'I do. Is there anywhere we can talk privately?'

'Aye. You can come through to the office. That's no problem.'

Finn nodded and they went to find the lad. He wondered briefly why the police wanted to speak to Clare and Lottie, but then realised it was probably just a formality. He knew from his previous cases that the police had to speak to lots of witnesses and took files full of statements to build a case, so it was probably just that.

Niall was cleaning feeding buckets along with some of the other staff and sorting the feeds out for evening stables.

'Now then Mr McCarthy. How are you? Do you have any news on Tom?' He looked anxious and Finn realised he was probably bracing himself for bad news. He couldn't resist putting him out of his misery.

'They are bringing him out of his coma but it's too early to see about his spinal injuries just yet. Shall we have a chat in the house?'

Niall nodded, clearly relieved.

The office was comfortable and well organised. He knew that Rosie usually did the books but was helped by a secretary a couple of days in the week. Niall looked at him uncertainly. The shelves were stacked with Timeform books, and the walls were decorated with photographs of their many winners. They were a yard on the up and things were promising. Niall's problems were the one blot on the horizon, so far this season.

'I've popped down to see how you are. It's not an easy thing being involved in an incident like the one at Wetherby, especially coming so soon after the drink driving.'

Niall nodded. 'I'm doing alright, but I can't concentrate, yer know, and I'm finding it hard to sleep at the minute. I keep apologising to Clare but she's real upset and keeps on at me. S'pose I can't blame her.' He looked tearful and so much younger than his 17 years. Finn waited for him to compose himself. 'And wi' the court case coming up, it's all getting a bit much, yer know?'

'I hear you've been drinking a bit too?'

'Not too much, but it's messing with me weight. It's the stress of it.' He gulped and looked broken.

'Well, just to let you know, no one is blaming you for what happened, in fact, Tom's family have put in a complaint to the authorities about the meeting even going ahead.' He paused, wondering how to phrase the next bit. 'In the meantime, it might be helpful if you don't talk to the press. The BHA want a unified response and would like all statements to go through their press office. It's up to you, of course, but that's their advice and mine too.'

Niall nodded. 'Sure, I've no problem wi' that at all.'

'Good. But in the meantime, I do have some contacts that might be able to help you, a psychologist, Tara Regan, and you can always talk to a dietician about your weight, though, you don't need me to tell you that it's probably to do with the beer.' Niall nodded and took the cards Finn handed him. 'And, of course, you still have a few months before the matter is at court, so you can fit in lots more rides, but not if you can't make the weights.'

Niall nodded. 'Guvnor wants me to ride a few, but I'm a bit spooked, so I am.'

'I can understand that. I'll pop down soon and put you through your paces.'

Niall grinned. 'Grand, thanks. And thanks for these.' He waved the cards about that Finn had given him.

'Just make sure you ring them. It's a service via the PJA so you won't have to pay a thing. They're all first class people and are there to help you. Everyone needs help, Niall, so don't feel you have to manage everything on your own. And if you ever feel like a chat, then ring me, you have my number.' He surveyed Niall steadily. 'I really do mean it.'

Rosie and Seamus promised to keep an eye on Niall, Clare and Lottie and ring if there were any concerns. Finn knew they would do their best.

'And Lottie, how is she doing now?'

Rosie frowned. 'Well, she's riding but I think she's a bit spooked about the accident too.'

'Good job you are both so understanding what with the three of them, Niall, Lottie and Clare, you've certainly got your work cut out.' Finn suddenly thought of something. 'Are you going to the opening of The Stagecoach? I think all the horsey locals are invited and it might cheer you all up.'

Rosie smiled. 'Ah, the place that Christian Gerrard is involved with? We might just do that. It might be just the job. I'll always do me best for them all, as you know...'

Finn smiled. Of that, at least, he could be sure. He made his way home with a heavy heart. At least he knew they were in good hands. Then he switched his mind to the search for Maclaren and was just about to search for towns in the Peak District beginning with LE, when he decided to see if Admiral Jervis was declared anywhere. He googled the declarations and found to his surprise that the horse was listed to appear at Haydock early next week. He was now trained by someone called Stan Denton, a middle sized trainer in Newark. The owners were listed as RHB Holdings but he assumed that was a partner or relative of Maclaren's and that he still had some ownership of the horse. He grabbed his phone and texted Hattie.

Fancy a day out at Haydock? Admiral Jervis is down to race. Nat coming today for a couple of days if you want to pop round. Finn

He then found a text from her reminding him about The Stagecoach Hotel opening tomorrow night. He usually hated those sort of bashes, but things being what they were, he and Hattie had decided to attend. He knew from experience that social gatherings were often good for finding out key pieces of information. Then he worked his way through his mail, noticing that he had some packages and found that the books by Ross Maclaren had arrived. He sat down to make a start reading them and wondered if the elusive author could resist seeing his horse race? If it was Finn, he'd certainly be there.

Nat turned up when Finn arrived back home from work. Harriet arrived shortly after with a large carrier bag full of food.

Nat kissed her and looked her up and down. 'How's my favourite redhead then? Someone looks good. New man?'

Harriet blushed. Nat was always so perceptive. 'Yes, but it's early days.'

Nat nodded. 'And you, Finn? Are you still going out with the actress?'

'No, she's long gone. I've just started seeing someone but before you ask me, I'm not saying anything else as I don't want to jinx things.'

Nat grinned and winked at Harriet. Interesting, she thought, thinking it was bound to be a certain jockey's sister. She had already noticed how Finn flushed when he spoke about her.

Harriet waved her bags about. 'I've brought steak and salad for dinner and some low cal stuff for pud.'

Nat beamed. 'Bless you. Can't wait.'

'So, what brings you to York?'

'Ah, I need to see a man about a horse,' Nat replied cryptically.

'You're not riding then?'

'Not racing. I got a two day ban for careless riding.' Nat shrugged, unabashed.

'And did you ride carelessly?'

Nat grinned broadly. 'No more than usual but you win some, you lose some.'

It was a good philosophy and one that had stood him in good stead so far. Harriet noticed that Nat always pushed and lived on the edge but just managed to stay on the right side of things. He was a risk taker, it was part of his personality and a characteristic that helped him become one of the best national hunt jockeys in the business. She had a genuine fondness for the man and was pleased to see him.

Over dinner, with a smaller, low calorie version served for Nat, they caught up with one another.

'So, are you guys doing any work for the BHA?' Nat asked. He knew all about their roles and had even been involved in some of their investigations, so they knew they could trust him.

Finn nodded. 'Well, not as such. We've been asked to track down an owner and a horse for a trainer. The pair had a row because of debts owed to the trainer. The owner then removed all his horses but sent round a painting in lieu of the training debts.'

'Hmm. Sounds interesting. What sort of painting was it?' Nat caught sight of Finn's shocked expression. 'What? I do know about art, a bit anyway. Well, Livvy is the collector and I have sort of picked it up. She's always getting catalogues from galleries.'

'It's a Gideon Moss painting.'

Nat sat back and stared at then both. 'Really? Livvy keeps going on about Gideon Moss, it seems his paintings are really popular these days. I was given a Daniel Jacobs piece when I won the National on Goforit, you know, that modern artist. I bloody hate the thing, but someone called Christian Gerrard has asked me to loan it for an exhibition up here.' He shook his head. 'Damn, I should have brought it with me.'

'What's it like?'

Nat pulled out his phone and scrolled through his photographs. 'Here, I thought I had a pic somewhere.'

Both Harriet and Finn peered at the photo. It was a painting of a bay horse, suspended in an ethereal background that gave the painting a modern, fantasy feel.

Harriet similarly pulled out her phone and showed a photo of the Maclaren painting to Nat.

'Now that I do like.' He frowned. 'Hey, isn't that Red Navajo from the 1910's? His markings were so unusual.' He peered at the photo of the painting. 'Wow. I know everyone talks about him in the breeding world but there are very few paintings of him.' He scratched his head. 'But I have seen one somewhere, but I can't just recall...'

Finn and Nat went on to explain to Harriet that Red Navajo's progeny almost without exception went on to do very well, and many of the excellent horses racing today could trace their ancestry back to the unusually marked chestnut horse.

'So, who has employed you two?' asked Nat.

'Jeremy Trentham. One of the horses he wants us to find is Admiral Jervis.'

Nat gasped. 'Now, I've certainly heard of him. In fact, I'm riding him at Haydock next week. My agent has just confirmed the ride. He's trained by Stan Denton now. He's a Gold Cup winner if ever I saw one, no wonder Trentham is pissed off.' He looked from one to the other. 'Has he changed hands then, because the owner was the author chappie, wasn't he?'

'Ross Maclaren, that's right.' Finn went on to explain what they knew.

'Hmm. Interesting and Maclaren has left his painting to cover the debt, has he? You know, I think I've seen a similar painting to Maclaren's like I said. I noticed it because of Red Navajo.' He tapped some keys on his phone. 'Here, I knew I'd seen it before. Look, it's for sale in a gallery in New York. Livvy went to look round as she's modelling there.' He frowned at the painting. 'In fact, it's very similar to the other one.'

'What?' Both Harriet and Finn crowded in and studied Nat's phone. There it was as plain as day, the self same painting. It was even labelled, 'Red Navajo in the Sovereign Stakes at Newmarket by Gideon Moss.'

94

Finn looked at Harriet. 'Christ, what the hell is going on? Is it a print of the same picture?'

Nat read the brochure online. 'No, it's definitely described as an original painting.'

Harriet was busily comparing the painting on Nat's phone with the photograph of the painting on her phone. 'They're absolutely identical, look.'

Nat studied the two paintings. 'Well, one of them must be a fake, but which one?'

The thought that Maclaren's painting might be fake had never entered Finn's head. 'Looks like this whole thing just got a whole lot more complicated.' He turned to Nat. 'Listen, why don't you come to this bash of Gerrard's tomorrow. It's the opening of his hotel, The Stagecoach. Gerrard knows about paintings, perhaps we can ask him?'

Harriet smiled. 'What a great idea!'

Nat rubbed his hands together, his eyes sparkling. 'Yes, I'll come. Sounds interesting and as you know, I do love a party. I only know Gerrard slightly and he was full of his wedding barn and how me and Livvy might like it. Just fill me on who's who, will you, and I'll keep my ear to the ground. People do seem to tell me stuff, Christ knows why.' He shook his head in exasperation.

Harriet had to admit that was probably true. She had noticed on many occasions that Nat exuded charisma and people did indeed unburden themselves to him. They became ever so slightly star struck and somehow unguarded and more inclined to reveal their secrets. This could be very useful.

Harriet thought for a minute. 'But Gerrard has already valued Jeremy's painting and believes it to be an original. He is supposed to be knowledgeable, so for all we know he might be in on the forgery. I mean, we don't really know him or even if he knows what he's talking about, whereas I could ask my uncle Sebastian, who is an expert, to have a look.'

'Good idea,' added Finn. 'That's settled then.'

'I like a bit of intrigue,' added Nat, rubbing his hands together, his eyes gleaming. 'And you two never disappoint. I'm glad I came now.'

Finn and Harriet exchanged a glance. Finn realised that he was too. He'd noticed that his old friend was like a catalyst; he made things happen.

He had always envied Nat his easy charm and self belief. And Nat had a surprisingly analytical streak and for all his bravado, his insight into things was often invaluable.

Chapter 11

As soon as Hattie followed Finn and Nat into The Stagecoach Hotel reception, she knew it was going to be one of those stylish events. She was glad she'd made an effort wearing her new bronze, maxi dress with black boots which just escaped being clumpy and looked Victorian and fashionable. Her auburn hair was in a side bun, and she'd borrowed a long amber necklace from her mother, taken care with her makeup and was wearing her new Cristal perfume. Finn, as ever, scrubbed up well and Nat had borrowed a suit jacket from Finn, tousled his hair and exuded good health and masculinity. Like horses being preened for a show, they shone and gleamed. It was as if they were entering the Best Turned Out horse competition which took place in the paddock before most races, thought Hattie wryly. Of course, they had watched the progress of the hotel refurbishment over the last year and knew no expense had been spared, so seeing the entrance hall, high chandeliers and glimpsing the waiters circulating with champagne and hors d'oeuvres, she was very glad they had gone all out.

'Just keep your eyes and ears peeled,' Finn had advised, 'listen to anything about Gideon Moss's paintings, Maclaren, art fraud, any snippets of information that might be useful.'

Nat did a mocking salute.

'And, of course, we mustn't forget to enjoy ourselves,' added Harriet.

'Absolutely.' Nat winked at her. His eyes gleamed. He spotted a waiter circulating with glasses of champagne and scooped up two and handed one to her.

Hattie's friend, Daisy, wasn't there, she was down south competing along with her fiancé Neil, but both had asked her to have a good look at the new wedding barn and pick up some leaflets for them. They still hadn't settled on a venue and were getting fed up with looking, so this might be just what they needed.

The foyer was packed with all the great and good of Walton society, dressed in their finery. She noticed several trainers, Jeremy Trentham talking to Christian Gerrard, their host, flanked by his wife and daughter, Pandora. Dottie Mitchell, who ran the Singing Kettle and Tristan Davies, Jeremy's main jockey and his girlfriend, Poppy. Hattie waved at them and vowed to talk to them later. There were also local dignitaries like the area MP, and a handful of councillors. Seamus, Rosie, Niall and Clare were also there. Clare looked ashen and like she would rather be anywhere else than at the party. Harriet also saw Vince Hunt together with his wife. She was used to being with Nat nowadays, but even she had forgotten what a star he was and never more so than within his own community. All necks were craned to catch a glimpse of him, Christian Gerrard was delighted he had come, and everyone was desperate to have a word with arguably, the best ever national hunt jockey. Harriet was aware that Finn commanded a great deal of respect, but Nat's star status was on a different level, almost like being in the presence of a rock god. Nat and Finn were swallowed up in the crowd, with so many people desperate for a word, so she made her way over to talk to Clare who looked pale and stressed.

She had met the girl before when she had disclosed being sexually assaulted by a conditional jockey. What awful luck to get over that, meet someone nice, like Tom Kennedy, only for him to be seriously injured in a fall, one that Niall was involved in too. Clare smiled wanly when she saw Harriet approach.

'I'm so sorry about Tom. How is he?'

She shrugged. 'He's out of the coma but there's still no movement below the waist. Spinal injuries can be like that.' Clare struggled to compose herself. 'I'm just trying to stay strong. He's going to Jack Berry House, you know the rehabilitation centre nearby, but we don't know if he will regain full mobility unfortunately.' Her eyes filled with tears.

Harriet had heard of Jack Berry House. It was a state of the art centre set up by the ex jockey, Jack Berry, and was renowned for its excellent work in the rehabilitation of injured jockeys. It was funded by the well regarded charity, The Injured Jockeys' Fund.

Harriet patted her arm. 'I suppose all you can do is take one day at a time and pray he recovers. He's in the right place, anyway. I hear it has all the latest equipment for spinal injuries.'

Clare nodded. 'Yes, I suppose so. Tom is so lovely. We have only been going out about 4 months and he wants to end things, says I have no obligation to stay with him, but I can't do that.' Her eyes filled with tears. 'Those few months have been the happiest of my life, you see.' Clare turned to look at Niall, her body turning rigid, presumably with resentment and something else as well, was it fear?

Harriet followed her gaze. 'It must be so hard working with Niall too...'

'You could say that. Listen, I might slip off early and go and check on the horses. I'm afraid I'm just not good company at the moment...' Before Hattie could answer and persuade her to stay, there was a clapping noise and then Christian Gerrard stood up to address the crowd. He looked relaxed in his dinner suit and supremely confident.

'I'm so pleased to welcome you all here today to the official opening of The Stagecoach Hotel. I want you all to enjoy yourselves and have a look at our facilities. There's the spa, the wedding barn and, of course, a first class hotel. Our aim is for this hotel to support the people of Walton and the thriving racing industry. Also, I'd like to tell you about a new project of mine. I will be sponsoring an exhibition next door in the museum of racing of a subject close to my heart, equine art. You can see,' he waved a hand, 'my friends from York Art Gallery are also here and will help curate the art exhibition which should open in a couple of weeks' time. And several of my fellow collectors have agreed to loan their paintings of horses, which is very generous of them.' Then he paused and looked at his watch and with a smile and a quick nod from someone in the crowd he added. 'And now my guest of honour the marvellous and distinguished actress, Caroline Regan, will do the honours and officially declare The Stagecoach open.'

Caroline was an ex Bond girl and still a sought after actress. She was renowned for her beauty and trademark rich, fruity voice. She stepped into the foyer resplendent in a long gold evening frock, complete with gloves and, as always was effortlessly elegant. Her trademark blonde bob was immaculate, and she looked far younger than her years. The crowd began cheering and Caroline smiled her dazzling smile.

Christian gestured for everyone to be quiet, and he led Caroline over to the double doors into the main building which were tied with a gold ribbon. Caroline took the proffered outsize scissors and smiled.

'Friends, I'm so honoured to be here and opening this divine 'otel. I for one can't wait to sample the spa.' There was a ripple of laughter at this and then she added, 'so without further ado, I declare The Stagecoach officially open.' She gave a coquettish smile. 'And I know with Christian at the helm, it will be a roaring success. Go and enjoy the evening everyone. Mingle and have a good look at everything this wonderful place has to offer. You won't be disappointed.'

Poppy Ford, Tristan Davies's girlfriend, tapped Harriet's shoulder. 'I hoped to run into you! So, how are you?'

Poppy was a social worker and had met Tristan when she had a young lad on her caseload, Kyle Devlin, at the yard. Kyle was a conditional in his own right and was likely to ride out his claim this year, so things were looking up for him. Hattie had watched Tristan ride with Poppy in the stands and she knew, first hand, the anxiety partners and relatives of jockeys suffered when they were competing. National Hunt racing was especially dangerous, and jockeys accepted that there could be serious falls, like the one experienced by Tom Kennedy. The pair exchanged gossip and agreed to meet up sometime for a coffee.

'We've double booked,' added Poppy quietly. 'We're having to go early so we can have a meal with Tris's parents.'

'Sounds like things are getting serious,' commented Hattie. 'Maybe you should have a look at the wedding barn, you should certainly enter the competition.'

Poppy flushed. 'Maybe. We're not thinking about anything like that. It's great that Nat Wilson's here too. How are you? How's your love life? Are you seeing anyone?'

Harriet blushed. 'Well, I am actually. It's early days, so we'll just have to see what happens.'

Poppy gave her friend a hug and they arranged to meet up the following week.

'Oh, Pandora Gerrard's here,' Poppy added, her gaze following the girl.

'Do you know her?' asked Harriet.

'Oh, not really. I've just heard of her,' Poppy added. 'Catch you later.'

Harriet wondered how Poppy knew Pandora, but then again, she had probably met her at the races, she decided. She dashed off. Hattie noticed Nat talking to Christian, whilst Pandora hovered nearby. Hattie saw the photographer, Lofty Ballard, taking photos and the journalist, Topper McGrew, scribbling away in a notebook as usual. They stood next to a man and a woman who Gerrard had indicated were from York Art Gallery. Finn appeared and nodded towards a couple of artistic looking types. 'Those pair might be worth talking to. I just need to catch up with Jeremy.'

Hattie didn't need telling twice and walked towards them. Topper and Lofty were close enough to be listening.

'So, you're from York Art Gallery? Tell me, do you know my uncle Sebastian Lloyd? He runs a gallery in York, Ebor Art.'

The woman with the pink hair smiled broadly. 'Oh yes, I know Sebastian. He has quite a nice little place. I'm Pixie Henderson and this is Kevin Taylor.' Kevin nodded, looking down his long nose and over his trendy, tortoiseshell eyewear. Harriet immediately started to ask questions about the exhibition. Pixie explained that she and Kevin worked as art restorers.

'I bet that's a fascinating job. How do you restore pictures?'

Kevin looked to grow in size and assumed a smug expression. 'With great care and skill. Pixie does five layer cleaning using solvents of various sorts and I repair holes and tears and do any overpainting.'

Hattie nodded.' Oh, so restorers have to be good at painting too?'

'Many of us are artists, we restore to earn a steady income,' said Kevin.

Pixie joined in. 'I love my work. I use UV light to study the surface of the artwork and then assemble possible solvents and do patch tests before I begin because each work is different. The component pigments vary as artists often used to mix their own. I'm a big fan of Gainsborough cleaning products but I do use others.'

Soon the conversation was becoming quite technical, Pixie had a great deal to say about her job as an art restorer and cleaner. Hattie wanted to move the conversation on. She was tempted to ask about Gideon Moss's paintings but knew she had to keep quiet about that. It was just as well as she couldn't get a word in edgeways anyway. If Pixie did pause for breath, then she could ask about art fraud in general, she decided.

101

'I'm working on a Degas at the moment. Painstaking work using q tips...' Hattie interrupted her before another tedious description of cleaning techniques. She vowed never to bore people with too many details about the work of a dietician.

'What about art fraud, do you uncover fakes like the TV programme, Faking It?' She noticed Topper listening intently, probably thinking that there might be a story in there somewhere.

Kevin smirked at Hattie. 'Oh yes, we do. In fact, about a quarter of new finds sent to us are fake. One prolific faker even knocked up paintings in his garden shed.'

'Yah. One forger's work is even highly collectible now. We work closely with the experts to check them. It's hard to pull the wool over us though.' Pixie was looking smug now.

'But fakes do get confused for the real thing. It must happen?'

Pixie nodded. 'There's two works of the same subject by Michelangelo. One in Paris, one in London. Both galleries swear that theirs is the real one and neither will back down, but who knows?'

'How interesting,' added Topper McGrew who had joined them clearly very interested in the discussion. 'Are there any suspicious paintings in the UK at the moment?'

'Oh, one or two that we are worried about...' She was about to say more when Kevin rolled his eyes and tapped Pixie on the arm. 'Christ, come on Pixie I need a drink.'

Topper caught her eye. 'Hmm, interesting reaction.' He tapped his nose. 'Kevin wanted to shut her up, I wonder why? I think there might be a story there, don't you, Harriet?'

Hattie nodded. 'Well, their behaviour was a little odd. Kevin definitely didn't want Pixie to say anything else, did he?' She liked Topper having got to know him in their last case when he had been surprisingly helpful. She felt like confiding in him about their work for Jeremy but knew that would be seriously unwise. He couldn't resist a scoop and before they knew it, the whole thing would be blown sky high with headlines in lots of papers. She could find out what he knew, on the other hand.

'I've been reading about art fraud and it's fascinating. If you find anything out, then I'd love to know.'

102

Topper smiled. 'Of course, you'll be the first to know if I do. Any particular reason you want to be kept informed?'

'Not really. It's just an interest of mine.' Harriet smiled. She had been bright and breezy, hoping to pass off her interest as just that. Topper gave her a quizzical look and she wasn't at all sure he was convinced.

The journalist scanned the room. 'And Penny Teasdale and her son have just arrived. Now that is brave.' He inclined his head towards a slight, blonde woman accompanied by a much younger, dark haired young man. 'I heard a whisper that her son is a conditional and that Finn is mentoring him.'

Harriet decided to come clean, after all it was public knowledge. 'Yes, I believe that's right.'

'Finn has clearly been holding out on me.' Topper looked hurt. 'I mean there's bound to be some prejudice against the lad because of his father and I could have written an article about him, smoothing his way, had I known...'

Harriet could see Finn approaching. 'He's only just started but it might be worth mentioning that to Finn. He's here so you can ask him.'

Finn had joined them and went on to explain about Freddie Mercer. 'An exclusive interview could be good, but let the lad get settled and get himself established, there's nothing much to report at the moment. Of course, he and his mother had nothing to do with Henry's activities and the boy deserves a chance. He can't have any contact with his father but that shouldn't present a problem as Penny is divorcing him.'

Topper raised an eyebrow. 'Hmm. It's not going to be easy for the boy once people realise who he is.' He frowned. 'It's still a tall order asking the lad not to see his father, though, isn't it?'

Finn shook his head. 'Freddie knows the rules and I have his word that he will not break them. Of course, he is a victim too, but I'll ask him about the interview. It might be better once he's more established though.'

Topper nodded. 'Alright. You're very trusting if I may say so. Isn't Penny an artist too?'

'She is, that's right.'

'Interesting. Animal portraits if my memory serves me correctly. I hear she is rather good.' Topper went on to explain about an exhibition that Christian was arranging.

103

Jeremy Trentham appeared with Laura and Finn made his excuses to go and talk to them.

'Christian's persuaded all the great and the good of Walton and racing to lend their horsey masterpieces. I see Nat Wilson's here too. Quite a coup for Gerrard. Caroline Regan's lending a work by George Stubbs and Sir Guy Montague has a Munnings. Should be quite an exhibition.' Topper smiled. 'I'm going to do a piece about it and this evening's opening, of course, and a friend of mine is going to take photos. It's supposed to cover equine pictures from 1800 to now, even introducing new artists.' He leaned closer and whispered. 'Penny's art is being exhibited and Gerrard's daughter, Pandora, has completed some daubs too. Anyway, excuse me, I've people to interview.'

Topper always knew the latest gossip and obviously on a mission to find out some information for his column.

After that Hattie drank champagne and ate some canapés and scanned the crowd unsure who to talk to next. She noticed with a pang that Clare had left and saw Rosie and Seamus deep in conversation with Nat. Niall and Pandora were standing either side looking awkward. Harriet decided to introduce them.

'Lovely do, Pandora, Niall, how are you both. Do you know each other?'

They both shook their heads, so Hattie introduced them.

Niall shook Pandora's hand, and they exchanged a polite nod. Pandora smiled.

'How are you, Harriet? It's brilliant that you brought Nat Wilson with you. Dad was really keen for him to come.'

'Yes, he's staying with Finn for a few days. He says he has a painting that he's going to loan for your dad's exhibition. How are the preparations going? I heard you are showing some of your paintings too.'

Pandora flushed. 'Yes, that's right. Mine are a bit more modern than those dreary old paintings, so they should stand out.'

'Are you interested in art?' Harriet asked Niall.

He shook his head. 'Nah, not really. I only like the horse ones, sort of.'

'We were just talking to the York Art Gallery, people who work with your father about art fraud, and they seem to think that about a quarter of new finds are fake. Imagine that!' Harriet couldn't resist throwing a grenade into the conversation to see what happened.

Pandora screwed up her face and laughed. 'Pixie and Kevin, you mean? Well, I think they're exaggerating.'

Harriet took this in. 'Maybe. I suppose it could be very lucrative.' She noticed Sian walked past and caught a whiff of her heady perfume. 'Your stepmother looks well.'

Harriet noticed that she looked different somehow, younger.

Pandora scowled. 'Had more botox, silly cow. She'll do anything to hang on to Dad.' Niall flushed and looked embarrassed, so sensing further inappropriate disclosures, she decided to steer Pandora off the topic.

'I'd love to see the wedding barn, if you don't mind showing me round?'

Pandora led her into the sumptuous surroundings. The wedding barn was a beautiful, spacious area with a ceremony room with characterful wooden rafters and French doors opening out onto a beautiful terraced area for photographs. There was another area for the wedding breakfast with a glorious courtyard leading off it. Hattie thought Daisy would love it and hastily scribbled a ticket with her details, which would be put into a draw to win the venue free of charge.

'Well, it's lovely. I'm sure it will be very successful. Are you nervous about showing your paintings?'

Pandora flushed. 'A bit. It's like exposing a part of your soul, really. God, that sounds stupid, but you never know what people will think.'

Harriet remembered the lovely flowing lines and distinctive style of Pandora's paintings.

'Well, I think they're very good. I'm sure people will like them.'

Pandora grinned. Harriet sensed a talented, vulnerable girl underneath all that dyed hair, piercings and dramatic makeup. Today she was dressed in a tight red dress, black fishnets and Victorian style, buttoned boots. Harriet realised that if you peeled away the layers of spikiness and truculence, she would look quite stunning.

'Do you live with your dad and Sian?'

She nodded. 'Had to, really. My mum's not too well, mental health stuff. I think Dad broke her heart and Sian too. Sian sort of made a play for

105

him whilst Mum was ill. Honestly, it was awful.' Pandora scowled and Harriet could sense some real animosity towards her father and Sian.

'How is your mum now?'

Pandora's lips trembled. 'She recovered from her breakdown but then she was heartbroken when Dad divorced her.' Her eyes filled with tears.

So that was where the loathing of Sian came from and the bitterness towards her father, thought Harriet. Interesting. She sensed waves of unhappiness from the girl.

They wandered back into the main building. Christian beckoned Pandora over.

She smiled at Harriet with genuine warmth. 'I'd better go. Thanks, it was nice to speak to you. Dad probably wants to introduce me to someone.'

'Well, he has loads of contacts in the art world. That could be very helpful to you.'

Pandora grinned. 'Maybe. I hope you're coming to the exhibition; I'd really like you to come, you've given me so much confidence.'

'Of course.' Hattie realised that underneath the spikey façade, the girl was really deeply insecure and unhappy. 'I'd love to.'

Harriet was surprised when Pandora hugged her and then disappeared into the crowd.

Back in the function room Finn was talking to a small, blonde woman in her forties and a young man. He made introductions.

'This is Penny Mercer and her son, Freddie, who is a conditional at Trentham's. Penny's just telling me that she's been doing some art restoration for the exhibition.'

Hattie noticed that Penny looked rather bruised around the eyes and had a wary, embarrassed expression. She had wavy blonde hair and was slim and attractive. She was well dressed in a grey coloured knitted dress, with tasteful makeup and beautifully painted fingernails, but seemed anxious and withdrawn.

'It's nothing much. Look, I must be going. I only popped in to support Christian.'

Hattie smiled at Freddie. He was a pleasant looking young man with dark hair. He certainly looked like his father, which would not really help him, she decided, as people would certainly associate him with his father's actions.

'Congratulations on your role with Jeremy. I hear he is one of the best trainers in the area.'

Freddie smiled. 'He is. I'm so pleased to get the chance to work for him after everything that happened, you know...'

Hattie felt she had to come clean. 'I do know. I was with Finn when everything happened with Sam Foster.' He was the conditional who had been asked to pull races by Henry Teasdale, Freddie's father.

Freddie smiled. 'Don't worry, I know. I feel really bad at what happened to Sam and all the other stuff with Dr Pinkerton. I was away at school at the time, so couldn't really help them.' He looked deeply troubled.

Harriet touched his arm. 'You mustn't blame yourself. I know you can't see your father as he's warned off, won't you find that hard?'

Freddie flushed. 'Not really. Mum and Dad are getting divorced. We both think what he did was terrible.' He nodded at his mother. 'Besides, I've always been a lot closer to Mum.'

Just then an older couple, who Hattie did not recognise sidled past them, glaring at Penny as they went.

'Come on, Giles. We really ought to leave,' the woman hissed, loud enough for everyone to hear. 'Who on earth let this riff raff in?'

Freddie blushed and looked at his shoes. Harriet's heart went out to him but when she looked around, she noticed that the crowd around had dispersed and she felt waves of hostility being directed at the young jockey and his mother. A stable lad, Jack Bishop, who had been close to one of the victims in the scandal, Paddy Owen, walked past glowering at Penny. He deliberately nudged her arm, making her glass of red wine spill all over her.

'Hey, look where you're going,' Finn shouted to the man's disappearing back. 'Oh, just ignore them. Everyone will soon forget about Henry...'

Penny's eyes filled with tears. 'I know, I know, but to be honest Finn, I haven't seen some of these people since then and the stares and gossip are hard to take. Harder than I thought they'd be, actually.'

'Do stay,' added Hattie. 'Just ride it out. You've every right to be here.' She pulled out a handkerchief from her bag and gave it to Penny to wipe her dress with. Penny dabbed at the wine mark and handed it back. She shook her head and seemed to come to a decision.

'I'm sorry, we shouldn't have come.' Penny smiled apologetically and made her way through the crowd and out of the hotel. Freddie followed her.

Finn waited until she was out of earshot. 'Such a shame. People certainly have long memories round here. It's hard on them both and I really feel for Freddie.'

They saw Seamus and Rosie as they were leaving. 'Have you seen Niall?' asked Rosie. 'Clare left earlier to look round the horses, but Niall was still here, but he seems to have gone too.'

'Maybe he's popped out with some of the other jockeys?'

Rosie smiled. 'I'm sure you're right.'

Finn arranged to see them later in the week.

The party petered out and after prising Nat away from a long discussion with Caroline Regan, they made their way back to Finn's where they pooled their information.

'Freddie seemed really sweet, actually and Penny,' was Harriet's verdict. She explained what had happened to Nat. 'I felt really sorry for them.'

'So, what else did you find out?' asked Finn

Hattie explained about her conversation with the restorers. 'One of them said that about a quarter of art finds are fakes, so that's interesting but Pandora, Christian's daughter, says that that's rubbish.'

'Hmm. The mind boggles,' added Finn. 'I suppose there's lots of money to be made in art fraud though.'

Nat looked thoughtful. 'You've got some interesting conditionals, that Niall Byrne and Freddie Mercer. You've got your work cut out there, I read about Byrne and his drink driving and as for Mercer. He's the spit of his father, Teasdale,' remarked Nat.

'I know, I know. He seems a decent enough lad, but you never can tell.'

108

Nat looked thoughtful. 'As they say, the apple doesn't fall far from the tree. Let's hope that's not true in his case. Pandora's an interesting girl. Underneath that Goth get up, she's actually quite pretty. She seems to be an accomplished artist in her own right, and I hear that Penny Mercer is still painting. She did some lovely pet portraits.' He sipped his drink. 'Anyway, are you any further forward in working out if the Maclaren painting is genuine? What are your plans?'

'My uncle Sebastian is something of an expert. I'm sure he'll be able to help. We can certainly ask him to look at the painting.' Harriet smiled at Finn. 'You'll like him, he's a real character.'

'Good idea. Of course, Ross Maclaren will know where he got the painting, so he'll know the provenance and all that,' added Finn. All roads seemed to lead back to Ross Maclaren. They needed to find him sooner rather than later.

Nat nodded. 'What are your thoughts about where he might be holed up?'

Finn and Harriet looked at one another. 'Well, we do have an idea, but hopefully he'll be at Haydock to watch Admiral run.'

'Let's hope so, if he still owns him. You know, Livvy is still in New York. She could express an interest in the other Red Navajo painting there and have a nosy around at it. She has a girlfriend whose husband is a collector who knows a thing or two about art. Chap called Will Molyneux. He could certainly give us his opinion on that painting. He may not be as expert as your uncle, but it's worth a shot.'

'It certainly is.' Finn frowned. 'We need to know so the gallery doesn't sell their Gideon Moss as the real deal, assuming Maclaren's is the original.'

'Christian was trying to get Jeremy to add the Maclaren painting to the exhibition. People can buy them, you know, so we need to know which one is the original,' added Nat.

Harriet looked thoughtful. 'We certainly do. Perhaps, Uncle Sebastian can liaise with this Will Molyneux person in New York then? When is the exhibition?'

'In two weeks,' replied Finn. 'So, we need to get a move on. Mind you, if we can speak to Ross Maclaren then I'm sure he can verify the painting.'

With Nat leaving the next day, they all arranged to meet at Haydock and keep alert for any information in the meantime. Nat was keen to be helpful too.

'I'll ask Stan Denton if he knows anything about Admiral's new owners and let you know.'

Harriet nodded. 'Brilliant. Well, we've scattered a few firecrackers, that's for sure, let's just wait and see if there's any fall out.'

Chapter 12

Finn settled down with his morning coffee and toast and started to read Ross Maclaren's first book where the reader is introduced to the hero, Robert Miles Banks, an ex SAS soldier who went rogue. He looked at the blurb on the back about the author and wondered where on earth he was and what he knew about the painting. He studied the thumbnail photo of the author, trying to commit his patrician face to memory so that he'd recognise him if he did turn up at Haydock. He was usually good at recognising faces, so he thought he'd be able to pick him out of the crowd. Next on his list was to visit his conditionals and check on their progress and the best place.

It was great to go to the communal gallops in Walton. Finn found out so much by watching his conditionals ride. It blew the cobwebs away just being outside in such a lovely spot, even on a cold morning, and if he kept his ear to the ground, he could find out exactly what was going on in the racing world. It was a large area bordered by huge oak and beech trees set just on the outskirts of the town with laybys on the road and a small parking area for horse boxes. There was a trail for 4x4 vehicles, and some trainers used this to drive up onto the gallops and see the horses at close quarters. Most of the local trainers used the facility although some had their own gallops, especially those who lived further away whose horses would require transporting here. The facilities were excellent though, with at least four tracks of different distances, all on an incline, and one an all weather track and with a range of hurdles and larger chase fences at one side. Trainers arrived throughout the day, usually the morning and the streets of Walton were often ringing with the sound of horses' hooves as the strings made their way to the gallops. This morning the place was a hive of activity as usual, with strings of horses in their yard's jackets, and matching hat silks making their way up the tracks. Finn had parked his car in the layby and enjoyed the stroll up onto the gallops, enjoying the winter sunshine as it flickered through the trees. He had arranged to meet Freddie there to put him through his paces, but also cast his eye over his other conditionals if they were riding. Jeremy had his own gallops at home but did transport some of his horses by box to use the facilities from time to time for a change of scene. His own gallops were being currently resurfaced, so were out of use.

Jeremy was in a Land Rover near the fences and was instructing Freddie to warm up. He smiled at Finn as he arrived. Finn decided not to say anything about the other painting for now until they knew a bit more.

'When will your own gallops be finished?'

Jeremy shrugged. 'Oh, in a couple of days, but in the meantime, it's helpful to bring the horses here for a change.'

Finn nodded, his eyes scanning the horses and riders. He spotted Freddie riding a bay horse. 'So how is he doing so far?'

'Very well. He's a nice lad, hardworking and a decent rider although he has been struggling with the shorter stirrup lengths.'

Finn laughed. 'I suppose that's to be expected making the transition from eventing to racing, but I'm sure he'll get there. Are you OK if I ask him to do some jumping, is the horse up to it?'

'Yep, be my guest. The horse is called Tenacious, a fair hurdler, so he should be fine. '

Finn went to talk to Freddie who smiled.

'Everything alright?'

'Great. I just need to get used to riding with shorter stirrups and balancing over fences, that's all.'

'Fine. Do you want to have a go at the hurdles, maybe have a longer stirrup length to begin with and then put them higher.' Finn adjusted the stirrups to a mid point between an eventing and racing length. 'Try these. Do a couple of circuits in trot and then canter and pop over these fences when you're ready.' Finn pointed at a row of brush hurdles.

He ran back to Jeremy and climbed into the passenger side of the Land Rover. They watched as Freddie warmed the horse up and then jumped over the row of hurdles. The lad wobbled alarmingly over the first two but settled down to a better position over the last few fences.

'Go again!' yelled Finn.

This time, the lad did better but was insistent on positioning his horse for each fence rather than letting the horse see the stride.

112

Jeremy tutted. 'He's not bloody showjumping. I loose school all my horses so he doesn't need to hold him up!'

'I know. I'll have a word.'

Loose schooling was the practice of putting the horse in an arena without a rider and getting them to jump on their own, so they learn to trust their judgement about striding, and therefore not lose speed whilst positioning themselves. Most quickly picked up what was expected of them. It worked well and taught the horse to sort itself out over fences and become proficient at the striding, which was one less problem for the jockey to worry about. Not all trainers did this, but it certainly did help the horse and Finn approved of this practice, having been the beneficiary of it many times.

Finn ran back out of the vehicle towards Freddie. 'Right, I'll put the stirrups up to almost racing length so you can have another go, and this time give Tenacious his head. He knows what he's doing, and he doesn't need riding so carefully. I know you're used to showjumping and those huge cross country fences but these are smaller, the top part is flexible, you're not going to get any faults. The aim of the game is speed. The horse knows what he's doing and doesn't need you to interfere. OK?'

Freddie nodded and tried again, this time managing much better. Tenacious flew over the fences far more quickly with minimal intervention from his rider. By the end of the session, both Jeremy and Finn praised Freddie and were feeling much happier and discussed his progress in the Land Rover.

'Next time we'll concentrate on positioning within a race. Freddie's used to riding without other horses around him, so that is something we'll need to work on, but so far so good.'

Finn fed back to Freddie and then made his way back to Jeremy.

'Did you see that Admiral is running at Haydock. Nat Wilson is riding him.'

Jeremy frowned. 'I bloody well did! Seems the owner is now RHB Holdings whoever they might be. I can't think Ross would have sold him though, he'd be a fool if he has.' He shrugged. 'I suppose it depends how much debt he's in. He certainly earned a lot but was always a bit of a spendthrift though, so who knows?' He fidgeted, clearly intensely irritated. 'I don't know this other trainer, but honestly, I just want to smooth over this

113

argument and have Admiral back where he belongs! Have you made any progress in the case?'

'Well, Hattie and I are going to Haydock to see if we can see Maclaren because he might be there.' Finn was unsure how much to reveal. 'We are making progress, but if he still owns Admiral, I'm sure he won't be able to resist seeing him run.'

'Good point. Just tell him he can come back!' Jeremy sighed. 'I'll wait to hear from you.'

Finn had spotted Vince Hunt and went to talk to him about his conditional, Jamie Doyle. He spotted Jamie riding Limoncello, a horse that Vince had high hopes of. A nice looking bay gelding, he appeared to be working well.

'How is Jamie doing? Is he ready to race ride yet?'

'Getting there, though he seems a bit distracted and forgetful. He's on Limoncello as you can see. Him and Gregorian are owned by a new chap, Eugene Casey, an Irish man. He likes the set up in Walton and wanted a smaller trainer for his horses, so they could have the human one to one input that they just wouldn't get in a larger yard.'

Sometimes horses in larger yards didn't always get the same level of attention, Finn knew of one horse who was barely ridden for several weeks as his name had been rubbed off the whiteboard in the tack room by mistake. This was far less likely to happen in a smaller yard, so he could quite understand the owner's point of view.

'Is it alright if he has a go over the hurdles?'

'Sure. He's been in lots of point to points in Ireland and Limoncello should be fine, so no problem.'

Finn went to meet Jamie and gave him some instructions over hurdles and suggested that if things went well, then they could try the steeplechase fences.

Jamie grinned enthusiastically.

'Grand.'

After warming up, Limoncello jumped effortlessly over the row of hurdles. Finn had him jumping at angles and coming from different directions.

'We can leave it there or if you want you can try the steeplechase fences?'

Jamie grinned, his face lighting up at the prospect.

'Well, they're obviously larger so you'll need to maintain your position and prepare for take off, so you don't give him a jab in the mouth.' Finn studied the fences for a moment. Some of them were much larger, wider and more solid than the hurdle fences. 'You don't need to jump them; we can always have a go another day.'

'Nah, I'll give it a go, right enough.'

'Great.'

There was a ditch and a couple of tall brush fences. Jamie circled then set the big bay over the fences but struggled to maintain his seat over the last two. Finn wanted to end on a high, so advised him to prepare his seat better before the fences and asked him to go again. As he was watching, he saw out of the corner of his eye, a couple of men advancing up the gallops to where the vehicles were parked. They were dressed smartly and had warm overcoats and smart shoes, clearly professional. Then it came to him. They had a confident air, so much so, he knew that they were police officers. He wondered what they wanted as they seemed to be heading towards where Vince was parked. He flicked his gaze back to Jamie when there was a shout and a thud and then Limoncello came galloping past without his rider. Finn jogged after the horse as the reins were caught in his forelegs and thankfully caught up with the animal when he slowed down to a trot.

'There, there boy. Come on now, no need to gallop off. Let's check you out.' The horse shivered, his ears pricked. He neighed but allowed Finn to stroke him, unravel his reins from his forelegs and lead him back to where Jamie was standing, pale but holding out his wrist. It was bent at an odd angle and looked broken. The two smartly dressed men were talking to Vince and Jamie. They flashed their warrant cards.

'We're here from the police. Can we have a word with you about Niall Byrne?'

Finn noticed Jamie's pale face and the fact that he was clutching his wrist. He decided to take charge.

'I'm afraid gents, we'll need to take Jamie to the hospital to get his wrist checked out, so your interview will have to wait.'

Jamie nodded and looked forlorn. 'I'll pop into the station right enough when I've got this sorted.'

115

'Mind you do sir,' added the taller of the two men. 'We really need to speak to you, and you've not responded to previous calls. We also need to speak to Lottie Henderson.'

'I'm Jamie's jockey coach so I'll make sure he does come in, but for now he does need to get to hospital.' He explained that he also worked with Lottie and gave them directions to Seamus's yard. The two men didn't look at all happy but had no choice to agree to postpone their interview. Vince had called another rider over and arrangements were made to transport Jamie to hospital. Finn watched as the two police officers made their way back down the track. A strange thought occurred to Finn. Jamie had done pretty well over the larger fences and there had been no indication that he was going to fall. Limoncello had been jumping cleanly too. Had Jamie realised that the two men were police officers and thrown himself off the horse to avoid being questioned by them? Did he have something to hide about what happened that night when Niall was arrested? Surely not.

He was still deep in thought when he arrived home, grabbed a shower and ironed a clean shirt. Maybe he was overthinking things, he hadn't actually seen the fall, so it could have been due to anything, maybe the horse was spooked, or had swerved and who in their right mind would engineer a fall from a horse to avoid speaking to the police? Jamie was keen to be riding, so it didn't make sense at all. He was just being fanciful. He concentrated on getting ready, applied a splash of aftershave and chose a warm coat, his anticipation building for the date with Theresa.

Theresa looked gorgeous, her complexion glowed, and her dark curls were worn loose around her shoulders. She wore a red and black patterned wrap dress which showed off her slim figure. They had arranged to meet at a French restaurant in York which served really authentic cuisine. Theresa tucked into her beef bourguignon with real relish. Like Harriet, she enjoyed her food and did not pick at it unlike some of the women he had taken out. Not that he was one to talk. In his racing days he'd had to be very careful about his weight due to his near 6 foot height and tended to eat snacks throughout the day and then one larger meal later. These days he ate better, enjoyed his food but still weighed just a stone and a half over his riding weight, now a much healthier weight for a man of his build and size.

'So, I presume Niall is more settled now?'

Theresa smiled. 'I think so, though of course he's still got the court case, but I think he can see beyond that now.'

'Good. The police came to talk to Jamie Doyle today on the gallops about that evening, but he had fallen off so had to go to hospital.'

Theresa smiled. 'Oh, I'm sure it's just routine. So, do you think Niall could make it as a jockey?'

Finn considered this carefully. 'I think so, he has talent that is for sure, but you need a good work ethic, a bit of charm and a bit of luck too. Fingers crossed, he'll get there.'

He was rewarded by a huge grin.

'So, what have you been up to? How's work?' he asked.

'Oh, busy, you know. There's an awful lot of sorting the kids out, doing disciplinary stuff, liaising with social services, that sort of thing.'

'Do you actually do any teaching?'

'A bit.'

'And what is it that you teach?'

'Art and design, so I keep my hand in.' Theresa smiled.

'Wow.' It was so strange, suddenly his whole life seemed to be full of artists and paintings. He was tempted to tell her about their search for the missing author and Jeremy's dilemma, but he decided against it. It was better to tell people on a need to know basis. He thought he could talk about the artist in general terms though.

'Have you heard of the equine artist, Gideon Moss.'

Theresa laughed. 'No, I haven't. I like more contemporary artists, Lydia Jamieson is very good animal artist and I also like Hockney, Hirst, Klimt, Banksy.'

'Do you paint yourself?'

'Just the odd daub.' Theresa smiled. 'I did think I would be famous when I was at University, I was so enthusiastic, thought everything I did was so original. But, in the end, you grow up and that's that. Even with talent, it would be so hard to make a living from art, you'd need to be discovered and nurtured and that was never going to happen, so I did what everyone in the same situation does, teach!'

There was self deprecation in there, but also real regret. Finn stretched his hand out and held hers.

117

'That must have been hard.'

Theresa laughed. 'Ah, it has its compensations. Long school holidays with lots of trips abroad, the kids are great and so funny, and you never know I may teach a budding Banksy or Damien Hirst, so I'll settle for that. But that's why I want to help Niall follow his dreams, as I couldn't achieve mine.'

'Very laudable. Niall's so lucky to have his big sister look out for him.' Finn suspected that Theresa had made a great many sacrifices to help Niall and it made him all the more determined to help him.

The conversation progressed on to future plans and past loves. Finn told her about his relationship history and the fact that he had never been married.

'Oh, I was married, but it didn't work out and we divorced after a couple of years. We just ran out of steam although me mammie said it was because he was English, of course. He didn't pass the Byrne test apparently, no Irish heritage to speak of. Now, with a name like Finn McCarthy, you've got to have some Irish blood, haven't yer?'

'I have. My paternal grandfather and maternal grandmother were Irish for starters.'

Theresa laughed. 'Irish blood on both sides! I think you'd pass the Byrne test, though, right enough.' She seemed very pleased, and Finn thanked his lucky stars for his ancestry.

They finished their drinks and got a taxi home.

'Are yer coming in?' Theresa looked at him steadily.

Finn gazed at her later, noticing her creamy skin and the slight bruising under her eyes. He knew he was really falling for her. They had so much in common. She showed some vulnerability and he really wanted to help her and Niall. She smiled at him, a slow, sexy smile and he was lost.

He had an early start and decided to creep out of bed without waking Theresa. He struggled into his clothes in the hallway and decided to leave her a note. He wandered around downstairs and opened a random door which he thought led to the hallway. Instead, he found it was a sort of studio which was full of paintings, a wide variety of canvasses, paints and piles of old picture frames. His gaze rested on a pad of notes, written in a small neat hand. Presumably they were for students, feedback probably. He felt a rush of affection for Theresa. Bless her, all that effort. He felt uneasy to look at more, as though he had wandered into her private space. So, he pulled out a piece of paper and pencil and scribbled her a note which he left on the kitchen table.

It was only later when he plugged in his phone in his car that he saw he'd had lots of messages and missed calls. Several were from Harriet and some from Rosie and Gabriel Taverner. He rang Harriet first. She sounded like she had an awful cold then he realised to his horror that she was crying.

'Oh God, oh God, it's Clare!'

Finn listened, his blood running cold with a terrible foreboding.

'What? What about Clare?'

'There's been an accident. She wasn't in work this morning and then they found her, she's dead...' There was a muffled sob. 'She was in one of the stables, she'd been kicked by a horse several times.' Harriet blew her nose. 'I just can't believe it, the poor girl. After everything she'd gone through and then after Tom's accident...' she wailed.

'Oh Christ! Bet it was that mare Sweet Pea or whatever her name is. Are you OK? Do you want me to come round?'

Harriet sniffed. 'No, it's alright. I'm just talking to Mum and having a coffee. Gabriel is on the case, and I think he wants to talk to you too.'

'OK.' Finn took this in and instantly wondered if there was more to Clare's death than met the eye. Obviously, the police would investigate any sudden death but still what on earth was she doing in the stable at night? He'd ring Gabriel and see what he could find out. 'Listen, do you still want to go to Haydock today? It's fine if you want to miss it.'

Harriet seemed to rally. 'Of course, we can't bring Clare back and I need to think about something else. It's just one of those tragic accidents, I suppose.'

'I suppose so. I'll pick you up in about an hour then?'

He rang Rosie and Seamus, Seamus answered sounding absolutely broken. 'Missus has taken it hard, she was so fond of the lass, we both were...'

'Which horse's stable was she found in?'

'Sweet Pea's. She came back from the do at The Stagecoach and must have gone in there to check on the horse. She loved that bloody mare,

119

too!' He fought back tears. 'That policeman has been round, nice fella he was. I can't believe it, Finn, so soon after Tom! Who'll tell him for God's sake, poor wee fella!'

Finn imagined that horrible task would fall to the police, probably Taverner. As he clicked off the call, the man himself rang.

'Ah, Finn. I presume you've heard about Clare Hudson. It's an awful thing to find a girl like that dead. I know you had dealings with her and encouraged her to report her rape to the police.'

'Me and Hattie both spoke to her, as you know. I presume it was an accidental death and she was killed by Sweet Pea?'

There was a pause. 'Sweet Pea, oh the horse. Well, there will be a post mortem of course. Can I ask you, is it usual to keep the headcollar on a horse in a stable?'

Finn felt the cold finger of alarm creep down his spine. 'It's not usual at all, but Sweet Pea was stroppy. In fact, I suggested they keep a headcollar on her as she could be head shy, so maybe they decided to leave it on.' Finn sighed. 'She had a leather one on, so it would break if it caught on anything inside the stable.'

There was a long pause. 'And what about the top stable door, it would be unusual for that to be closed, wouldn't it?'

Finn stiffened. 'Definitely. Was it closed and bolted?'

'Jammed with a lead rope.'

'I suppose the wind could have blown it closed but usually they are hard to shift. There's usually a hook on the back of the top door that fits into an eye attached to the main stable to keep it open. 'A horrible thought occurred to him. 'Do you think her death is suspicious?'

Taverner sighed. 'We're in the early stages of our investigation, but it could also be a tragic accident. Can I ask you to keep your ear to the ground and let me know if you hear anything?'

He hardly needed to ask. 'Of course.'

'And keep an eye on Hattie will you, she's dreadfully upset and as this is now my case, I'm going to be really busy.'

Finn assured him that he would and rang off deeply troubled. Was it an accident? He hoped so but he couldn't help but wonder if their probing about paintings, fakes and the like, had somehow led to Clare being murdered? Then he dismissed his gloomy thoughts. It was bound to be an accidental death, of course it was.

Chapter 13

They both travelled to Haydock in something of a contemplative mood. Finn noticed Hattie wiping away tears from time to time and tried to cheer her up.

'Look. If you're not feeling up to it, I can drive you back home, we've plenty of time, you know.'

Harriet smiled. 'It's fine. I'm just shocked and upset for Clare, that's all. She'd been through so much and just when things started to go well for her...'

'I know. I feel the same. Rosie is absolutely in bits.'

'What will happen to the horse?'

Finn had wondered that himself. 'I'm not sure. She's a talented mare by all accounts, but if she's so hard to handle then safety has to be a major consideration. On the other hand, if she just kicked out and kicked Clare accidentally, then it's a tragic accident. There will be a post mortem, of course.'

Finn didn't mention the anomaly of the stable door being closed, which suggested something far more sinister. As for Sweet Pea, horses were herd animals, and their instinct would be to kick out if they saw a suspicious movement behind which frightened them. Then again, Clare was an experienced horsewoman so she would have known to exercise caution.

'Anyway, let's try and focus on the day and see if we can find Ross Maclaren, shall we? It's no use speculating about Clare's death, we just have to let the police do their job.'

Harriet smiled slightly at this. 'Yes, we do. I have memorised Maclaren's face and don't forget his height, he's 6' 3'' plus so he should be hard to miss.'

'Absolutely.' Finn smiled back, he was pleased that Harriet's mood seemed to have lifted which was something. Although she looked pale and tired, she was, he knew, a resilient character and calm in a crisis.

The first person they saw at Haydock Park was Topper McGrew. He greeted them both effusively.

122

'Bit of a story brewing here, I reckon,' he tapped his nose. 'Admiral Jervis is the favourite in the big race, and I reckon that writer chap, Ross Maclaren, is going to be kicking himself selling such a good prospect. I can't believe he's sold the gelding, and no one seems to know anything about RMB Holdings, so I'm sensing something of a mystery. Your pal Nat Wilson's on board too.' His eyes roved over Finn and Harriet. 'You don't know anything do you?'

Finn laughed. 'Not much. Nat thinks he's on to a winner, but you never can tell.' Finn had studied form. There were some good horses in the race. 'Reformed Character stands a good chance too.'

Topper nodded sagely. 'Worth an each way bet, I reckon. I'll catch you in the bar after the race and buy you a drink. ' He lowered his voice. 'It's a pity Jeremy fell out with Ross Maclaren. Still, maybe Ross didn't sell Admiral Jervis after all.' His eyes gleamed. 'I'll keep an eye out for Mr Maclaren. Let's see if he turns up. He'd be a fool to sell such a good horse and I'm betting he hasn't.'

Hattie grinned at him. 'Well, if you see him then do tell me. My dad is a great fan of his books and he'd love an autograph from the man himself.'

Topper raised his hat. 'Certainly, my dear. Anyway, must dash, people to see, stories to sniff out. Oh, terrible shame about the young stable girl who was killed at the Ryans' yard, by the way. Still, I suppose horses are wild beasts underneath everything. A tragedy for the poor girl and her family though.'

Finn wondered how he knew about Clare, but then stories, news, scandal and all the rest was his business. He suspected that Topper was fishing for information. He wasn't about to mention what Taverner had told him. He merely nodded. 'It certainly was a tragic accident and awful. The Ryans are devastated, of course.'

'And after her boyfriend was injured too, such a pity.' Topper shook his head, musing on the vicissitudes of life. 'Anyway, best get on.' He tapped his nose and was gone, disappearing into the well dressed afternoon crowd. Hattie looked around the place, pleased to be back at one of her favourite courses with its leafy rural surroundings, the trees ablaze with colour, autumn sludgy greens, yellows and oranges.

'He doesn't change, does he?'

'Not a bit. He's always sniffing out a story. He's as sharp as a tack but it was a good call telling him about your father's passion for Maclaren's books. With three pairs of eyes looking for him, if he's here then we're sure to find him.'

They had decided en route on a strategy to search Haydock Park and find Ross Maclaren. Hattie was going to look in the bars and restaurants whilst Finn was going to check out the jockeys' areas and parade ring. Nat had promised to ask a few questions of Admiral's trainer. He'd yet to hear from him.

'He has to put his phone away and can't use it until after the last race, so we'll just have to wait.'

Hattie looked at her watch. 'Plan B is to go to his cottage if we can find it, I suppose, but it's a lot further to drive and he may be evasive. It might be easier to catch him here. Anyway, time for a drink and something to eat, I reckon.'

Finn grinned. 'Yep, let's go.'

Hattie followed Finn, heading towards the members' bar in the main stand. There was the usual crowd of smart enthusiasts on this blustery October day. As they moved inside along a corridor decorated with racing prints, Hattie stopped.

'Look Finn, there's a hunting painting.' She pointed to a scene depicting horses jumping over a fence. In this painting the riders seemed to adopt the leaning back position and were more stylised in format. They both studied the card underneath the painting.

'A lovely painting circa 1850 by an unknown artist,' read Finn. He studied the canvas closely to see if there was a signature but couldn't find the distinctive G Moss squiggle. On reflection, the composition was different those of Gideon Moss, even to his eyes. The horses were less well defined, and the conformation not as well depicted. He stepped back to take a photo with his phone and nearly collided with a man in a wheelchair who was wearing a greenish tweed suit and had a trilby pulled low over his face. He was also wearing dark glasses.

'Oh, I'm so sorry,' said Finn and stepped back further to let the man pass.

The man waved the apology aside and wheeled on without a backwards glance.

124

At the restaurant, munching hot pork and apple sauce baps Hattie glanced around the small bar. 'So, what are we looking for? We know Maclaren's characters like disguises. I mean the main protagonist in Maclaren's books is described as wearing a bush hat, camouflage trousers and jacket, so that doesn't help us.'

Finn studied a photo of Maclaren from the jacket of his last book on his phone. 'Well, we know he's tall and slim with angular features. Reckon he would just wear a trilby and hide out in the stands, hiding behind binoculars. That's what I'd do. '

'Mmm, this is lovely' said Hattie through a mouthful of pork. 'Maybe he'd go into the other public enclosures, thinking he was less likely to be recognised. I'll nip over there when I've finished my coffee. What do we do if we see him, approach him, take photos?'

Finn considered this. 'Tail him and try to make contact if possible. But we don't want to scare him, just talk to him about Admiral. If needs be, we could follow him to his car, at the end of the day, if you've time. I'm sure he'll be here.'

They split up and Hattie went over to the Grandstand and Paddock areas away from the County Enclosure. She glanced here and there trying to spot anyone who resembled Maclaren, maybe in disguise. She spotted an unusually tall woman, but she noticed that her jaw and nose were different, when she turned around, softer and not at all like the craggy, patrician looks of the author. Then she went into the bar and pretending to be waiting for someone, slowly eyed the occupants but found no one who looked remotely like Maclaren.

Hattie also paraded down the row of bookies, but most tall men were fatter than the author and didn't fit the bill. If he's in disguise, it's a good one, she thought, wondering if the author would go to the trouble of padding himself out or wearing a fat suit. But she rejected the idea as somehow it seemed too theatrical for a former soldier.

Back at the parade ring Hattie caught up with Finn. The horses for the main race were now making their way down to the start.

'Anything?'

Finn shook his head. 'No one came to stand with Nat and the trainer for instructions. Maybe he really has sold the horse and the new owners couldn't make it.'

125

Hattie frowned. 'Or he's watching from home. That's what I'd do on a cold, windy day like today.'

The race began and it turned into a ding dong battle with Admiral Jervis disputing the lead most of the way round with Beginner's Luck. At the final jump Nat got a huge leap out of Admiral Jervis and his lead was in no doubt. In the end, he won comfortably by about six lengths. They both rushed to the winner's enclosure and had a good look around but again could not see anyone who resembled the author waiting to congratulate the jockey and trainer.

Nat posed for photos and as he made his way back to the weighing room, Finn congratulated him.

'Thanks Finn. I'll try to catch you later. As I said I've been asked to loan a painting for the exhibition in Walton, so if you could drop it off? I've brought it with me.'

Nat had already mentioned this, and Finn was happy to oblige. 'Sure, no problems.'

Hattie pulled her green scarf around her neck as the wind was blowing up and there was a crispness to the air which suggested a frost later. 'I'll get us a drink, Finn. I don't think he's here.'

'Meet you in there. I'm just going to ask around in the paddock to see if anyone has seen him.'

In the members' bar Hattie ordered two whisky macs then found a table. Finn joined her a few minutes later.

'So, I think we'll have to have a rethink. He's proving pretty elusive this Maclaren guy, isn't he? No one seems to know anything,' said Finn.

As they were drinking, Nat appeared with Topper. The two had had a rather strained relationship in the past when Topper had written some critical articles about the jockey, but now they had clearly resolved their difficulties and were on more cordial terms. Nat ordered coffee for them both and then joined Finn and Hattie.

'Great win,' said Hattie. 'Admiral won easily in the end.'

Nat grinned. 'Cheers, he's as good a horse as I've ridden in a long time. My next ride's been scratched. Got a leg, so I thought I'd come and see you before I head home.' He stretched out his legs and nicked a chip off Harriet's plate. He was in good spirits, the very picture of health and contentment, Harriet couldn't help but notice.

'So, you've never seen Admiral Jervis's owner?' asked Finn. 'No congratulatory phone calls or anything?'

Nat shook his head. 'The trainer, Stan said the horse arrived and all contact with RMB Holdings is by email. Fees arrive promptly and he's never tried to find out more. I mean, who would? Good horse like that, you'd just take the money and enjoy training him.'

Topper was listening intently. 'Mmm. I have asked about and can't find anything about the new owner, nothing at all.' He stood up. 'Anyway, I just need to see what's happening in this next race. I'll see you later.' He raised his hat and was gone.

'Odd though,' said Finn thoughtfully. 'Mind you, this is his first win for the new trainer, and he only left Jeremy's recently, you'd had thought the new owners, if they exist, would have turned up today.'

'Walk out with me,' said Nat, 'I want to give you that painting I mentioned.'

When they reached Nat's car, he opened the boot and picked up a painting covered in a horse rug which looked none too clean. Hattie moved the rug aside to have a peek.

She laughed. 'Christ, Nat. Have you just bunged it in your boot?'

Nat shrugged. 'Yeah. As I said, it's not my cup of tea at all.' He wrinkled his nose. 'Awful bloody thing. Anyway, I give Livvy free rein with the décor and all that malarky and she hates this painting. She prefers Lydia Jamieson's stuff.'

Finn had heard of Lydia Jamieson, a young artist who was gathering a considerable reputation in the world of art. Trust Livvy, he thought, she always did have impeccable taste. He looked at Nat's Daniel Jacob's painting. It was modern, stylised and had much more impact in person that when he had seen the photo of it on Nat's phone.

Hattie studied it carefully. 'It could be worth a bit though. You'd have had to have used white glove transport then.'

Predictably she had to explain what it was.

Nat laughed. 'No way. The rug will do just as well. Hey, maybe I'll even sell it.'

'Are the paintings at the exhibition for sale then?'

'So Gerrard said.' He rubbed his hands together. 'Might need it with everything Livvy has planned for the wedding. I suggested the barn at The Stagecoach as a venue, but it didn't end well.'

'Have you set a date then yet?' asked Harriet.

'No, but we're working on it.' He grinned and ran his fingers through his hair. 'If it were me, I'd just have a quick ceremony in a week or so, with a handful of people and pop down the pub later, I can't be doing with all the fuss. I'm worried she'll change her mind the longer this goes on and then she realises what I'm really like!' He chewed his lip and looked downcast.

Harriet laughed. 'Course she won't change her mind, Nat.'

Nat grinned. 'I hope not.' He suddenly looked vulnerable.

Harriet was about to reassure him when they heard a shout.

'Finn, Harriet!' Topper McGrew jogged towards them from the racecourse. He looked excitedly at them. 'Listen, I think I have just spotted Maclaren. I reckon he put a heavy bet on Admiral, and I saw him pick up his winnings just now.'

Harriet groaned. 'How did you manage to find him?'

Topper grinned. 'He was in disguise as a chap in a wheelchair. I called after him and he bombed off and I saw him practically run the last few strides to his car, fold up the wheelchair and drive off. Disabled, he certainly was not! He headed off towards the motorway in a Land Rover, but with the queue to leave, he'll be long gone.'

Hattie and Finn exchanged a stunned look as they cast their minds back to the punters they had studied.

'Christ, he was the man looking at the painting! We'll never catch him now. Damn! I can't bloody believe it!' exclaimed Finn.

'A wheelchair was the perfect way to disguise his height,' added Harriet glumly. 'I suppose we were so concerned to move out of the way, we didn't really look at him.' She remembered that he was wearing a trilby and sunglasses, so it was a good disguise all in all.

'Anyway, it's too late to follow him but I think that tells us all we need to know, doesn't it?' Topper raised his hat. 'Anyway, I'll be off, see you all anon.'

Nat waited for Topper to disappear and looked at the pair. He had an air of suppressed excitement about him.

128

'Listen, I've just thought of something. Livvy likes Maclaren's books; she says that she's surprised that he's never won an award for his writing. She loves them. Anyway, it made me think how you could easily persuade him to break cover.'

'How?'

Nat grinned. 'He's been nominated for several prizes but hasn't actually won any of them.'

'And?'

Nat shook his head incredulously. 'All you have to do is pose as a member of an organisation doling out a prestigious award and then say you need to meet him in person to discuss it. Then bob's your uncle!' He looked from Finn to Hattie. 'He won't be able to resist coming to meet you, I guarantee it!'

Harriet bounced up and down and could not resist giving Nat a hug.

'That's brilliant, utterly amazing, Nat! Why didn't I think of that?'

Nat flushed, beaming with pleasure. 'Because clearly you are not as devious as me.'

'Hmm. It might just work,' added Finn.

They said their goodbyes. Finn promised to take Nat's painting to Gerrard, and they made their way home.

After discussing how they have missed the man in the wheelchair and how stupid they had been to not spot him, they settled down in silence. Hattie pulled a novel from her bag. It was one of Maclaren's and then she spent some time googling things on her phone. Eventually, the flurry of activity came to an end.

'I've got it. Listen, I did some research on Maclaren and like Nat said he has been nominated for The Golden Gun thriller award three times but has never won it.'

'OK.'

'Well, supposing I rang his agent or wife, probably both and claimed to be from The Golden Gun's award's panel and said I needed to meet him urgently, arrange something and then we turn up. The result for the proper award is due to be announced in a few weeks' time, so the timings fit and it's open to books published within the last few years. So, his last book would be eligible.'

129

'Hmm. Do you know anyone on the award's panel. I mean, we'll need to get everything as accurate as possible.'

Harriet smiled triumphantly and showed him the Google page on her phone. 'Yes. Look, the secretary who has been arranging the panel is a Madeleine Frost.' She held up her phone to showed Finn a photo of the woman from her Facebook page. 'She's mentioned in articles about the nominations as a contact person.'

Harriet suddenly threw back her head, getting into role. 'I mean how hard can it be? I bet she'll say something like, 'Yes, darling. Your book is a tour de force, a literary masterpiece,' she added in a breathy voice.

Finn laughed. 'How do you know Madeleine would speak like that?'

'Because literary people all seem to, haven't you noticed.' Her mood was buoyant. 'Fancy Nat thinking of that. He really is one of my favourite people.'

'Mine too.' Finn meant it. He was so glad that Nat was back in his life. At least they had made some progress in their inquiries and Harriet had something positive to focus on rather than Clare and her tragic accident. A slight feeling of disquiet gnawed away at Finn about Clare's death, but he dismissed it. The post mortem would rule that her death was a horrible accident, he was sure of it. Or was it just the alternative was just too awful to contemplate?

Chapter 14

Topper was washing up the dinner things after he and his sons had had a takeaway pizza. In fact, Topper had made his own healthy pizza using pitta bread, tomato puree and a little cheese for himself whilst letting the boys feast on the real deal. He had rustled up a fruit salad for pudding. The boys were getting ready for bed, and he was due to take them back to school tomorrow afternoon, after an early morning fishing session in the nearby anglers' lake.

As he washed the dishes, Topper ran through the events of the last few days centring on the death of the stable girl Clare Hudson, which by now was big news. He was due to write a piece about it for tomorrow and as usual found himself mentally planning what to write, where to find information and trying to judge how much of the facts to take at face value. Was it really just a tragic accident? On balance he thought, probably 80% yes. But there were nagging doubts. He could not stop himself replaying the events of the last few weeks, as he scrubbed at a particularly stubborn ketchup stain.

A kaleidoscope of images played though his mind. Tom Kennedy's accident, the stupidity of Niall Byrne fleeing from the police, the posh opening of The Stagecoach Hotel with Christian Gerrard, urbane, charming and ever so slightly smug. He wondered how a Toxteth lad could become a self styled art expert? Then there was the blatant disguise of Ross Maclaren at Haydock races, where he'd clearly seen his horse, Admiral Jervis, win. If he still owned the horse, of course. But try as he might Topper had so far failed to trace RMB Holdings and find out exactly who was involved. It had to be Maclaren but why go to all that trouble to hide his ownership? What was he concealing? Something felt wrong somewhere, but he couldn't exactly place what. But he was Topper McGrew and if there was a story to be had he would find it. He resolved to do some research when he'd said good night to the lads.

He crept upstairs and found Tim spark out asleep in his room, snoring softly. Topper leaned down and pushing back the mid brown hair, gave the lad a peck on the cheek. Topper looked at his sleeping son and felt a surge of happiness. His relationship with them was a highlight for him.

He tiptoed across the landing and found Giles watching a You Tube clip on his tablet whilst sketching out a cartoon in his notepad.

'What's that you're watching, son?'

Giles grinned impishly. 'We're doing about Michelangelo in school, and I found this You Tuber who reckons there's a portrait in a Milan gallery that a forger from Bolton says he did in his garden shed...'

'Good Lord,' Topper leaned down to watch the clip where a punky looking young man with nose and face piercings was expounding the theory. Topper stared at the young man.

'Who's he?'

'Dunno. He's called Fakerr. He does a load of art stuff online. It's quite cool.' Giles smiled. 'Imagine, if someone from Bolton could fake a Michelangelo, anyone could do it Dad, couldn't they? You know I might not be a cartoonist Dad, I might vet pictures for a living.'

Topper knew better than to betray too much interest in the subject, otherwise he'd never get Giles into bed.

'Well, you'd better settle down now, Giles, there's a good fellow. It's an early start tomorrow, I'll call you at 7. And another time we could visit some art galleries and find out about this sort of stuff, if you like.'

'OK. Night.' Giles stifled a yawn and Topper went downstairs and took out his laptop and notebook. His head was buzzing with possibilities. Just supposing Gerrard had a side line in art fraud? It might explain how he'd got so much cash and he employed artists to do restoration work, so why not use them to recreate paintings? He remembered what the two employees of Christian had said at The Stagecoach opening about the amount of forgeries that had come to their attention. No, that was ridiculous. It was a million miles from knowing about crime to committing it, and if they were involved, then why mention it? He must not let his imagination run away with him. Steady on, old chap, he told himself.

Topper allowed himself a half glass of red wine and set to work surfing the internet. He was definitely onto something though. He didn't know quite what but if he followed his nose, he might chase down a story, probably snuffle along a few false trails but capture some juicy details along the way. Something else bugged him about Maclaren or rather Finn

132

McCarthy and Hattie. Why were they so keen to find the author? Was it just about Admiral? He knew that there was something they weren't telling him but what? Trainers lost horses to rivals every day of the week, Admiral was an especially good horse, but even so, they seemed to be taking an excessive interest in finding Maclaren.

As often with Topper when searching down a story, he took an instinctive detour. First, he googled infamous art fakes and came across the forger Giles had discussed, Archie Todd, and found that he was serving a prison sentence. He had claimed that he had not known that his business partner was selling his work as legitimate masterpieces, but this mustn't have cut any ice with the jury. Topper took in the thin, unprepossessing face as he stood next to a work in the style of Van Gogh but with yellow carnations not sunflowers. Interesting, the work looked good to him, and he supposed it was different enough not to be confused with the original. He had also knocked up some sculptures in his shed which had been sold as ancient antiquities for breathtaking sums of money. If there was so much easy money to be made in art, then it would certainly attract criminals. He would like to bet that Gerrard was not kosher. He had a sixth sense about such things, and he was dissatisfied with what he knew about how he had acquired his wealth. It rang false to him. Besides, it would make an excellent story. It just might take a while to untangle all the elements and run them to ground. He'd put the word about, keep his eyes and ears open and see where it went. He sent a quick text to Lofty asking him to listen out for any gossip about the Gerrards and Freddie and Penny Mercer or whatever they called themselves now, because he wasn't sure about them either. People didn't change their spots and there was a good chance that Penny had known what Henry was up to. Lofty Ballard was always a good ally when you were chasing a story. Time for bed old son and a fresh look at things tomorrow, he decided with a yawn.

Chapter 15

DCI Gabriel Taverner glanced at his colleague, DS Anna Wildblood. They were at the post mortem of the poor unfortunate stable girl, Clare Hudson. The pathologist, Dr Tony Ives, a bear of a man with a penchant for fine wines and French cuisine, repeated his verdict in his thick Scottish burr.

'She was clearly hit on the temple and has various other wounds consistent with being kicked by a horse with shoes. He pointed at the horseshoe shape on the left of her body. 'But that kick there is the one that ruptured the spleen and was the fatal blow. But the hands, more importantly, the wee lassie's nails tell a different story...'

The Edinburgh accent was much in evidence as he turned over the victim's hand and pointed to the fingernails. 'There are miniscule particles of wood that match those taken from the stable door under the nails on both hands. From what I saw of her at the murder scene, it's clear that she was trying to get out of the stable and these scratch marks are consistent with those on the top part of the stable door.' He waited for this to sink in. 'So, detectives she tried to get out, but the door was jammed. If it was done so deliberately, then she could have been murdered.'

Wildblood exhaled and had turned rather pale.

'And the time of death?'

'Between 11 pm and 3 am, I'd say.'

DCI Taverner frowned. 'She had been to a party earlier, some opening of that new hotel in Walton and had left early. She must have come back to the yard and checked on the horses, gone into Sweet Pea's stable. And the top stable door was jammed shut as a lead rope was caught in it, but perhaps it was put there deliberately. The horse must have kicked her repeatedly...'

'Aye, well, the trainer will know better about the horse, Sweet Pea, was she called? A real misnomer because she certainly kicked out at the wee girl, kicked her to death, in fact. There are horseshoe marks all over the lassie. Who would close the stable door, any suspects?'

Ives loved to theorise and help the police solve their cases. Initially, Taverner had been irritated even undermined by it, but over the years he had come to respect and admire the good doctor. He even wanted to know what Ives thought about suspects.

'Well, the trainer said the mare was much calmer when she could see everything so closing her stable door would have certainly unsettled her causing her to kick out. So, we are looking for someone who knew that, someone who followed Clare and closed the top stable door when she was in it.' Ives sighed heavily. 'The poor lassie.'

Wildblood had managed to compose herself. 'Couldn't the stable door have been closed accidentally and got jammed? Have we checked?'

'SOCO will have established that. The door was held back by a hook attached to the door which fitted into an eye which was drilled into the brick. I suppose it could have become detached. We'll need to check it didn't become warped so that the door jammed in the frame, but it's all a bit co-incidental. A lead rope just happening to become wedged in the door, just when she was in the stable. I don't buy it.'

Ives nodded. 'It must be someone who knew the horse's reputation. I note she was sexually assaulted a wee while ago and came in for a forensic medical.'

'Yes, that's right,' Taverner confirmed.

'And her boyfriend was paralysed in a riding accident recently,' added Wildblood.

Ives tutted. 'The poor, wee girl. Some people have awful lives, don't they?' He contemplated this then suddenly nodded. 'Well, I'd better let you get back and find out what happened to the lassie then, hadn't I?'

Taverner's mind was in overdrive as they drove to the Ryans. Who would want to harm a stable girl? And what an awful way to die at the mercy of a vicious horse.

Wildblood hated post mortems, well, anyone in their right mind would, but she usually fainted, so he had a quick glance in her direction. She had lost the shell-shocked look but was quiet as she contemplated poor Clare's last moments.

135

'So, what do yer think, guv? Poor lass, it were a terrible end for her. Jealous boyfriend, ex lover, it's usually a bloody man, isn't it?'

Taverner had to agree. Sometimes, he despised his own sex as he had ample examples in his line of work of the horrors perpetrated by males and Wildblood was right, most murderers of females were males they had been in an intimate relationship with. There were still on average two murders in the UK every week, despite changes in domestic violence laws and a greater number of prosecutions.

'Hmm. It could well be. We'll see Mr Ryan and see what he has to say. He might well know something about Clare's love life, if she had any admirers certainly.'

'It's not often we get a death caused by a horse, is it guv? They always seem such lovely creatures, petted over and treated better than a lot of children these thoroughbred racehorses.'

'That is certainly true, but I suppose there's bound to be the odd one that can turn nasty.'

They rounded the corner as they came into Walton and neared the Ryans' place.

'Isn't this the yard where the conditional jockey were done for drink driving?' asked Wildblood.

Taverner remembered ringing Finn McCarthy, his jockey coach having been tipped off by his opposite number in traffic. They pulled into the yard and watched as a lot of horses put their heads over their stable door, ears pricked as they watched the new arrivals.

Wildblood parked the car. 'It is. I rang Finn about the lad, Niall someone or other. I wonder how that case is going?'

Anna gave him a sidelong look. 'Looks like we'll be needing to contact Finn again and Harriet Lucas. How are things going with her anyway, guv?'

Taverner grimaced. 'Good, but now we're on this case, I'll be a bit tied up, so that won't help.'

Wildblood gave him a sympathetic look. 'Gi' over, will yer! Her father was a policeman and her brother is a serving one, so she'll know the drill.'

'I suppose so. Come on, we'd best look lively and see what's what.'

136

Seamus Ryan's eyes filled with tears as he talked about his deceased stable lass. His wife was equally emotional but that did not stop her making cups of tea and handing out slices of delicious carrot cake.

'We're besides ourselves. The poor wee lass. We'd all gone to the do at The Stagecoach. Thought it might cheer the lass up after what happened with her boyfriend.' Seamus wiped his eyes and rallied. 'She must have come back, so she did, and checked on the horses. We don't know what led her to go into the stable on her own, and she didn't tie Sweet Pea up neither. Horse must have kicked out and that was that.'

Rosie's eyes streamed with tears. 'Sure enough, the lass had no luck and then she met Tom Kennedy and they were proper lovebirds and then he had a serious fall. Would you credit it? Mary, mother of God, what had she done to deserve such hardships, I'd like to know!' she demanded.

Taverner was struggling to catch the Irish accents which were more pronounced as they were thick with emotion.

'So where is the boyfriend?'

'In Jack Berry House, it's a rehab place for injured jockeys, see?' Seamus explained.

'Does Tom know about Clare?' Taverner was dreading the answer.

Rosie frowned. 'I don't think so, her mother was told and may have gone down there, but I don't rightly know.'

Taverner thought he ought to check it out and hoped someone had told the poor man otherwise the job would fall to him.

'So, the horse, Sweet Pea, was known to be aggressive, I understand. What steps did staff take to protect themselves?' Taverner hoped they had taken precautions.

Seamus sighed. 'She was a bit marish, to be sure, but manageable, I'd say. We left a headcollar on her in the stable, a leather one so we could grab her and tie her up. Finn suggested that and we thought it was a good idea. That's what we had to do, but she weren't so bad as long as she could see out the door and see what was going on.' He scratched his head and his eyes glistened with tears once more. 'That's the strange thing, officer, I don't mind telling you I don't know how it happened but when we came back from the do, the mare was squealing because the top door were closed. There was a lead rope jammed in there. That mare hated a closed top door more than anything else, she did. I don't rightly know what

137

happened. The door's fixed to the wall with a metal hook and the dammed eye had come out the brick work, so the door must have swung loose and became jammed by the lead rope which was hung on a hook outside.'

Taverner noticed that Wildblood was eyeing up the carrot cake. It all sounded a bit too convenient, the door coming loose and just happening to become wedged with the lead rope. He could think of other explanations.

'Could someone have pulled the metal eye out of the brickwork, do you think?'

Seamus glared at him. 'Why? Who'd do such a thing?'

'We're just thinking of all the possibilities, that's all,' added Wildblood soothingly.

'Well, I don't think that's any sort of possibility at all.' Seamus drew himself up to his full height. 'That girl was loved by everyone, she really was, she were grand and no mistake.'

SOCO had already examined the stable, but Taverner wanted to have a look himself. It sounded most unlikely that the eye had fallen out of the wall and the door closed on a lead rope which just happened to be there, which only left one possibility. SOCO had not ruled out foul play.

'Mind if we have a look?'

'Be my guest.'

Wildblood asked about the mare as they made their way outside.

'Oh, her owner's taken her off to be a brood mare, we didn't want her round the place. Maybe it'll settle her,' added Rosie sadly.

The stable was taped up with police tape. Taverner pulled on his plastic gloves and examined the hook and the metal eye which had come loose from the wall of the stable. The wall was in a good condition and the eye, a U shaped piece of metal that the hook from the top door slid into, had been pulled out of the wall. There were scratch marks either side of the drill holes of the eye which looked to Taverner like the screws had been prised out with a metal object like a screwdriver. The row of brick built stables had all been constructed at the same time, so Taverner studied the next stable. A bay horse put his head over the stable door and whickered at him curiously.

'Steady there,' murmured Taverner. The stable was similarly built. The top door was held in place by the same style of hook and eye attached to the wall. Taverner gave the hook a good tug but there was absolutely no give in it. He shooed the horse into his stable and gently closed the top stable door by lifting the hook. The door fitted properly but opened easily enough. He reached his own conclusions. In his mind there was no shadow of a doubt that the stable door of Sweet Pea had been tampered with. Someone had followed Clare and locked her into the stable, knowing full well that Sweet Pea would kick out and harm the stable girl. They had prised the hook off the wall to make it look like the door had slammed shut, and no doubt closed it on the lead rope to make sure it was jammed.

Taverner looked at Seamus and Rosie, trying not to give anything away.

'OK, then. Thanks for your time, Mr and Mrs Ryan. We'll be in touch as the investigation unfolds.'

Seamus looked at him suspiciously. 'Yer think it was deliberate, don't yer?'

Taverner certainly did think that but needed to be circumspect at this stage. 'I wouldn't like to speculate, at the moment, but we do need to keep an open mind. I'll get some staff round to take formal statements from you.'

The couple watched as Wildblood drove out of the yard.

As usual, the police officers debriefed on the way back.
'Well?'

'There's no doubt in my mind that the stable door was tampered with, so from that I conclude that Clare Hudson was murdered.'

'Christ! From what we know, things were going well for her, after her sexual assault, new boyfriend and all that.' Wildblood wiped away tears. 'Mind you, it can't be the boyfriend what did it, can it, wi' him being injured.'

Taverner nodded. 'No, that's true. We will still need to rule him out of our inquiries as he could have got someone else to do the deed, and of course, I bet no one's told him yet.'

Neither wanted that job, but someone needed to do it. It was a task for a senior officer. Taverner, of course.

Wildblood sighed. 'Rather you than me, guv. What were the name of the place he's convalescing at again?'

139

'Jack Berry House, it's not far from the centre of Walton.' Taverner typed the address into the sat nav and Wildblood wearily turned the car round.

Chapter 16

Finn was absolutely appalled to find out that the police thought Clare's death being deliberate. Taverner popped around to tell him in person much later that evening.

'Oh Christ, are you sure? That's awful. Does Harriet know?'

'Yes, I just told her, and she was pretty upset too.'

Finn sighed. 'Just when things were going well for Clare too. I thought things turned a corner when she met Tom and then he was injured in an accident, and now this! Christ, does *he* know?'

Taverner sighed. 'I've been to Jack Berry House to tell him myself. One of the perks of being promoted, not.'

Finn couldn't imagine what it would be like to have to tell people bad news on a regular basis, the worst news imaginable. At least DCI Gabriel Taverner was a decent human being, the empathic face of the police.

'Does Clare have any family?'

'Parents and a sister. They're all aware.' Finn poured them both a whiskey from the sideboard and handed Taverner a glass.

'I'll get one of the other officers to take a statement but off the top of your head, do you know who would want to harm her?'

Finn sipped the whiskey and shuddered. 'Why do you think it is a murder anyway? Couldn't it just be a tragic accident?'

Taverner explained about the hook and eye on the door and how the eye had been forcibly removed.

'So, someone tried to make it look like the eye had fallen out and the door slammed shut. It was jammed because a lead rope was caught up in it. But the eye in the wall had definitely been prised loose. There were scratch marks consistent with someone levering it off with a screwdriver or something similar and it's too coincidental for a lead rope to get jammed in the door. The rope was stored outside on a hook but what are the odds of a sudden gust of wind causing it to rise up precisely at the same time as the door closes? I just don't buy it. So, it has to be someone who would know about the mare being aggressive which could be pretty much anyone.'

Finn frowned. 'I agree when you put it like that, it does sound rather unlikely. I think she had an aggressive ex boyfriend a few years ago before the sexual assault, but why wait until now before striking? Maybe it was a member of staff who had a crush on her, and it wasn't reciprocated, something like that.'

Taverner put down his glass in a decisive manner. 'Niall Byrne works there too, doesn't he? How is he doing?'

'OK. He's obviously worried about the court case coming up, but he's coping, riding well, I'd say. The Ryans are pleased with him.' Finn didn't mention the collision with Tom Kennedy which had caused his injury, not that it was Niall's fault, of course. Still, trouble seemed to follow the youngster around. Besides, Niall seemed to respect Clare though from all the interactions he had seen between them, there certainly wasn't anything to worry him unduly. Obviously, Clare wasn't happy about the riding accident that led to Tom's injuries, but she seemed to think that it was accidental, so didn't blame Niall.

Taverner looked thoughtful, buttoned up his coat and stood up to leave. 'I heard that Niall was riding the other horse that collided with Tom Kennedy's mount, maybe even causing the fall.'

As usual, Finn had underestimated Taverner. 'Yes, that's true, but visibility was poor, and Niall was trying to find a gap. It could have happened to anyone. Besides, Clare could blame Niall and want to take it out on him, not the other way round, don't you think?'

Taverner nodded. 'True. If you hear anything from the racing community, anything at all, I'd appreciate a call.'

'Of course.'

Harriet sounded very down when he rang her the next day.

'Want to meet for lunch in The Blacksmiths? We can discuss Nat's idea about ringing Ross Maclaren's publisher about The Golden Gun award. I've got Maclaren's mobile number from Jeremy, not that he's picking up, of course. Surely, he'll answer the phone to his agent or publisher though?'

'Hmm, OK.'

When they met up, it was clear that Harriet had been crying and had hastily applied some makeup. She looked rather pale but rallied as soon as she saw Finn. He had bagged a table next to a roaring fire which was very much needed on such a bitterly cold day. There were a few familiar faces, stable staff and the odd trainer in the popular pub. Finn raised his hand to a couple of his current conditionals. They ordered food, a baked potato with ham and cheese for Finn and a panini and chips for Hattie.

'So, how are you?'

Her lip wobbled. 'Shocked and upset about Clare. To think that we are living amongst murderers,' her eyes scanned the crowd. 'It's horrible.'

'It is but we must let Gabriel do his job and try and carry on.'

'I know.' She let out a long, sorrowful sigh. 'How are Rosie and Seamus taking it?'

'Not well.' Finn has phoned them earlier. Seamus sounded hollowed out and Rosie had taken to her bed. 'I think they feel responsible, but of course, that's nonsense. They thought a lot of Clare and they were very good to her.'

Harriet shook her head. 'They mustn't think that. She was like a daughter to them really. But who would do such a thing? She was such a lovely girl!'

'I know. Gabriel asked us to pass on any information we might pick up and the police will need to interview us too.'

The food arrived and after initially seeming reluctant, Harriet rallied and tucked into her panini which was a good sign. He had never known a girl with such a hearty appetite, and she never seemed to put on an ounce either. Thank goodness he wasn't riding, otherwise it would seriously annoy him. She seemed to have perked up, so Finn felt able to make plans.

'About the phone call to Maclaren? He's not answering the mobile to Jeremy, but maybe he's changed his number. Shall we try it anyway?' Finn pulled out the piece of paper on which Jeremy had written Maclaren's number.

Harriet dialled it, poised for action with a kind of steely purpose, but there was no response.

'Damn. I couldn't even leave a message. Anyway, I've got the agent's number, someone called Louise Briggs. So, I'll try her. It's amazing what you can find out on Google.' Harriet tapped away at the keys on her phone in a determined fashion. Finn recognised that his friend was back, pragmatic and keen to do something useful rather than mooch about.

'So, have you thought about what you need to say?'

Finn was about to say something further when Harriet met his gaze and grinned.

'Good afternoon. I'm Madeleine Frost, the administrator of The Golden Gun award. I would like to speak to Louisa Briggs, agent for Ross Maclaren.'

There was a pause and eventually Harriet said. 'It is extremely important that he contact me on this number as soon as possible. Can you give a message to Louisa? We have decisions to make, and I don't mind telling you that an early meeting with Mr Maclaren could make all the difference.' Harriet rolled her eyes at Finn as she listened to a staff member making various excuses about where Louisa Briggs was and how Ross Maclaren's details were strictly confidential.

'I understand that, but there's no harm in passing on my details, surely? He can ring me on this number but please do not give this out to anyone else. Time is of the essence so arrangements can be made, so I must ask that this message is passed onto Mr Maclaren as soon as possible. I'm sure Louisa and Mr Maclaren will want to hear what I have to say. How can I put this, let's just say that he will learn something to his advantage.'

Harriet finished the call, her face lit up by a huge grin.

'And? Did they take the bait?'

'Hook, line and sinker.'

Chapter 17

Topper arrived at Market Rasen races keen to see how his tips would perform. Set in a sleepy Lincolnshire town, it was one of his favourite little courses. He loved that one could see the course, the paddock and the bookies in a glance, so cosy was the layout. Today was a jobbing weekday meeting with a smallish but, he knew from experience, knowledgeable crowd of real jump racing enthusiasts.

It was a crisp, cold day and Topper paused to take a few lungfuls of fresh Lincolnshire air, before making his way over to the bar for a coffee and a bite to eat. Since his epiphany which caused him to stop whining about his misfortunes, he no longer drank too much and had made a commitment to eat healthily and exercise. Now, he felt rejuvenated, like a new man. He'd even given up smoking, mostly, just having the occasional vape. Three stone lighter, he had now had to buy a new tweed racing suit which he was wearing for the first time. He even sported a green moleskin waistcoat and had had a decent haircut. As he strode purposefully across the course, he cut a trim and much younger looking figure. He even noticed with surprise that middle aged women eyed him speculatively, whereas before they did not seem to notice him at all. He was seeing Jane from Boxercise tonight for a tentative second date and things were going well. Life, thought Topper, was good.

The bar was filling up. Topper recognised several trainers, Vince Hunt, Alister Broadie, a few familiar owners and some fellow journalists. He ordered a coffee and a sandwich to eat before the first race when his tall photographer friend, Lofty Ballard, sidled up beside him. Topper ordered him a Scotch.

'What have you done with the old Topper? You look like some tit off the telly ...'

It was the usual remark which Lofty never failed to make since Topper had taken himself in hand. Lofty in contrast looked his normal, crumpled self. His cream mac was in need of a wash, he had huge bags under his eyes and would have benefitted from a shave, haircut and trim.

As usual, his camera was slung around his neck. Topper grinned good naturedly with the zeal of the new convert.

'Healthy living, old son, you can't beat it. You should try it. Now how're things?'

'So so, ' Lofty took a slug of Scotch and flicked through his racecard. 'Should be a good day. I was at Catterick yesterday. Got a few pics you might be interested in...'

Topper took a swig of coffee and a bite of his ham salad sandwich and tried not to look too keen, otherwise Lofty would notice and try to sell the pictures to him instead of simply handing them over.

'Right. Anything special?'

'Well, I don't rightly know. There's some of Christian Gerrard and others of that new conditional you mentioned, who was it, Freddie Mercer.'

Lofty eyed Topper closely, looking for signs of interest and a crafty look spread across his face. Topper maintained his casual, relaxed expression but his curiosity was certainly piqued.

'Oh that. I was just getting carried away, you know me, not really interested now, just nosing around you know what I'm like.'

Lofty downed his Scotch looking disconsolate. 'Well then. I'd better be off...'

'Course you could just email me them while I get you another drink and maybe a sandwich?' This was slipped in casually. Lofty paused and then gave an almost imperceptible nod.

'Sure, cheese and pickle and a double please, single malt.' Lofty brightened and got out his phone as Topper made a quick order, specifying a Glenfiddich and another coffee for himself. Of course, Lofty wasn't stupid, he watermarked all his photos, only removing the mark and improving the quality of the photo when payments were made in full.

They munched away companionably and presently Lofty fiddled with his phone, emailing the photos to Topper. Intrigued, he had a quick look at the photos whilst Lofty sipped his drink and munched his sandwich. One showed Christian Gerrard, at Catterick races and he was pictured coming out of a bar with another man and they were talking. Topper enlarged the photo. Who was his friend? He stared at the thin, unprepossessing and yet strangely familiar middle aged face. He thought back but still couldn't quite place the man, but he knew it would come to

146

him. Then Topper swiped over to the next photo and found a picture of the new conditional, Freddie Mercer, standing closely to another man. He recognised him as Peter Teasdale, a corn merchant locally. This was Henry's brother and therefore uncle to Freddie. There was nothing illegal about this, it was only his father that Freddie couldn't have contact with. But the two brothers had always seemed very close. If Freddie was meeting Peter, then was he in contact with Henry as well? Had they just met by chance or was this a planned meeting? Topper felt uncomfortable with this knowledge and wasn't sure what to do next. It wasn't enough to alert anyone, but it certainly piqued his interest. He spoke genially enough to Lofty, but didn't buy the photos, there wasn't any point just yet. He hinted that Lofty was on the right lines and asked him to keep his wits about him, which was code for him taking surreptitious photos of the people he'd mentioned. He slipped his friend a couple of twenties, just to keep him sweet and went on his way.

He had a busy day ahead. He had people to interview and quotes to get and he would have to leave this for now and come back to it. Something smelled wrong to Topper, but he didn't know yet what it was. He forced his mind back to the task in hand and wandered off to watch the first race, the cogs of his brain whirring way as the well oiled machinery tried to work out a strategy. So what if Freddie was meeting Gerrard and then his uncle? He'd certainly know Gerrard well and there was no problem with the lad meeting his relative but just supposing Peter was visiting his brother and passing on messages to Freddie? Suppose they were carrying on some criminal enterprise? But what?

He reached no real conclusion and decided to shelve the matter for now. He spent a productive afternoon, watched all the races, carried out the required interviews and had plenty of quotes and information for his articles.

Back home, he noticed the mess his lads, Giles and Tim had made when they'd stayed over. He took in the room, his horse painting he had inherited from his family, a good one, well painted which he was fond of. He squinted at it and wondered if it was valuable with all this talk of paintings and exhibitions. It was a study of a hunting scene at the turn of the century. He had inherited it, along with a few others, from his father who told him that it was valuable. The painting depicted a hunt scene. Men in red coats and ladies in black riding habits and top hats were sailing over a post and rail fence with enthusiasm. The painting was well executed, the flowing lines representing the fast and exciting movement of the horses and riders. The horses were captured beautifully, every muscle and sinew were perfect. He studied the painting for a signature but couldn't see one at all. What a pity it wasn't a Gideon Moss, thought Topper. He'd been alerted to the artist's name at The Stagecoach opening and in his usual manner had stored the information away. He'd even heard that Gerrard had a few. Gideon Moss's old paintings were now very valuable. He googled Gideon Moss's distinctive signature on his phone, studied it and went through his sideboard drawers where he found a permanent fine marker in black. Seized by a sudden impulse, he practised the signature on a piece of paper and once satisfied he had got it right, he copied it onto the right hand lower corner of the painting with the permanent marker and then stood back to admire his handiwork. Not bad, he thought. He was fired up by all this talk of valuable Gideon Moss paintings and the prolific number of fakes that the art restorers had talked about. He could pretend it was an original, it was good enough in his eyes. Not that he was thinking of selling it, he'd leave the painting to the boys. Why shouldn't they profit from it? That would set the cat amongst the pigeons, he decided, pleased with himself. He'd actually done a pretty fair copy of Moss's signature and maybe in the future, the painting might be confused with a real Moss which could do his boys no end of good. And no one need ever know. It was, he reasoned, hurting nobody.

Then his attention drifted as he wandered around the house. The bathroom and bedrooms were a mess, and the sitting room was strewn with pizza boxes, crisp packets and other food debris. Still, he didn't want to nag them, it had been hard enough anyway getting the visits arranged. He felt hugely proud of his sons. He had a bit of a tidy round but longed to continue his writing. The book, a racing thriller, was coming along well. Then he had a genius idea. He was far too busy and talented to do the cleaning, so he'd employ a cleaner. He was earning a good wage now, far more than he had previously and at long last he had prospects, a book coming out, a new column. Everything was coming up roses for him and not before time!

After a quick tidy up, he poured himself a small dram of Scotch and googled local cleaners in the area. He remembered that Penny Teasdale, Mercer, as she called herself now had a cleaning business, he'd overheard people talking about it at the opening of The Stagecoach, what had she called it? Spick and Span, that was it. He felt a pang of sympathy for the poor woman, once respected and revered within her community, having to clean for a living. So, he'd help her out and at the same time he might be able to see what her son, ex husband and brother-in-law were up to. He found the agency and sent them a quick email. Feeling buoyed up, he sipped his Scotch and wondered what his main character, a journalist called Charlie Galbraith, was going to do now he'd come across doping allegations in a particular racing yard. Then it came to him, and he began to type feverishly.

Chapter 18

As Hattie settled herself at her desk in the dietician's part of the PJA offices in Walton, her mobile phone rang. Hattie answered expecting it to be a friend, or her family or Finn.

'Hi!'

There was a pause and then a quick fire, but well spoken voice said,' Is this Madeleine Frost?'

Remembering her fake call the other day pretending to be something to do with The Golden Gun awards, a startled Harriet attempted to recreate the haughty, over confident voice of Madeleine Frost she'd feigned before.

'Ah yes. Who is this please?'

'It's Louisa Briggs from Hanson's Literary Agency. You left a message for me about my client Ross Maclaren being put forward for an award.'

'Yes, that's right. We wanted to meet him to discuss it further, so needed his phone number.'

There was a long silence. 'Well, that's as maybe, but the thing I'm struggling with is that I know Madeleine Frost from the award's committee, the real Madeleine Frost, and she assures me that she hasn't left a message for me, and that Ross isn't being considered for an award. So, you can see my problem.' There was an icy silence as Hattie tried to compose herself. 'I presume you're from the press desperate to find out where Ross is, but you will not be successful. If you contact either of us again, I won't hesitate to report you to the police and the real Madeleine Frost will also take action too. Have I made myself clear?'

With that she ended the call, leaving Harriet gasping and feeling mortified, as if there were ants crawling all over her skin. Christ, they should have thought of that. All literary people knew one another, of course they did, and now their plan just looked foolish and ridiculous.

She quickly texted Finn.

We've been rumbled. Just had a call from Ross's agent threatening me if I try to contact them again. Any ideas?

Finn arranged to meet her at her house and go through the options. It looked like they were going to need to search all the cottages for rent in the Peak District after all and try to piece together Maclaren's address from the information they had already.

After work the pair met up at Harriet's. Phillipa and Bob, Harriet's parents were away. Harriet had prepared a steak and salad together with a good Merlot.

'Mum and dad will be so sorry to miss you. They've gone away on a minibreak to Edinburgh for a few days.' Harriet tossed the salad and poured Finn a glass of wine.

Finn smiled. He genuinely got on well with them. 'I'm sorry to miss them too. How are they?'

'Same as ever. Mum's part time at work now, Dad's busy playing golf and in the garden and likes to discuss crime, punishment and policing with Will and now Gabriel.'

Finn laughed. 'Is there any news on how Gabriel is getting on with the investigation into Clare's death?'

Harriet shook her head. 'No, not that he'd tell me anyway, of course. I think he'll be tied up investigating everything for a while anyway. How are things with Theresa?'

Finn stifled a broad grin. He felt heady with the sheer thrill of hearing her name but settled for a mundane response.

'Good, going well actually.'

'Great. I'm pleased for you. Right, we'd better get on.' Harriet was happy to move on to other subjects. It felt strange talking about their romances with each other, she wasn't sure why exactly. She pulled out a pad and some pens. 'So, here's what we know, Ross is staying somewhere in the Peak District at a place called Rock Cottage near a town starting with the letters LE. So, if we search all the holiday rentals online, there will be loads of websites though, then we can narrow it down.'

Finn produced a map and leafed through to find the Peak District area.

'Right, I'll go through the towns beginning with LE.' He stared at the map, making a note of anything relevant. Finn made a list of villages Longcliffe, Litton, Littlemoor, Leek. Then it came to him.

'Hey, there's only one town beginning with LE in the area, Leek.'

Harriet typed 'Rock Cottage, Leek' into the various websites. Eventually, she narrowed the search down to three cottages. The website had an online booking system and a calendar which showed when the cottages were booked up.

'Let's look at their availability, shall we? It's October, so not peak season.' She stared at the screen; her expression animated. 'Bingo. Of the three listed only one is occupied at the moment. Rock Cottage, described as being near Leek and close to the Roaches, a beautiful, rock formation in the heart of the Peak District. I can't believe it, I thought we'd never find it!'

Harriet clicked on the images which showed a fabulous stone cottage situated down a gated drive, with mullioned windows and amazing views of the Roaches, an impressive rocky ridge. One part was called Hen Cloud and another Ramshaw Rocks. The scenery was dramatic; rockfaces set in moorland and heather, utterly wild and breathtaking.

'Wow. What a fabulous place in the middle of nowhere. Where better to finish off your book? He won't be disturbed there. What do we do? Just turn up?' Harriet frowned. 'He obviously doesn't want to be found.'

Finn looked thoughtful. 'Maybe we just knock on the door and tell him the truth, that Jeremy is sorry and wants Admiral back.'

'And that his painting might be a fake,' added Harriet.

'Mmm. Well, Ross might well have some vital information about how he acquired it which could be really important. What's it called, provenance, that's it? We should have heard from Nat by then about the painting in New York. So, when shall we go?'

'Sunday?'

'You're on. It's about three hours away, so I'll pick you up at nine.'

Harriet smiled. Finally, things were coming together. It was like a strange synchronicity, something she'd noticed during their other cases, somehow the two of them worked in concert. She didn't stop to analyse it, but she was sure that they were on the right lines.

Chapter 19

Taverner surveyed his team and summarised the information on the links board. His staff, DS Anna Wildblood, DC's Ballantyne, Patel, Haworth and Cullen all studied the photos, arrows and scribbles on the big board in front of them.

'Heck, what a way to go, being kicked to death by a bloody horse,' quipped Haworth, staring at the frankly horrible photo of Clare's injuries. There were several horseshoe shaped injuries on her body where she had literally been kicked to death. 'Poor lassie.'

'Thank you, Haworth. It certainly is a way to go. And as we have discussed, Clare Hudson had tried to get out of the stable as evidenced by the fragments found under her fingernails and the positioning of the body. The top stable door showed evidence of having been tampered with, at least the eye which the hook on the back of the stable door clipped into, had been clearly prised loose from the wall. Probably done to make the door closure look accidental, but worse than that the edge of the door had been wedged in place by a lead rope, so it couldn't easily be pushed open. It took the trainer a good few minutes to open the door and he wasn't being attacked by a vicious horse.'

The officers contemplated the images of Clare's battered body in grim silence. After a while, it was broken by DC Natalie Cullen,

'Couldn't it have just been an 'orrible accident? After all the lass would have needed a lead rope to tie the horse up, so what's to stop the door just jamming in the wind?'

Taverner shook his head. 'No. There are recent scratch marks on the wall and eye fitting where the screws were loosened and the whole eye fitment prised from the wall, so it has to be deliberate.'

'Christ, who would do such a thing?' asked Ballantyne, shaking his head in a mournful fashion.

Taverner sighed. 'I don't know. Clare was at a party beforehand, the opening of The Stagecoach Hotel in Walton, but left the event early. The trainer is Seamus Ryan and his wife is Rosie. Both seem to be devastated and had gone out of their way to support Clare. We have a list of stable staff here and I'd like you to go through them and take statements from them all. Niall Byrne and Lottie Henderson are conditional jockeys there, both coached by Finn McCarthy. Clare had a boyfriend, Tom Kennedy who was seriously injured in a race and is currently in rehab having had a nasty accident which has left him paralysed. Niall Byrne has recent form and is awaiting sentencing for drink driving and assault. He was also riding the horse that collided with Tom Kennedy's, causing the fall. There is nothing else on any of the staff there.'

'What does Finn McCarthy say about Niall's driving charge then?' asked DC Cullen. 'He's bound to be in the know and what about Niall running into Clare's boyfriend's horse?'

Taverner shrugged. 'He thinks it was just stupidity and immaturity on Byrne's part, the drink driving and the riding incident. He's a talented rider and Seamus and Rosie Ryan are standing by him and will support him even if he gets a prison sentence.'

'Prison sentence for drink driving?' commented DC Haworth. 'It's a bit stiff, isn't it?'

Taverner went through the details of the offence. Haworth whistled.

'I was involved in investigating that Irish mafia chappie in Yorkshire, he were a Byrne, weren't he?'

Taverner shrugged. 'That was before my time, but if he's serving a prison sentence he can't be involved. Besides, Niall is a young man and Byrne is a very common name in Ireland, as I'm sure you know.' Haworth looked suitably chastened. 'But I'll chase up the drink driving investigation with colleagues. Niall is also reported to be distraught and had no reason to harm Clare, in fact they got on well, despite the incident with her boyfriend,' added Taverner.

'Did you say the boyfriend was paralysed in a riding accident?' asked DC Natalie Cullen. Gabriel nodded. 'So, it can't be him then.'

Taverner frowned. 'There is another aspect to this, Clare Hudson did report a rape last year by Joel Fox, you remember, the conditional jockey, but Joel is languishing in prison for that and other offences, so it can't be him.'

DC Ballantyne scratched his head. 'I thought I recognised Clare's name.'

DS Wildblood frowned. 'Unless it's one of Joel Fox's associates on the outside, seeking revenge.'

'But why would they wait so long to do her in?' asked Cullen.

'Maybe they were biding their time and waiting for the right set of circumstances to present themselves, like a vicious horse? Whoever did it must have known the mare would kick out when the stable door was closed,' replied Taverner, letting the team absorb this information. Their expressions were grave, and he could almost hear the brain cells whirring into action.

'So, Cullen and Patel, can you chase up Joel Fox's associates, any regular prison visitors and so on, and don't forget his father, Lloyd, too. I'll speak to DI Johnson about Byrne and establish the status of the investigation and the rest of you, go through the staff list and consider who was at the party, seize CCTV footage of anyone following Clare when she left and take statements. We need to find if someone had a grudge against her, someone who had a reason to kill her. Fox seems the most likely, but we could be missing something.'

'What's the horse called?' asked Haworth, smiling at the scowls from his colleagues. 'Just askin', that's all.'

'Sweet Pea. She is a talented horse by all accounts,' replied Taverner.

'Sweet Pea! Right bloody name that is!'

'Isn't it just!' agreed Ballantyne.

'What's happened to her now?' asked Cullen.

'She's been taken out of training to become a broodmare. She could calm down if she's in foal, so they say,' replied Taverner.

Wildblood looked up from her notes. 'What did Ives say was the time of death?'

'Between 11 and 3 in the morning.'

'And do we know why Clare left the party early to go and check on the horses?' asked Cullen.

Taverner nodded. 'According to the Ryans, she told them she'd do the last minute rounds that Seamus normally does. He said he usually fills up hay nets and their water buckets. They said it was like she was wanting an excuse to leave as they were going to do it later anyway.'

Haworth looked thoughtful. 'Maybe she saw someone at the do that she knew, someone that she wanted to avoid.'

It was certainly a possibility. They all wondered who? Had that person murdered her?

Despite the many shocking things they had seen in their job, the image of the slight stable girl being kicked to death by a thoroughbred racehorse with the added information about the victim's sad history, had left them all reeling. Grim faced, they all set about their work and promised to feed back later.

Taverner was called to a meeting with his Superintendent, Lewis Wilson, a well coiffed officer who seemed approachable. He was Taverner's direct superior with his boss, DCI Sykes, being off sick after an operation. Taverner was in a temporary, acting up position.

'Ah, Taverner, how are things going?'

He brought him up to speed with their latest inquiries regarding Clare's murder. The Superintendent listened intently.

'So, you have various lines of inquiry it seems, and the press have been briefed?'

Taverner explained that rather than have a press conference, statements had been issued to the press and the local media briefed.

'Hmm. As a stable girl, I suppose if there's something going on, someone in the racing community will know what's what.' He flattened down his hair and glanced at his watch. 'Well, I'm sure you have everything in hand. DCI Sykes speaks very highly of you, so I'll let you get on. Keep me updated. I've a meeting with the Police Commissioner about now, so I've got to go.' He smiled and nodded at Taverner. 'Do find me if you need anything, won't you?'

Taverner left his office feeling surprised that DCI Sykes had spoken well of him but also quite deflated. DCI Sykes always made an effort to attend briefings and was sure to have lots of theories of his own to add to any inquiries. He hadn't always agreed with these theories and Sykes tended to seize upon the most likely suspects, in his opinion, but quite frankly he'd rather have this than the Superintendent's seeming indifference. He suddenly felt the investigation weighing heavily on his shoulders and found to his surprise that he rather missed Sykes' sometimes pugnacious and uncompromising input, as at least he was interested in solving crimes and bringing the bad guys to justice. Superintendent Wilson had a reputation for being good on the PR side of policing, and he knew whose approach he'd rather have. Troubled, he set about reviewing the evidence yet again and felt a renewed determination to find who exactly had murdered Clare Hudson.

Chapter 20

Finn spent a couple of days in London for his mental health course. It was great to catch up with some of his contemporaries, Marcus Neave and Colm Lawson, especially. Marcus worked more in the Midlands and Colm in the South East. It was helpful to compare notes on conditionals. One thing they all agreed on was that youngsters nowadays were more troublesome than they were. Mind you, Finn had to admit that they had got involved in some scrapes themselves.

'I can remember the stuff you and Nat Wilson got up to,' added Colm with a twinkle in his eye.

Finn nodded. 'Maybe people were more tolerant of youthful high jinks then.'

Colm agreed. 'I'd say so, so don't be too harsh on your charges.'

They reconnected over lunch and in the bar in the evening after the course. It was sobering to consider the impact of mental health difficulties on youngsters and scary that boys and men tended to show few signs of depression. Not even loved ones knew of their intentions until they'd committed suicide. They were reminded of the signs and signals to look out for, how mood could be affected by alcohol and drug use and the support services they could call upon to assist anyone who was at risk. Marcus and Colm both told him stories about their conditionals, some were taking drugs, some were struggling to make the weights, and several had had brushes with the law. He shared details of Niall Byrne and his drink driving charge.

Colm was from Limerick in Ireland. 'Whereabouts is Byrne from?'

Finn wasn't exactly sure. 'God knows. You don't know of him, do you?'

'No, there are a great many Byrnes in Ireland, of course, some good, some bad, very bad indeed, actually. I wonder why the lad did such a stupid thing as to drive off from the police?'

Finn had to admit, it had always bothered him too. 'Just a rush of blood to the head, he didn't engage his brain, I suppose,' was the best excuse he could come up with. 'But like you said before, maybe we're forgetting our own misdemeanours.'

Colm laughed and went on to talk about some of their scrapes.

In the end after an interesting couple of days, Finn came back to York with lots of ideas and resources he could point people towards if needs be.

He completed some paperwork and drove out to Walton to see a couple of new starters, made arrangements to watch Freddie Mercer ride in his first race and then called in to the Ryans to see how things were there.

Niall, Lottie and Seamus were out at Market Rasen leaving Rosie at home. She was delighted to see Finn and invited him in for tea and cake.

'There's no one we can trust to stay with all the horses. We've yet to replace Clare, you see,' she added sadly, explaining why she hadn't accompanied her husband.

'How are you all doing?'

Rosie sighed. She looked pale and still had huge dark circles under her eyes. 'Sure, we're just plodding on, what else can we do? The tide will turn but we've had a spate of nasty things happen, to be sure. We still don't know when Clare will be buried, the police are continuing their inquiries. That nice Taverner chap says it may be a while yet.'

Finn wondered how the investigation into Clare's death was going. Maybe Harriet might know.

'How's Niall? Any news on when his case comes up in court?'

Rosie shook her head and stirred her tea. 'No, strangely enough Taverner was asking about that too.' She frowned. 'Oh, by the way, Lottie wants to speak to you.'

Finn was sitting in the cosy kitchen yet even with the warmth of the red Aga belting out, he suddenly felt cold.

'Hmm, Sounds ominous.'

Rosie nodded. 'I should let her tell you herself, but I think we've all had enough nasty surprises...'

Finn bit his lip. 'Yes, we have. I'm all ears...'

'She's leaving, Finn. She'll explain it all, but she has lost her nerve over fences and wants to go to a flat yard in Newmarket.'

Finn sighed. Sometimes, jockeys did move around, and it made sense in a way as she wouldn't have the weight issues that some males

159

would have if they swapped to flat racing where the weights were so much lower. Still, he couldn't help but feel disappointed.

'I suppose it's the incident with Niall and Tom that spooked her.' He remembered Lottie's expression and her vomiting before she rode after watching Niall and Tom fall. And of course, Clare's death would have weighed heavily on her too.

Rosie patted his arm and poured him another cup of tea. 'Well, I can't say I blame her with everything that's gone on here recently. She's really quiet but she's a nice lass and I'll miss her.' Rosie dabbed at her eyes. 'I just pray to God, that things settle down. First Clare and all that bother, then Niall and then Tom and then Clare's death. It's almost as though we're jinxed.'

Finn sighed. 'I'm sure that things will get better.'

Rosie managed to smile. 'I'm sure they will, God willing. Now don't forget to look surprised when Lottie tells you.'

Finn nodded in agreement and arranged to come back when Lottie was going to be around.

He was driving home, deep in thought when he received a text from an unknown number.

Can you come and see me asap? I need to tell you something. Tom

Finn had called into see Tom when he was first moved to Jack Berry House, a state of the art rehabilitation centre built by The Injured Jockeys' Fund, near to Walton. He had called in on spec as he was passing and had missed Tom as he was having a physiotherapy session. To his eternal shame he hadn't found the time to come back but he had left his phone number.

He was directed to see Tom in his room. He was lying in bed with monitors and wires connected to him but at least looking alert and recognisable as Tom. Finn thanked his lucky stars that he had never had need of such a facility when he was riding. It was where people with stable but more long term issues came for rehabilitation, but it still freaked him out. Despite the homely appearance of the place, the telltale medicinal smell lingered and there were health staff in formal uniforms. Tom was leafing through The Racing Post, a hard habit to break for a jockey, no doubt.

'I'm so sorry about Clare, Tom. It's truly awful.'

Tom nodded. 'I know. She was a lovely girl.' His eyes filled with tears, his voice quavering. 'I told her we would need to finish when this happened because I didn't want her to feel obliged in any way, but she wouldn't hear of it.'

Finn shook his head in genuine sorrow. 'How are you anyway?'

Tom attempted a smile. 'Oh, I'm getting there, I have some feeling back in my legs which is great, but it'll be a long job, that is for sure.'

'Great, that's really good news.' Spinal injuries were unpredictable, Finn knew, that Tom's spinal column had not been severed and temporary paralysis could result from bruising, and with a bit of luck, full mobility could still be achieved.

Tom shook his head ruefully. 'I'd just found out that I would make a full recovery, on the same day that Clare was killed.' He blinked away tears. 'And she never got to know.'

Finn touched Tom's arm, unsure how to react. 'I know things may seem impossibly bleak just now, but you do have everything to live for. Just try and take one day at a time, mate.' Tom nodded and gulped. 'So, what did you want to tell me?'

'The copper came and told me about Clare and asked me to think about anyone who might hate her or have a grudge against her, if she had ever discussed anything with me. I was so shocked I didn't think about it, but I've had nothing to do here but think and I've thought of two possibilities.'

'OK?'

'I think there was something because Lottie and Clare were always gossiping together, but they'd shut down if Niall or I asked them what they were talking about. Now I think about it, Clare must have said something to Lottie. Clare seemed wary and watchful, but she'd say everything was fine when I asked her. I know about her being attacked and that lad being put away because of it. Clare never felt safe. She always looked about her, always tried to fade into the background. I wonder if she was scared that someone would be after her because she gave evidence at Joel Fox's trial. '

Finn considered this. Clare had been through an awful ordeal and maybe her lack of trust and wariness were all part of the healing process. Or perhaps, there was a good reason why.

'Did she actually say that?'

Tom shook his head. 'No, not as such, but she'd make remarks about rich people having the money and the contacts to do anything, anything at all.'

Finn wondered if that included getting someone murdered.

'So, do you have any other suspicions about who might want to harm her?'

Tom looked thoughtful. 'Well, I did wonder if there was something else going on the night Niall was pulled by the police.'

'How do you mean?'

'Well, there's always been rumours of drugs circulating in and around Walton.'

Finn had heard these rumours before but then again, the police had struggled to find hard evidence. Mind you, he had wondered if the incident with Niall was actually about something else, it was just such an extreme reaction, to try and speed off from the police.

Tom looked thoughtful. 'All the rumours seem to centre around one person.'

'Niall?'

Tom shook his head. 'No, Jamie Doyle.'

Finn took this in and tried to compose his features into a neutral expression.

'Really? Are you prepared to speak to the police?'

'Yes, of course I am.'

Later Finn was about to ring Jamie Doyle, when he got a call from Vince Hunt, the trainer who the conditional jockey was apprenticed to.

'How strange, I was just about to arrange a visit to see Jamie.'

'Jamie? Didn't you get my message? He's gone. Just cleared out. He's taken all his stuff, the useless article. I was just ringing you to see about getting a new conditional and how long it might take, that's all.'

'Where on earth has he gone? He must have told someone?'

Vince sounded irritated. 'I presume back to Ireland. His mother's supposed to be ill, and he's worried about her or so he said in the note he left. I'd have given him time off for a visit, so I think that that might be an excuse.'

162

Finn was beginning to think this was hugely coincidental, just as Tom was recovering and now able to speak out.

'Have you heard any rumours about him?'

Vince paused. 'No. He's too fond of his phone but I told him about that. He was actually shaping up to be a decent rider truth be told, and he was a good worker too.' He paused. 'Anyway, what have you heard?'

'I just wondered whether you'd heard anything about him using and dealing drugs?'

Vince laughed. 'No. Nothing at all, in fact when he had a fall and sprained his wrist, he wouldn't even take a painkiller, so I doubt he's into anything like that. Still, it's annoying he's gone. How soon can you get me another, someone that might just stick around?'

Finn said he'd been given some new conditionals so he'd see what he could do. His head was buzzing. He decided to ring Taverner and tip him off about what Tom Kennedy had told him and he'd add the comments from Vince Hunt into the mix too. He supposed that Jamie could still be a drug dealer without using himself and if he had drugs in the car, it would certainly explain why Niall drove like a mad man to lose the police. Surely, the arresting officers would have searched Niall and the other passengers and the car? Maybe Clare had become aware of his drug dealing and he killed her to keep her quiet? Even if that were true, it was a very extreme reaction, unless an organised crime group was involved. Christ, he wondered, what the hell was going on? Just when he thought he had it all worked out, other curve balls were thrown into the mix to derail his theories, leaving him with precisely nothing.

Chapter 21

Topper was about to drive out to Wetherby, one of the local courses but decided to have brunch first and continue planning his book. He had to admit after a flurry of enthusiasm, he was finding the plotting difficult and was trying to plan it without killing his creativity stone dead. I always reserve the right to go where I want to go in my writing, he told himself. Sometimes only really good plot devices came to him as he was actually typing or at odd times like when in the shower. It was a strange old business novel writing, he decided, so different to his racing reports which were based on facts, quotes and his knowledge about racing. Now he had to rely on the latter with a liberal helping of characterisation not to mention the plotting and he was struggling. He made some notes, read The Racing Post and looked up from his paper and glanced around the room. His cottage looked very clean and tidy. He was pleased with the cleaner he had engaged from Spick and Span, the cleaning agency run by Penny Mercer.

Appointing the cleaner, who he had never actually met, they came to an arrangement about the key and payment, fulfilled two aims. One was to actually keep his house clean, but the other objective was to find out a bit more about Penny Mercer's business. He was still suspicious about Finn taking on Penny's son, Freddie, as a conditional jockey. He was also wary about Christian Gerrard but had shelved that for now. Freddie was a more interesting prospect. His father was serving a prison sentence at HMP Lindholme near Doncaster. He was also warned off which meant that his son could have no contact with him if he was involved with racing, no one from the racing world could. It was like being sent to Coventry, being a complete social pariah in the racing fraternity. Any evidence to the contrary would certainly blow things for Freddie and he'd lose his licence. To date though, he'd not found out too much about the business, Spick and Span, except to say that Penny ran a tight ship and had sounded cool and professional when she'd rung him after he'd emailed the company. He'd signed a contract and saw that the business had insurance for damages and Penny had explained that the cleaners had to complete training. She also said that she did spot checks on properties to ensure the very highest of standards and invited him to ring her immediately with any concerns he might have.

The whole enterprise was well run, and he had to admit that his cottage was looking pretty good even after he'd had the boys for the weekend. Tim and Giles were lively, talented lads and they'd messed about with Nerf guns for much of the time, Tim deciding to count their bullets on target more accurately by covering the end of the foam bullet with paint which left lurid blue marks on the walls and themselves. Topper laughed at the memory. But his cleaner has sorted out the debris, the crisp packets, school uniform, rugby boots and pizza wrapping and she'd even popped everything in the dishwasher and tidied up so that the cottage was gleaming. She'd even dealt with the blue dots and cleaned them off the walls. He looked around his sitting room again with satisfaction. Amazing! Then his heart sank when he noticed the telltale blue dot on the gold frame of his painting, the one he had signed himself. His Gideon Moss. Damn, but at least the boys hadn't hit the actual painting. He fished out some paint stripper from the cupboard under the stairs which had been left over from when he'd done the cottage up, diluted it and rubbed the blue mark. It came off easily enough, the only trouble was it took the gold gilt off the frame with it, leaving a lighter section underneath. Still, never mind he'd patch up the gold bit later. He glanced at his watch, saw the time, drained his drink and decided to set off to Wetherby. He'd think about Gerrard and Freddie Mercer as he drove and hoped to get some inspiration for his book from his day at the races, maybe from even what happened to the conditional himself. His mood rose as he drove. He'd got another date with Jane from Boxercise, his career was on the up and if he could finish his book and get it to a publisher then he was sure they'd love it. Onwards and upwards Topper, he told himself.

Wetherby was an old racecourse dating back to 1891. It was a National Hunt course but changed in 2015 to include flat racing. It was a friendly, unpretentious course and the punters and staff were solicitous, yet down to earth. Topper popped into the press room to avail himself of the food and drinks which didn't seem that healthy to him. How times had changed. He sipped a coffee and picked at a sandwich, ham salad on wholemeal bread, before deciding to walk around the enclosures, study the horses and write his pieces. He relied on technology these days and was holding a tan, leather man bag with a state of the art laptop and fancy work mobile, with which he could record conversations with jockeys and trainers. He saw that there were a few trainers from Walton, Vince Hunt, Alistair Broadie and Jeremy Trentham. He wondered if Jeremy was ready to put his latest conditional Freddie Mercer up, but decided it was probably too early. He wondered why Jeremy had felt compelled to take him but decided it was probably because Penny Mercer and Laura Trentham were friends, so she would have had some sympathy with Penny. She might even use her cleaning services too, for all he knew.

He mooched about, interviewed some trainers and jockeys who he managed to catch, then decided to follow his friend Lofty, whose large frame he had spotted sauntering into the main bar. He looked dishevelled and was wearing his customary cream raincoat, which had clearly seen better days. Topper sat on a bar stool next to Lofty, winked at his old friend and ordered a couple of whiskeys.

'Now then, Lofty. How are you?'

Lofty raised his glass and took a sip of his drink.

'Nice one. I'm good, but not as good as you appear to be by the look of you.'

Topper grinned. 'Well, things are on the up. New job, lots of things in the pipeline, you know.'

'Got any tips for today?'

Topper looked at him thoughtfully. 'How about I mark your card and if you're ever in the environs of HMP Lindholme when the visitors are coming and going, I'd be grateful for a few photos. And anything of this lad.' He showed Lofty a recent photo of Freddie Mercer.

Lofty scratched his dishevelled head. 'HMP Lindholme as in Hatfield near Doncaster?'

Topper nodded.

Lofty narrowed his eyes. 'Now what might be your interest there?'

Topper shrugged. 'Oh, just following a hunch, that's all.' He refused to be drawn further.

Lofty studied him and then shrugged. 'Might be able to do it, but I think it's worth a bit more than a few tips, mate.'

Topper pulled out a few twenties and handed them over. Lofty counted them, sniffed and put them in his pocket.

'Right you are, then.'

'Got anything else I might be interested in?' Topper was aware that Lofty frequented a strange universe where information was currency and Lofty as a freelancer picked up and stored all sorts of random information. He took an awful lot of photos too, and not just of horses. He could be very useful as he was a quiet man and he sidled in and out of places, listening and taking everything in.

'Heard about the girl who was kicked by a horse at the Ryans' place. A bad business.' Topper waited for more. It was a bit like dealing with a clairvoyant listening to Lofty he decided, he had to wait for the information to come through from the other side. Eventually Lofty added, 'heard it wasn't an accident exactly.'

Topper tried not to look surprised. So far, this information hadn't been released to the general public, but no doubt would be shortly. He struggled to compose his face into a neutral expression. He didn't want to spook Lofty by betraying too much interest.

'Who's in the frame for that, then?'

Lofty shrugged. 'Not sure. I just heard a whisper. She was killed to keep her quiet about something though, I do know that.'

Topper tried to look nonchalant.

'Quiet about what exactly?'

Lofty shrugged. Topper listened some more but there seemed to be no further information that he was prepared to divulge. He glanced at his watch and saw the bar crowd start to thin out as punters went to watch the next race.

'I'd better get off then, Lofty. Places to be, horses to back, you know. Keep me posted, old fellow, will you?'

Lofty nodded and tapped the side of his nose. 'I will.'

It was a few days later when Lofty sent him an email with several attachments. He made a note to look at them later but tonight he was off on another date with Jane and didn't have time to check them out. It was only when he picked up his keys and paused to smooth down his hair, then rummaged around to find some gel to style it, that he noticed something

167

different about the Moss painting. He studied it carefully. The rubbed out section on the frame, where he'd used the paint stripper to remove the blue paint from the Nerf gun bullets, was no longer there. In fact, there was now no sign of the area he'd rubbed with paint stripper, none whatsoever. The picture frame was restored to its former glory. He studied it closely and found he couldn't even see where the pale area had been at all now. Maybe, he'd imagined the lighter smudge on the frame, but he didn't think so. How strange.

Could the boys have come back, and fearing their father's wrath repaired the frame? No surely not, the logistics of being transported here by their mother and gaining entry to the house made it highly unlikely. Besides, he wasn't angry, he was just glad to see his boys and they would know he'd not make a fuss. What the hell was going on? He pondered on the painting and its mysteriously repaired frame. He knew it was significant, but he hadn't yet worked out why. Think on, old son, he told himself. It'll come to you; it always does, sometimes when he least expected it.

Chapter 22

Anna Wildblood motioned to Taverner as soon as he came through the door. He was still frowning, trying to understand her meaning. It soon became clear when DCI Sykes trundled into view. Taverner noted he looked pale, slimmer but otherwise well.

'Now then, Sir. Good to have you back.'

Taverner found that he actually meant it. It was quite hard running a team and taking instructions from Superintendent Wilson, who was an experienced officer but the polar opposite of Sykes, on the surface at least. His softly, softly approach, addiction to police PR campaigns and 'empathy' with victims were all very well, but not to Taverner's mind, that helpful unless crimes were actually solved, and the bad guys put away. The Superintendent's major preoccupation seemed to be looking as though they were doing something for the public, but he didn't seem so bothered about solving crimes. At least, Sykes was keen on apprehending suspects and getting convictions, and Taverner much preferred his approach.

'Well, I'm back part time after Christmas.' He had some papers in his hands. 'Just popped in to pick up some work. I'll go mad with just daytime TV.' Sykes' gaze slid over the links board. 'Hear you have another suspicious death, a stable lass killed by a vicious horse.'

Taverner nodded and was glad now that he hadn't moved into Sykes' office, preferring to remain in his own much smaller one.

Sykes nodded. 'Who are your suspects?'

Taverner gave him a summary of the case.

'Mmm.' Sykes appeared to be about to ask more then decided against it. 'And thanks for the Scotch, much appreciated though, I have had to hide it from the wife.'

Taverner smiled. It was actually Wildblood who had organised the whip round and Haworth and Ballantyne who had suggested an expensive bottle of Scotch for the boss, a somewhat strange present for someone who had just had heart surgery and probably not what the doctor ordered.

'And the surgery was a success?' added Taverner.

Sykes nodded. "Twas. Anyway, I'll be off. It'll be business as usual in the New year.' He nodded. 'Good luck with everything.'

'Thanks. You look after yourself.' He found that he actually meant it.

The team who had appeared suspiciously busy whilst Sykes was there, suddenly looked up from their desks ready for their morning briefing. The inquiry into Clare Hudson's death was progressing slowly. They were still in the preliminary stages and information was being gathered, it would take some time to come in and be sifted through and cross checked. What Taverner was struggling with was a motive for the attack on Clare. A quiet, hardworking stable girl, popular with those she knew well, adored by her employers and family, it was a puzzle. The only lead was the link to Joel Fox who had raped her and another girl and was currently serving a prison sentence. Joel's father, Lloyd Fox served a short prison sentence then sold his yard and was rumoured to be living abroad. There was no evidence that he had even been in England at the time. If Joel had orchestrated an attack on Clare as vengeance, then he must have relied on a third party to carry out the attack.

He sifted through the information they had from Forensics. There were no fingerprints on the stable door, apart from those of staff who usually worked there, so unless it was one of them, the perpetrator must have been wearing gloves. Amongst the debris at the crime scene was a false fingernail, which had come off either Clare, or possibly her assailant. Surely that was significant? He couldn't imagine that stable staff wore such things, given the practical and hands on nature of their job. Maybe Clare had treated herself to a manicure for The Stagecoach party? But there was no evidence that Clare had worn false nails from the post mortem or from a search of her house.

He went through the statements so far from those who had attended the event at The Stagecoach, Harriet's amongst them. No one had noticed anything peculiar. It was clear that Clare had decided to head home and check on the horses before turning in and she had told a few people at the party, one of whom may have followed her. He went into the main office to find that Haworth and Ballantyne were sifting through their interviews, Cullen was studying phone records and Patel was hunched over a computer screen.

'How's it going?' he asked. 'Is there anything from the CCTV from the hotel?' Taverner had high hopes of the CCTV given that there had been no expense spared on the building, it was bound to be of a high quality.

Patel shrugged. 'Bloody thing wasn't switched on as the place isn't officially open until the end of the week. It's a high tech system...'

'But no use to us at all, if it's not switched on.'

Patel sighed in frustration. 'Exactly.'

'Anything else?'

Ballantyne turned to look at him. 'Well, we have confirmation that Lloyd Fox is living in Sweden doing some business deals there. He served a short prison sentence for his part in the crimes, sold up here and is trying to make a fresh start. Crucially, he was in Sweden when Clare died. Of the people at the party one or two have criminal records, Niall Byrne and Jamie Doyle.'

Taverner knew about Byrne. 'What's the information on Doyle?'

'Drugs, possession, possibly dealing...'

Taverner took this in. That might be significant, it was hard to tell.

Haworth gave him a meaningful look. 'But the other thing is that Doyle was a stable lad for the Foxes when they were in Walton.'

Taverner's ears pricked up at that. That reminded him he needed to chase up Byrne's case with DI Johnson too. Maybe there was some credibility in the theory that Joel Fox had something to do with Clare's death, after all? Maybe he had paid Jamie Doyle to do it?

'Right. I'm just trying to picture The Stagecoach. Aren't there some houses opposite? Maybe one of them has CCTV or one of the video doorbell things, they're quite good these days and work on motion sensors. Maybe someone over there picked something up unwittingly.'

Just then Taverner's mobile rang. It was Finn McCarthy. After a few minutes, Taverner turned to the team.

'That was Finn McCarthy. Guess who has upped and left without so much as a trace? Jamie Doyle, he's believed to have gone back to Ireland. And there's more, Clare's boyfriend, Tom Kennedy, told Finn that he thought there was more to that incident when Byrne was arrested for drunk driving. Remember that Doyle was in the car on the night. Supposing he had a large quantity of drugs and Clare knew about it and he threatened her?'

'Well, it would certainly be a motive, wouldn't it? But surely the police who arrested Byrne would have been through the car like a dose of salts? Stands to reason,' added Haworth.

It was routine to search a car following such an incident and Taverner was sure the traffic police would have done so.

'I'm sure they did, but maybe they missed it?'

Taverner left a message for DI Johnson and followed it up with an email asking for him to get in touch as a matter of urgency. He felt like the investigation was floundering and they really needed a breakthrough. Just keep going, he told himself. Whoever had killed Clare must have planned things, their actions must have been noticed by someone, somewhere. He knew they would struggle with a murder charge, after all, the horse had dealt the fatal blow, but it didn't do to worry about such things at this time. They just needed to press on. It was a bit like a ball of wool, all they had to do was find the end and pull, then the whole lot would unravel before their eyes. He wished it was as easy as it sounded.

Chapter 23

Ye Olde Starre Inne in York was an ancient pub with beams and an abundance of atmosphere including several ghosts apparently, one a Royalist officer from The Civil War, two black cats that may have been buried alive and an old lady who was often seen slowly climbing the stairs. Today it was still a popular place and had a good, wholesome menu. Theresa was already there sipping water and beamed as soon as she saw Finn. He kissed her lightly on the cheek. She was wearing a fitted red dress that showed off her figure and a black coat and red and black checked scarf. She looked radiant and full of health.

They chatted about their week. Theresa regaled him with tales of rowdy pupils and the funny things they had said. He filled her in on Clare's death which she knew all about from her brother Niall.

Theresa sighed and shook her head. 'Oh, that's awful. Being kicked to death by a horse. Niall's properly upset by it.'

'Well, the police are investigating, so we'll soon find out more.'

'Are they suspicious?'

Finn wasn't quite sure what was public knowledge so declined to say more.

'I suppose they have to investigate any unexpected death, that's all.'

Theresa shivered and clutched his arm. 'Let's talk about something more cheerful, shall we?'

They did. They swapped childhood stories and talked about family and friends.

'There's just me, my sister and mum. Jenny lives nearby and has two children, so it's nice to see my nieces who are both lovely.' It reminded Finn that he needed to contact them. Work was so absorbing somehow.

Theresa rolled her eyes. 'Oh, I'm the eldest and it was hell at home with so many of us and mammie being on her own.' She smiled. 'It's nice having a big family, but then again I've got to keep Niall on the straight and narrow and that's easier said than done.'

173

Finn considered this, noting that she still used the present tense, so he presumed she still felt that she was doing this.

'I suppose his court date will be coming up shortly. You know when it happened and he sped off from the police, was there anything else going on?'

Theresa looked puzzled. 'Like what exactly?'

'Well, it was just such a strange thing to do, to be stopped by the police and then him driving off like that. It's an extreme reaction.'

Theresa nodded and then rolled her eyes. 'I suppose, but then Niall was always an impulsive eejit, the things he did as a boy, well, I could write a book about him.'

'Do you know Jamie Doyle?'

Theresa looked steadily at him but shook her head. 'I don't think so, should I? I think Niall may have mentioned him, but in passing, that's all.'

'I just wondered.' He suddenly thought of something. 'Niall rang you that evening to sort out his car. Did you see anything else in the car, something he or one of the others was trying to hide?'

Theresa frowned. 'He rang me because he was upset but then you came, and I thought he'd be better talking to you. He asked me to sort out the recovery of his car and take his riding stuff back. To tell you the truth he was really worried about his job, so he wanted to talk to you.' She frowned and looked suddenly wary. 'Anyway, why are you asking all these questions?'

Finn cursed himself as he realised he had ruined the mood. He tried to reassure her.

'Look, I'm sorry, don't mind me, I'm just trying to get things straight in my head.'

Theresa sniffed and gave him a suspicious look. He could have kicked himself when later Theresa claimed tiredness and wanted an early night. She stifled a yawn.

'I've loads of marking to do. Teaching requires so much out of hours work. I have to assess the 6th form projects and it's taking me forever.'

Finn nodded. 'Oh, I think I saw them. I wandered into your study by mistake when I was leaving the other day and saw all the work, the canvases, and all those old picture frames. Your students have worked very hard.'

Theresa smiled. 'Oh yes, it was a project about art and, so they had the great idea of repurposing old frames. They got a bit carried away. I've to take them all back to school though now when everything's been graded.' She kissed him perfunctorily. 'I'm sorry, it's such a drag. The deadline is coming up, you see.'

Finn hid his disappointment. 'It's no problem. I'm tired myself and I have an early start tomorrow. Look, I'll ring you in the week.'

Theresa hugged him again. 'You do that, Finn. That t'would be grand.'

Finn went back home feeling rather bereft. He and Hattie were going to find Ross Maclaren tomorrow, so it was true that he had to be up early himself, but he couldn't help feeling irritated. Why had he asked so many questions? Theresa had not liked him probing deeper into the events surrounding Niall's accident and who could blame her. It made him look like he didn't trust Niall, which in some ways he didn't entirely. Why couldn't he have kept his big mouth shut? Never mind, I'll ring her in the week and make it up to her, he promised himself. If he got the opportunity, that was. Don't overthink things, he told himself, she probably was tired, and he was stressed, that was all. Yet he couldn't help but wonder if his burgeoning relationship was as promising as he'd first thought.

Chapter 24

Finn picked Hattie up from home the next morning and they made their way on the 'A' roads and motorway down to Leek in the Staffordshire Moorlands. As they travelled, they took the opportunity to talk about their strategies about how best they were going to approach Ross Maclaren.

'I think the easiest thing is to be honest and say we've been employed by Jeremy to find him, apologise on Jeremy's behalf and then ask him to bring Admiral Jervis back to the yard. What do you think?'

Hattie pondered this. 'I agree but I'm thinking how do we get a foot in the door to start with?'

'I think we'll have to play it by ear and go with the flow.'

Harriet frowned. 'Supposing he just locks the doors and ignores us? That's what I'm worried about.'

'Hmm. He'll certainly be wary, that is for sure. We'll have to think of something.'

Harriet had felt quite buoyed up when they found Maclaren's address, but now she began to wonder whether they hadn't been a bit naive. If Maclaren refused to see them, there wasn't a great deal they could do.

Finn looked thoughtful. 'We could do a recce of the situation and then have a think. I wonder if he has any animals? Maybe we could say that one if his animals is in distress and lure him out? I wonder if the locals know he's there?'

'Maybe we could call into the nearest pub and ask about?'

The motorway gave way to green fields, and they reached the Staffordshire Moorlands. They drove through Leek, which was a pleasant market town, and on towards Upper Hulme where the landscape was dominated by the huge rock structures of Hen Cloud and Ramshaw Rocks, and green fields gave way to moorland and heather.

Harriet had been reading a local guide on her phone.

'If we carry on past Upper Hulme on the Buxton Road, we pass the Winking Man.'

'What's that?'

'It's a rock formation like the profile of a face with a hole in it, like an eye. As you drive past it looks like the person is winking at you. Wow.'

Finn laughed. 'Don't get too excited. We probably won't have time to go sightseeing.'

'Ah there is a pub called Ye Olde Rock Inne in Upper Hulme, so we could call in there and they do food.'

Ye Olde Rock Inne was a beautiful traditional pub. It had a roaring fire and a homely atmosphere. They ordered a toasted sandwich and a coffee, the menu looked wonderful, but Finn was keen to get going and make the most of the daylight.

'Lovely place,' said Finn when the barmaid served them. 'The area is spectacular. I bet you get loads of famous visitors, don't you?'

The woman laughed. 'Not so you'd notice. It's pretty undiscovered around here and that's how we like it.'

Harriet tried again when she went to the bar for some sugar.

'What a place! I bet you get loads of writers and painters round here. The spectacular scenery is bound to inspire the creative types. Are there lots of holiday homes about?'

The barmaid nodded. 'A few. We do get mainly walkers and climbers. It's bad in the winter though, the roads are impassable in the snow, so it puts folk off.'

Harriet made polite conversation and made her way back to Finn.

'Hmm. I don't think anyone would know he was here. Think about it, he writes about disguises, and I bet he wears them himself, so no one will have a clue if he's here or not.'

Finn raised his eyebrows. 'Well, the locals don't seem literary types, so he's probably safe from discovery here,' he added drily.

They set off and followed the directions to Rock Cottage which led them through the village of Upper Hulme, through a ford and passed a disused mill. From here the countryside opened out. They drove on until they were at the foot of Hen Cloud, a huge rock formation and the scenery over the moorland and field beyond, was wild and exhilarating.

'Anyone would get inspiration looking at that,' added Harriet. Finn took in the view. The sky was flint grey, the stones forbidding, enlivened only by the earthy green and purple heather. It was truly majestic.

They continued down a narrow road with moorland and heather either side. There were a few sheep and farms but other than that the place was completely isolated. They came across a house in the distance. There was a hand painted sign attached to the wall which read, Rock Cottage, that showed them they had come to the right place. Down the long drive they could just make out a stone cottage at the end of it, set in rugged moorland and surrounded by sheep. There was a swirl of smoke coming from one of the chimneys, so it certainly looked like someone was in. Finn pulled into a passing place.

'Shall I just walk down there and do a recce and come back and get you?'

Harriet frowned. 'OK. What are you looking for?'

'Well, we'll knock first off and then if that fails then we'll need to think of something else.'

'Don't leave me here, Finn,' she hissed. 'Make sure you do come back.' She didn't want to miss out on all the fun. Finn gave her the thumbs up and darted down the track.

She waited, tapping her fingers in irritation. Honestly, she should have gone and then she could have claimed that she was lost if anyone came out. At least as a female she might be able to get away with being lost and a bit ditsy. After what seemed like an age, Finn returned. The skies had darkened, and rain was starting to fall. He had pulled up the hood of his jacket and jogged as he made his way to the car.

'What did you find?'

Finn shook the rain out of his hair. 'Well, there's a Land Rover there with the keys in the ignition so if all else fails then we could force Maclaren to come out by pretending to drive off with it.'

'I suppose that would work.'

There was a gap in the rainfall. 'Come on, we'll knock first and move to Plan B if that doesn't work.'

The track was poorly kept with huge potholes and Harriet was glad she had worn her sturdy boots. The drive seemed to go on for ever, but eventually they came to the house. It was a lot larger than it appeared from the road and quite grand, with a range of outbuildings, stabling and a cultivated garden at the back which had been tamed from the wild

178

moorland. There was a stone porch and beyond that a large oak door with a brass door knocker in the shape of a fox.

Finn nodded towards it, and they stood out of the rain under the porch. Finn lifted the door knocker and released it three times. The sound of it falling reverberated through the building. A dog barked and scratched at the door, but other than that, there was no sign of life.

Finn tried again, but apart from the dog whining and scratching there was nothing. Finn and Harriet listened intently. The dog whined again and then Finn heard it, a shushing noise, someone trying to quieten the animal.

'Is there anyone home?' called Finn. 'We just want to talk, that's all.'

There was silence. He tried again and again, but there was no response.

Finn jerked his head towards the outbuilding where the black Land Rover was kept. They ran towards it and opened the doors. Finn started the engine, deliberately taking his time so as to elicit a response from the owner. He reversed the car and revved up loudly to make sure that he was overheard. The rain started to fall heavily. Finn was about to set off down the driveway when suddenly there was a knock at the passenger window. There was a figure, blurry from the rain shouting at them. There was no mistaking the long narrow, tubular shaped object he was holding.

Harriet gasped. 'Christ, Finn. It's a shotgun!'

It had taken a long time for Ross Maclaren, for it was certainly him, to calm down.

'For God's sake, what the hell do you think you were playing at? Tell me why I shouldn't call the police?' he repeated once Finn has persuaded him to put the gun down.

'Well, we did knock on the door, and you didn't answer, so it was a way to get your attention,' Finn explained.

Ross scowled in recognition at Finn. 'Hey, I know you, don't I? Aren't you that jockey, Finn McCarthy? What the hell? Are you a bloody journalist now?'

179

'No. I'm a jockey coach and this is Harriet Lucas. She's a dietician. We only pretended to drive off with your car to make you come out,' explained Finn for the second time. 'You see we really need to talk to you.'

Ross nodded ruefully. 'Well, it certainly worked.' He was tall, patrician in appearance and had a slight Scottish accent. He was clearly the man they had seen in the wheelchair when Admiral ran. 'Well, as you can see, I'm never going to make a jockey and I don't need to lose weight, so what the hell do you want?'

'Jeremy Trentham asked us to find you.' Finn went on to explain about their work for the BHA. Harriet nodded and was glad not for the first time, that Finn's success as a jockey had helped them out of a tricky situation. Racing people still recognised him. Maclaren stared at them and seemed more relaxed, intrigued even. He gestured that they follow him inside into a large kitchen and quietly set about making tea. He handed mugs around and they settled on the spindle backed chairs around the scrubbed pine table.

Maclaren stroked his chin and looked thoughtful. 'So, Jeremy sent you, Finn McCarthy of all people. And you now work as a jockey coach but also do undercover stuff for the BHA?'

'Yes, we sort of fell into it really. It's a long story,' replied Harriet.

Ross studied her. 'Well, as an author I like stories, so do tell me, I'm intrigued. How do you fit into things?'

Harriet smiled. 'I used to work for the Racing to School project and Finn and I came across one of his conditionals after a race, who had been badly beaten up, he wasn't supposed to win, you see. I helped patch him up and as you can imagine there was a lot more to his story, blackmail, race pulling you name it. Finn and I worked together to find out what. I'm a dietician now and work for the PJA.'

Ross looked from one to the other. 'So, you work in and around Walton, both in different parts of the racing industry. Very clever, of the BHA I mean, you can quite legitimately ask questions, I suppose.'

'Of course, it's all hush hush,' Finn added.

'Naturally.' He steepled his hands and looked thoughtful. 'I won't breathe a word. 'He looked from one to the other. 'So, Jeremy hired you to find me?'

'That's about the size of it. He feels very bad about the argument you had and also concerned that the painting you left him in lieu of payment is worth far more than the debt you owe him. Gideon Moss's paintings fetch quite a bit these days and it is a very rare painting of that famous stallion, Red Navajo.'

Ross rubbed his eyes. 'Mmm. Ridden by Will Gibb in the Sovereign Stakes at York in 1912.' He studied them for a while, as if coming to a decision. Eventually, he appeared to come to a decision.

'Well, you have achieved something no one else has in finding me, I'll give you that much, but I must ask you to keep my whereabouts confidential, is that clear?' He studied them. 'Otherwise, I might change my decision about shooting you.'

Unsurprisingly, there was no argument from either of them, not being sure if he was joking or not. They both nodded. 'Of course.'

They waited for Ross to say more. He patted his dog, a border collie called Bracken, and sighed. They sipped tea and waited.

'I suffered badly from writer's block and no matter what I did, I couldn't overcome it, you see. It's been years since my last book. The publishers and my agent were all pushing me and that made it so much worse.' He shook his head in irritation. 'And then the money started to run out, we had creditors, I had to borrow to pay bills, the debts were piling up. I suppose we had been extravagant, rather I had. Fortunately, my wife, Sue, is a sensible sort of woman, she went back to teaching, streamlined the debts and booked this place so I could use the solitude and isolation to get on and finish my book without press, agents and the like bugging me.'

'Has it worked?' asked Harriet. 'My father is a massive fan, by the way.'

Ross smiled. 'I'm delighted to say it has. I am at the editing stage, but it is to all intents and purposes finished. And it's good, which is such a relief.'

'So, where is Admiral?'

There was a pause as Ross composed himself. 'When Jeremy started to push me about payments, that really was the last straw. I sold the other horses via an agent, they were mediocre anyway, and Sue set up a company and now she owns Admiral. You see, I was scared that creditors would take him, and I couldn't bear that. He is a wonderful horse, I'd never part with him. I found a small trainer, Stan, and made it look like he had been sold. He was really, but to my wife.'

'RHB Holdings, Robert Henry Brooks, the hero in your books,' added Harriet.

Ross smiled. 'Yes, you have done your homework. I couldn't resist that. Then I gave Jeremy another of my assets, the Moss painting of Red Navajo because I knew that it was worth a bomb, and I couldn't risk that painting being sold to pay creditors either.' He shrugged. 'I knew Jeremy well enough to know that he'd do the right thing and look after it and when my book is finished, I'll pay him every penny I owe him and take it back.'

Harriet bit her lip but decided to ask the question that she was dying to ask anyway.

'I suppose the Moss painting is genuine?'

Ross looked aghast. 'Absolutely. It's a family heirloom. I was bequeathed it by my grandfather when he died. His grandfather commissioned Gideon Moss to paint it as he owned Red Navajo. The horse was the best three year old in 1912 and went on to have a stellar stud career, as I'm sure you know. Strange markings, with his white leg though. Some people loved his flashy looks, others disliked them. My great grandmother fell into the latter category and sold the painting, and my grandfather bought it back when the extent of Red Navajo's prowess as a stallion was known. It is certainly genuine which is why I sent it by White Glove Transport, of course.'

Harriet looked at Finn. She hadn't the heart to mention the other painting in New York that Livvy was pretending to be interested in, that was being studied by her friend. The provenance for Jeremy's painting was cast iron, so that meant that the New York painting had to be a fake. Finn seemed equally hesitant to mention the other picture, now he had heard this. Of course, the presence of the shot gun made easier not to ask further questions.

'So, you'll pay Jeremy back?'

Ross nodded. 'Of course. I had a small advance because I have become something of a liability in writing terms. Historically, I had written so many books and was quite prolific, but after the writer's block, I became something of a risk. I am assured a larger sum once they have read this latest book. Then I'll pay Jeremy and take back my Moss painting.'

'Will you send Admiral back to Jeremy?' Harriet continued. 'Because that's really why Jeremy wanted us to find you.'

Ross paused. 'I'm not sure. You know we're second cousins, don't you? That's why I was so annoyed about him going on about the money, I mean family ought to count for something, shouldn't it? It just felt like the ultimate slap in the face, the last straw, him going on about the debt.'

Harriet nodded. 'But he is very sorry and he's one of the best trainers around.'

'And he has gone to considerable effort to find you, don't forget,' added Finn.

Ross grinned. 'Aye. I'll think on it. I would still want Nat Wilson to ride Admiral mind. I've nothing against Tristan Davies, he's a great jockey, but Nat, well, he's something else. He just clicks with Admiral somehow, and there's no one who can ride a finish like he can.'

Harriet knew that Tristan was going to be very disappointed, but that was racing for you. The owner still held all the cards in the sport of Kings.

Finn nodded. 'I know Nat very well, and I have to agree, he's the best in the business. I'll speak to Jeremy. I'm pretty sure he'll agree.'

Harriet smiled. 'Looks like that's settled then.'

Ross merely nodded. He pulled out a bottle of Scotch and three glasses and poured a healthy dram in each.

'I'll drink to that.'

They drove home in high spirits, considering their task was completed.

'Well, that's a job well done, what a relief,' Harriet concluded.

Finn agreed. 'He seemed like a decent chap, and we did get an invite to his book launch, so that is something to look forward to.'

Harriet beamed. 'I know, I can't wait.'

They stopped off en route to refuel. Harriet went into the services to buy some sandwiches and cake for the journey back. When she came back, Finn was on the phone looking confused and then worried. He ended his call abruptly.

183

'What is it?'

Finn frowned and seemed to take an age to compose his thoughts. 'That was Nat. You know Livvy has feigned an interest in the Moss painting in New York and asked her friend, Will Molyneux, to study the painting and he's examined it. He says in his opinion it's genuine!'

Harriet gasped. 'What? That can't be true, surely? Maclaren has cast iron provenance. He was bequeathed the painting, and there are all sorts of family connections. You heard him! And surely if he was left the painting in his grandfather's will, then they'll certainly be a record of that.'

Finn shook his head, bewildered. 'But if we look at it another way and the New York painting is genuine then the one at Trentham's must be a fake.'

Harriet frowned. 'Thank God we didn't mention the other painting to Ross!' Her face fell. 'Christ, Ross is never going to return Admiral to Jeremy's now. How on earth has this happened? Perhaps, Ross has made up all that stuff about his ancestors, him being an expert storyteller and all that? We could get Uncle Sebastian to have a look at the painting, that might be an idea. I'd trust his judgement.'

Finn looked thoughtful. 'That would be brilliant. I'm sure Jeremy will be as anxious to get to the bottom of things as we are. Maybe Molyneux isn't the expert he says he is, so your uncle might contradict him.'

Harriet nodded. 'He's very well regarded so I'd back Sebastian, definitely. He does all sorts of work for Sotheby's and he's even writing a book on some famous forger or other, Archie someone. He knows all the pitfalls. They can even do X rays and paint analysis these days. I remember him telling me about it.'

They pondered on the paintings the rest of the way home and came to no particular conclusion. Harriet reflected on their earlier high spirits. It was as though someone had popped their bubbles with a sharp needle and the air had fizzled out in a steady hiss. Neither of them had even countenanced the possibility that Maclaren's painting could be a fake despite the seemingly solid provenance. What the hell was going on? They'd have to explain about the New York picture to Jeremy to get Harriet's uncle to examine the painting. It didn't escape Finn's notice that rather than

184

improving the relationship between Jeremy and Maclaren, this was likely to have exactly the opposite effect.

Chapter 25

Haworth delivered his information with a flourish. 'Well, I've just been given intel about Jamie Doyle. He's got previous for drug dealing, cannabis and opiates! He was involved with the Irish equivalent of Youth Offending.'

'Oh, OK,' Taverner took this in.

Haworth looked disappointed with his reaction. 'The lass is shut in the stable and gets kicked to death by a horse, we're investigating. and he buggers off, a bit coincidental, isn't it? And now we find this out about Doyle. It's got to be relevant, by my reckoning.'

'Certainly is. I have just been speaking to Finn McCarthy, his coach. Seems there is a fairly high drop out rate in racing. He may just have decided that being a jump jockey was not for him, but I agree we need to investigate further. I have a next of kin address from Finn in County Cork, so get on to the guards there will you? Have them visit and get him to explain himself. We also need to know what he was doing on the night Clare died, got it?'

Haworth did a merry little dance, like a leprechaun. 'To be sure, to be sure,' he muttered in a passable Irish accent. 'I wouldn't mind a trip out to the Emerald Isle meself.'

Taverner gave him a stern look. 'Let's see how the guards do first, so don't get too carried away.'

DS Anna Wildblood caught his eye and smiled. Haworth was the joker in the pack, irrepressibly good humoured, he was a complete contrast to DC Ballantyne, the gloomy Scot, who was definitely a glass half empty sort of chap. Both were steady and experienced coppers though and stalwarts of the team. Anna looked animated which meant she also had information to impart. He looked at her and waited.

'Now then guv. I've been making some inquiries about Joel Fox's visitors. According to the nick, he's been a model prisoner, kept his head down. His father is confirmed as being abroad at the time of the incident doing yet more business deals, we think but he's in regular contact by phone and letter with his son. There's an aunt who visits him, Lloyd's sister and her daughter, Joel's cousin but apart from that there's nothing to suggest he has been in touch with anyone on the outside. In fact, the slimy sod wrote a letter to Clare expressing his sorrow and apologising for the attack.' Wildblood scowled at this.

Cynically, Taverner wondered if he was really remorseful or whether this was more about impressing the parole board when the time came for his case to be heard. It was hard not to be a sceptic in his line of work.

'Anything else?'

Anna smiled. 'Well, as we know Jamie Doyle was once employed by the Foxes, so they did know each other. They were said to be close, though. Great pals in fact.'

Taverner felt that now they were getting somewhere. Perhaps a plan to harm Clare had been hatched before Joel was sentenced, or maybe Doyle had taken it upon himself to harm the girl and acted alone to avenge his friend.

Anna looked up. 'What was the previous for Doyle again?'

Haworth checked his notes. 'Possession and dealing of cannabis and opiates.' Haworth suddenly looked animated. 'And there's intel that he once stuck a pitchfork into another stable lad when he worked in Ireland as a juvenile. The other lad didn't want to make a complaint though.'

Taverner raised an eyebrow. 'Mmm. So, he's capable of violence then. Interesting, very interesting.'

In the corner, Haworth was searching for the phone number for the guards in Cork whilst singing his own version of Danny Boy. 'Oh, Jamie boy, the net, the net is closing...'

Wildblood shook her head, tutted and rolled her eyes.

Taverner busied himself chasing up the Forensic reports and expressed annoyance that there had been delays. Patel promised to find out what the delays were. Later Cullen and Ballantyne came in looking buoyed up and flushed with success.

Taverner went to speak to them. 'Don't tell me you managed to find someone close to The Stagecoach with a video doorbell?' He still wondered if the murderer had followed Clare when she left the pub and was furious that the staff had not turned on their expensive CCTV for the opening night.

Ballantyne was grinning from ear to ear, which was a very rare occurrence and Cullen looked like a child on Christmas Eve.

'Even better,' added Ballantyne. 'The house opposite the drive to the Ryans has a dash cam on their expensive 4x4. It was parked opposite the driveway face on. The owner had it set to park mode, so it records in response to motion. It was parked there on the evening of the murder.' He brandished the dash cam in the evidence bag.

Patel rubbed his hands in anticipation. This was right up his street, he loved electronics and gadgets. He believed that the potential from them was limitless and that they were, to his way of thinking, an absolute boon to policing. There was a palpable spike of excitement in the office.

He held out his hand, his eyes gleaming. 'Come on then, let's see what you've got. Hand it over!'

Chapter 26

Jeremy Trentham was busy on the yard when Finn called in. Freddie was grooming a horse and raised his hand as soon as he saw Finn.

'I've got my first race at Catterick,' he added excitedly. 'I'm riding this fellow, KissMeQuick.'

Finn patted the huge bay and nodded. 'I saw you listed as riding in The Racing Post. Niall Byrne's riding in the same meeting. How are you feeling?'

Freddie raised his eyebrows. 'Ah, alright, I think. My mum's got up quite a crowd to cheer me on, Christian Gerrard, Pandora, I even think she mentioned it to that journalist, James someone or other.' The lad looked apprehensive, and Finn couldn't help feeling sorry for him.

'Are you sure that's alright with you? I mean, I can have a word with her if you like. Some conditionals would like to just get on with it without an audience, especially for their first race. I wouldn't like to think of you being under any pressure.'

Freddie looked uncertain then shook his head. 'No, it's fine. Mum always came to the eventing, and I'm used to having a few folks about. Besides, things are going well for us now. Mum's cleaning business is expanding and she's still doing restoration stuff for Gerrard. She says we have to celebrate all the positives after everything that's happened.'

Finn could see her point of view in a way, but it was Freddie's first professional race and it might make him feel tense, that was all. Things might not go according to plan as the lad still had a lot to learn and he could only do that by race riding, he knew. It might be a great deal easier without an audience.

'I'll be there myself, so I'll catch you before the race and talk you through it. If we're early, we can do a course walk.'

Freddie nodded. 'Great stuff. I'll see you there.'

Jeremy came into view and Finn nodded towards the house. Finn dreaded having to tell him about the painting but needs must. They had to get Jeremy to agree to it being assessed by Sebastian Lloyd.

189

'I have news, can we go inside?'

'Of course.'

Jeremy showed him into the room where the Moss painting was hung. It really was a lovely composition and each time Finn saw it, he noticed something different. The foreground was dominated by the bright chestnut horse with the white leg and white socks, Red Navajo. There were other horses, bays and greys in the background and the trees and foliage were painted to perfection. Surely, this had to be the real thing? The more Finn saw it, the more he admired the skill in the brushwork.

He brought Jeremy up to date with the investigation, how they had found Ross, the visit and his terms about returning Admiral to him. Then he told him about the identical painting in New York and how the art expert had declared it genuine. Jeremy's expression changed from surprise, absolute delight and then confusion.

'But I don't understand? If Ross's painting is a fake, then why didn't you just tell him?'

'Because the relationship between you both is still fragile, he has cast iron provenance, he was bequeathed the picture from his grandfather, and it was transported securely. But the fact remains that the identical painting in New York has also been authenticated by an expert and Ross gave this to you for safe keeping. He might have given you a fake, I suppose.' There was another possibility, but Finn wasn't quite ready to go there just yet.

'Well, really, he gave it to me to cover a debt...' harrumphed Jeremy. 'Surely, he'd never stoop so low as to give me a replica?'

'I don't know. What's good is that he can now repay you many times over. His book is finished, the publishers will release the money once they have approved it, so there's no problem on that score.' Jeremy looked a little mollified.

'Hmm. I can see what you're saying, but surely he wouldn't have gone to all the trouble to have a painting faked? He's a complex man, extravagant and eccentric in some ways but he's not a crook. I don't think so anyway.' He sighed. 'Christ, supposing he is?'

'But there's an easy way round this.'

Jeremy looked hopeful. 'Yes, what is it?'

'We can get Sebastian Lloyd to have a look at this painting. He's Harriet Lucas's uncle, he's an art expert in York, he runs a gallery and is happy to give us his evaluation. '

'Gerrard already has. He's happy enough with it and even had a buyer lined up but I would never do that until I'd spoken to Ross. It's lovely, I've grown quite attached to it actually.' He turned back to Finn. 'I'm thrilled you and Harriet have found Ross and he is considering returning Admiral. Of course, Nat Wilson can ride him. Tristan will be busy enough anyway as I've a yard full of good horses, but Admiral is something else.' He came to a decision. 'Are you off to see this Sebastian chap now? I'll come with you, then I can hear everything for myself.'

Finn was pleased at Jeremy's quick grasp of the facts. 'We are. Have you got anything we can wrap the painting up in?'

Jeremy nodded and rushed out coming back with an old duvet and a bin liner. Finn removed the painting from the wall, wrapped it carefully and then placed it in a bin bag.

'Ready?'

Jeremy nodded.

As they were about to leave, a young woman came into the room. She was wearing a cleaner's tabard.

'We've finished in here, if you want to come through,' Jeremy told her. 'It's the cleaner,' he added to Finn by way of explanation as they walked back into the yard, Jeremy tucking the picture under his arm.

'Ah, yes. Who do you use?' Finn wondered if they hired cleaners from Penny's company.

'What?' Jeremy looked surprised. 'Oh, Laura sorts them out. Our old one retired so we've had an agency one for a while. They're very good, if you want me to ask her?'

Finn laughed at Jeremy's vagueness.

As he was leaving, Finn noticed a small Micra car with a sticker in the back, Spick and Span Cleaning Services. He made a mental note to ask if this was the name of Penny Mercer's company.

Jeremy recovered his spirits. 'I'm sure all this nonsense of authenticating the painting is just a formality, you know,' he added breezily. 'It's too well done to be a fake and the painting of Red Navajo is perfect. Experts can be wrong. Is this Sebastian chap any good?'

191

'According to Harriet, he is one of the best. Sotheby's use him and he is also writing a book about art fraud.'

Jeremy appeared much happier. 'Well then, I'm sure he'll be able to put that other chappie right.'

Finn nodded. He really hoped that it was as simple as that.

They picked up Harriet and the three of them drove to Sebastian's gallery in York where he was waiting for them. The Moss painting was carefully wrapped and perched on Jeremy's lap for the whole journey. They reached the busy city and parked up. The gallery was tastefully decorated, with a shop front in gold and black lettering which opened out into a large space filled with beautiful paintings. There was a seascape exhibition on display with vivid, coastal scenes, orange skies and inky grey seas.

Sebastian was immaculately dressed in a stylishly cut navy suit, a crisp white shirt and red paisley cravat. Finn thought that a cravat was surely a crime against fashion, but Sebastian seemed to be able to carry it off. His eyes had a lively intelligence to them, and his frame was lean and muscular. His blond hair was swept back off his face. He kissed Harriet warmly on the cheeks, smiled broadly and shook Finn and Jeremy's hands.

'Well, I'm delighted to meet you both. I'm pleased that Harriet asked me to assess the Moss painting,' his eyes raked over the package that Jeremy was holding. 'But first, let's get you a drink, tea, coffee, wine, gin, we've the whole range. What do you fancy?'

He nodded at his receptionist, a frighteningly stylish blonde with a heavily pinned French pleat, a tight grey suit, red talons and sky scraper heels.

'Francesca, will you do the honours?' He then took them into an office, with antique bookcases, and a large desk and easel positioned in the centre of the room.

They chatted whilst they drank their tea. Then Sebastian stood up, flexed his fingers and made to take the painting from Jeremy.

'My dear chap, let me take that, then we can unwrap it and see what we've got!' He practically fizzed with excitement as he unwrapped the package like a gift and placed it on the easel. The trio watched as Sebastian pulled out a magnifying glass and examined the painting minutely. He turned it over and studied the back as carefully, his lips pursed. Eventually, he turned to them.

'So, who can tell me about the painting and how it came to be in Mr Trentham's possession?'

Finn relayed the tale and Jeremy added bits of relevant information. Sebastian listened intently and then wheeled in a large light, switched it on and continued to examine the painting. He picked up a notepad and made some notes in a flowing, cursive style.

He regarded Jeremy. 'So, the painting came to you about two months ago, and was sent by secure delivery from Mr Maclaren.'

'Yes, it was a surety on a debt incurred for racing fees.'

Sebastian raised an eyebrow at that. 'Really? How interesting and how did Mr Maclaren acquire the painting, what is its provenance?'

Sebastian made copious notes as Finn explained, looking impressed at the mention of the painting having been bequeathed in a will and the information about Red Navajo belonging to Maclaren's great grandfather.

'Hmm, excellent. Very solid provenance, in fact, you can't get any better than that sort of family history. Of course, if the painting was bequeathed in a will, then there could still be a record of that, so even better.'

Eventually, he picked up a new catalogue and leafed through it to a bookmarked page.

'Hmm, well this is the other picture.' He lifted up the catalogue and showed them a small image of the painting which was being displayed in The Attic Gallery in New York. Jeremy gasped at the image as although it was a miniature, it was identical to the painting in front of them.

Jeremy frowned. 'So, surely that is a fake, the one in New York?'

Sebastian sat down and looked at the assembled group.

Harriet smiled. 'Well? What can you tell us about this painting, Sebastian? Is it genuine?'

Sebastian hesitated. 'Hmm. It's a hard one to call actually. To be certain I'd need to take minute scrapings of paint, in particular the green and white paint and send them off for analysis. It won't harm the painting at all.'

Finn looked confused. 'Why do you want to examine the green and white paint specifically?'

Sebastian smiled enigmatically. 'Well, this is where it gets interesting. Forgers are very clever now. There's a chap currently languishing in prison, someone called Archie Todd, who made forgeries in his garden shed, and claims to have faked some famous paintings which have already been authenticated by a panel of experts. In fact, once that happens it's hard to get experts to contradict each other. It's about the loss of face, you see. Clever forgers use authentic materials, aged canvases, the proper paint and so on, so it's devilishly difficult to tell which is authentic or not.' Sebastian paused, making sure his audience were paying full attention. 'According to the painting itself, this was completed in 1912 but nowadays green and white paints have completely different chemical compositions.' He pointed at the painting. 'If this is genuine then Moss would have used a green paint of a different chemical composition to modern times. And the white paint would be different too.' He pointed at Red Navajo's white leg. 'In 1912 it would have been painted using paint with zinc oxide in it, but this changed to titanium white in the 1920's, so that should assist us.' He walked around to the rear of the easel and studied the labels on the back. 'And these catalogue labels are very interesting too and can be checked. It's a complicated business, but in the end, forgers do cut corners and it's actually very hard to get all aspects right. I can research the catalogue labels. It's not so hard when you know where to look. But I would really need to complete paint analysis. How do you feel about that? I'd need permission from the owner, of course.'

Finn looked at Jeremy. 'Well, as it's surety on a loan, I think that's you, so do you give permission?'

Jeremy nodded. 'Absolutely. I think we need to know what's what, so let's go ahead.'

Harriet frowned. 'Shouldn't we ask Maclaren?'

They discussed the pros and cons until Sebastian raised an eyebrow.

'Might I suggest that time is of the essence as the New York painting is up for auction shortly and the analysis will take a couple of days if I can hurry things along.'

Finn smiled. 'Well, that settles it.'

Sebastian seemed pleased. 'Splendid. I will need you to sign an agreement, Mr Trentham and then we'll get the paint chips, which are microscopic, sent to the laboratory.'

It was frustrating that they wouldn't get to know for a least a day or two. As Finn drove back to Walton, both Harriet and Jeremy were deep in thought.

'Well, it must be the original, don't you think?' Jeremy beamed. 'The provenance is cast iron and as you have explained it's an asset that Ross expected me to protect.'

Finn nodded. 'Of course. I'm sure you're right.'

Harriet was keen to reassure them about her uncle's credentials. 'Sebastian is a genuine expert. He's been asked to pronounce on lots of paintings. Sotheby's use him a lot. I'm sure he will authenticate the painting and that will be that. I suppose he'll need to contact the gallery in New York and put them right if theirs is the fake.'

'I suppose he will, 'replied Finn. 'They'll have to remove it from the auction and inform the police.'

'Cheats never prosper,' added Jeremy darkly. 'And quite right too.'

After they had dropped Jeremy and the painting off, Finn drove Harriet home. They discussed the situation and the likelihood of the Maclaren painting being the fake.

'I can't see it, myself,' added Harriet. 'Otherwise, why would Maclaren have it transported by secure transport?'

Finn considered this. 'Well, maybe he's cleverer than we think and has had a fake made and used the transport to give Jeremy the right impression.'

Harriet looked horrified. 'God, you don't think he's selling the original in New York, do you? He did say he'd been very extravagant, and we've only got his word for it that's he's actually finished his book.'

Finn considered this. 'Well, we'll know in a few days, I suppose. There's no point second guessing the outcome.'

Harriet looked thoughtful. 'Have you ever thought that something strange has happened to all the people who were in the car when Niall was arrested. Jamie and Lottie have both left, Tom was seriously injured, and Clare is dead?'

195

Finn considered this. 'Why don't we pop into The Blacksmith's for a quick drink, it might help us think.'

Harriet grinned. 'OK, you're on.' They both knew it would take more than a couple of drinks to stop them pondering on Sebastian's judgement and the strange coincidence of what had happened to the passengers in the car on the night that Niall was arrested. Was it a random set of events or something altogether more sinister?

Chapter 27

Topper had had a pleasant date with Jane, that was all going well, much better than he dared hope. In fact, he had stayed over at hers and things were moving on nicely. He'd invited her over in the week to cook for her. He wasn't a brilliant cook and in the end hoped to buy some ready meals and pass them off as his own, by putting them in his own dishes and using sleight of hand, as it were. He was sure he could manage it and it saved him having to learn another new skill. At least with his new cleaner, his cottage would look spotless, and he was thrilled about his foresight in thinking about it. He'd vaguely met the cleaner when he had to come back to pick up his laptop lead, a young fresh faced woman, her hair tied back and devoid of makeup she looked rather familiar. She had looked rather scared at the intrusion but brightened when he told her what a good job she was doing. He had to admit that so far Penny Mercer was running a tight ship. He still didn't trust the family though and thought that Finn was mad to put his faith in them too.

Before going out to Catterick, he'd had a brisk walk, measuring his progress on his smart watch. He aimed to walk 7 to 10000 steps per day. In reality, he had no problem achieving this when he went racing and combining this with a lower calorie diet by swapping foods, he'd lost weight. He'd had a chat with Harriet Lucas, the dietician from the PJA and found her advice really helpful. She was becoming the 'go to' person who jockeys went to discuss their diets, as she had really up to date ideas, which incorporated all the latest research and trends in weight loss, such as intermittent fasting, time limited eating and keto based diets. She'd really helped Nat Wilson when he'd been off for a year, and he had no hesitation in recommending her. Losing weight had given him far more energy and a new lease of life. Mentally he felt sharper too.

He worked on his novel for a while, drank water and then came to a natural pause. His eyes were again drawn to the painting he'd rashly signed as being by Gideon Moss and the strangely restored gilt frame. He knew he had over done it with the paint stripper, and had taken the gold paint off with it, but now it looked as good as new. He'd spoken to his ex wife Jacqui wondering if the boys had popped back when he was out, and fearing his censure had repaired the frame.

Jacqui had laughed. 'Don't be ridiculous, Topper! They know you wouldn't tell them off, so why would they bother? You spoil them and they can do no wrong in your eyes. Besides, I'd have had to drop them off and I can tell you I haven't. They've been away at school and far too busy with after school activities anyway. Maybe you thought you'd damaged the frame when you hadn't? Perhaps it dried and the damage wasn't as bad as you feared?'

Topper bristled at the suggestion that he was an indulgent father, but then he decided he rather liked the thought. His own parents had been distant and very preoccupied with their own lives. They were happy enough to send him away to school and were unsure what to do with him when he came home in the holidays. He'd tagged along to the races with his grandfather and that was how he had developed his interest in racing. He didn't want to be like that, and besides he was justifiably very proud of them. They discussed the boys, their progress, and changes to contact arrangements.

'It's very nice to be able to talk to you, Topper, like civilised adults,' Jacqui added.

He agreed. His hurt and anger over the separation had subsided to a great extent. He was getting on with his life, he could have adult conversations with his ex now things were improving, and life was good. She was always a sensible sort of woman; it was one of the things he had admired about her, and she would certainly know if the boys had sneaked into his house. Maybe she was right about the painting? He knew he hadn't imagined the whole thing, but he couldn't yet work it out. He would do, the answer must be there, he told himself.

He sipped his coffee and leafed through the photos he'd asked his friend to take of visitors to Lindholme prison, where Henry Teasdale was imprisoned. His bad feeling about Freddie Mercer still lingered and nagged away at him. The BHA were being far too lenient, in his opinion. He thought it was a huge ask for the boy to not see his father. He sipped a coffee and looked through the photos. Lofty had used a long lens and taken the

198

pictures in the early afternoon, before the light faded. He leafed through frames of young women with babies in pushchairs, parents, smartly dressed people who looked like solicitors and children being supervised by anxious mothers. He wondered what it would be like in prison and decided it would be a pretty awful experience. Lindholme was a Cat C prison for less dangerous inmates. Teasdale had not been charged with murder unlike his conspirator, Dr Pinkerton, but he still imagined that the visits would be supervised under the watchful but oppressive eye of prison officers. He flicked through the photos with an increasing air of dejection. He'd paid handsomely for them, and they hadn't helped at all. He looked back through them and felt despair. There was nothing really of interest, until his sharp eyes alighted upon an image of a young man, in a sweatshirt with the hood pulled up, wearing breeches, long socks and jodhpur boots. He was talking to a young girl who looked familiar. She had a wan complexion, mid brown hair and defined eyebrows. Still, young women often looked alike to him, so that was no big deal. His gaze turned to the young man again, specifically to his clothing. Over the top of the hoody, the man was wearing a padded jacket. It was olive green with writing in yellow on the left hand pocket. He scrutinised the writing which he recognised. It was a great pity he couldn't see the man's face which was turned away from the camera, but the man was wearing standard horse wear and he knew the coat could be really important. He googled well known equine outfitters and studied the logos of popular brands. With a rush of excitement, he saw it, the same yellow writing in a cursive script. It spelt out the word of a popular brand, Barbour. His spirits lifted. He knew it! How many prison visitors were likely to be riders, not many. It had to be Freddie Mercer visiting his father. Maybe the woman was his girlfriend? His instincts had been right all along. He'd take the photos to Finn McCarthy and hopefully that would be enough to convince him to check on visitors to the prison. He was sure the BHA would have contacts within the prison and probation service to establish who had visited Henry Teasdale. In fact, he knew that Mercer was going to ride in his first race at Catterick, so if he was sharp about it, he might catch the lad in his Barbour en route to the weighing room. With renewed zeal, he set off, his mood lifting.

Finn and Harriet were intending to go to Catterick tomorrow too. He wanted to watch Freddie Mercer and Niall Byrne ride, and Harriet had to be on hand for a media event where she and her colleagues had to hand out information to interested parties about the work of the PJA. There were also stands for The Injured Jockeys' Fund and the Retraining of Racehorses, a BHA charity which supported this. It was a hugely positive step towards horse welfare. Many ex-racehorses now had alternative careers as riding horses competing in eventing, showjumping and dressage events. Finn focused on what he needed to do today. He'd managed to contact his friend Nat Wilson and asked him to get Livvy to try and establish the owner of the Moss painting in New York. Livvy's request had been met by a polite refusal from the gallery who cited data protection, however.

Finn had slept badly; he was too wired up after the revelation about the New York painting and thoroughly confused. He also pondered on what Harriet had said. Was there a link between the incident when Niall was arrested and what had subsequently happened to the people in the car? He remembered what Tom Kennedy had said about Jamie Doyle being linked to drugs. Had that led to Niall driving off from the police? Maybe Niall was involved with the drugs, or they had all been taking them and knew the police would find them. Yet, Niall had been arrested for drink driving only, there was no mention of drugs and surely the police would have searched the vehicle? Perhaps, Jamie Doyle had intimidated Niall and made him drive off from the police? He remembered the police coming to talk to Jamie whilst he was riding on the gallops and how the lad had been involved in a fall just as the police had arrived. Was that intentional? He decided to speak to DI Taverner and ask him to investigate the incident. Maybe the drug issue had been a motive for Clare's murder? Perhaps, she had threatened to go to the police? Whatever had happened that night, was it a coincidence that of the people in the vehicle, Clare was now dead, Tom was seriously injured, Lottie had decided to throw in the towel and go to a flat yard, and Jamie had done a runner to Ireland? Were these events linked? Maybe, maybe not. It occurred to him that Tom's accident and Clare's death were so horrific, that maybe everyone wanted to distance themselves. He couldn't blame them, he felt like that himself.

He also had a personal matter to attend to. He had been slightly put out by Theresa disappearing early on their last date and had decided to invite her to the race meeting. He had tried texting her and then ringing, but he'd had no luck in getting through. He wondered if this was a brushoff and found that he minded, very much, so was pleased when he found she had left her diary at his from when she last stayed over. It was a pale, pink book which had fallen down the side of the sofa. He seized upon it as an excuse to contact her but was far too gentlemanly to look through it. He felt sure it must be important and decided to pop into the school she worked in, The York Academy, to hand it to her. He drove to the school. It was just after 9 am and the hordes of school children in their sedate grey and red edged blazers had reduced to a mere handful. He strode to the reception and was met with the politely raised eyebrows of a middle aged receptionist.

'I wonder if I could have a quick word with Theresa Byrne. I believe she's a teacher in the Art Department.'

The woman ran her fingers through her phone list then rang a number. After exchanging some brief words, she put the phone down and peered through the Perspex screen.

'She doesn't work here anymore. She left over a year ago.'

Finn hid his surprise. 'No worries. I think I might have got the wrong school, after all.'

The woman suggested other schools in the area, but none of them sounded right to him.

Except he thought he was right. Never mind there must be some explanation, perhaps there was a similar sounding school, that must be it. He went back to his car and drove to Walton his head buzzing. The he realised that he had missed some messages from Theresa stating that she'd love to see Niall race at Catterick, but she'd make her own way as she needed to get back for a colleague's leaving do. He must have got the wrong school, he told himself. He could make further inquiries but why would he do that? He realised he was falling for Theresa, and he was sure that it was he who was mistaken. He responded agreeing to meet her and saw that there were further messages from Harriet. The verdict was in from Sebastian. Finn immediately rang her.

'So, what does Sebastian think about the Maclaren painting?'

There was a sigh. 'I have no idea because he won't tell me over the phone. It's so not Sebastian's style. He wants to meet us tonight to go through his findings.'

'Christ, why not just tell us?

'Because Sebastian loves his theatrics, that's why.'

Finn sighed, curiosity nibbling away at him. 'OK. Where and when?'

'6pm at his gallery tonight.'

Finn mentally thought through his schedule. He had visits to undertake, conditionals to assess, but he could do all he needed to do and get back to York for 6 pm.

'Hmm. Do we need to involve Jeremy, do you think?'

Harriet paused. 'No, if it's bad news, we can break it to him later.'

Finn could see the wisdom of this. 'OK.'

Harriet was right about Sebastian's love of theatrics, Finn thought, whilst they waited for him to cut to the chase. He was dressed in a grey three piece suit with his trademark cravat, this time in yellow with a smattering of small black polka dots. He had explained the process of the paint analysis in painstaking detail and also went on to explain his research on the catalogue stickers on the back of the painting.

'I've cross checked them with past catalogues and there is absolutely no doubt of course.'

Finn thought he'd missed something. 'I'm sorry, absolutely no doubt about what?'

'That the painting is a fake, a very good one, but nonetheless definitely not original.' Finn and Harriet looked at one another in confusion. Finn had been sure that the New York painting was the fake and now they had the unedifying task of explaining this to Jeremy.

'What? Just run the findings past me again, will you?' asked Harriet frowning.

'Well, my dear girl, the paint analysis shows that the green and the white paint chips are definitely of a much more modern chemical composition. You see the white would contain toxic elements up until about 1920 and the chips removed from the painting of Maclaren's didn't. Also, the green paint used was also of a much more recent type.' Sebastian frowned. 'And the 2 catalogue stickers on the back are not right either. One is a different size to the stickers used by that auction house at the time and the other is the right size but a different design. Catalogue stickers are an important part of the history and can be checked, especially going back to the 1900's. So, in conclusion, it's a very good fake, but not the real thing.'

'So, what happens now? Do we tell Ross Maclaren that his painting, the one he's treasured all his life is in fact a fake? I thought you said he had cast iron provenance?'

Sebastian considered this. 'And so he does. Of course, there is another possibility and one you should carefully consider...'

Harriet and Finn glanced at one another and waited for Sebastian to elaborate.

'I am minded to think that the painting delivered to Trentham was indeed the original. After all, Maclaren sent it securely, his provenance about his relative owning Red Navajo checks out, his great grandfather commissioned it, it was sold and his grandfather bought it back when the progeny of the horse started to do well. So, it is possible that the original could have been stolen and substituted whilst at Jeremy's.'

Finn thought this through. It had never really entered his head, but now he was really beginning to wonder if this might be true.

'I suppose it's possible. I mean there's always someone at the yard but not necessarily in the house, they're preoccupied with the horses as a rule. Christ, how do we tell Jeremy?' It was beginning to look like they were never going to heal the relationship between Jeremy and Ross, after all. Ross would never forgive Jeremy if he thought the painting had been stolen from underneath his nose.

Harriet scowled. 'God knows.'

Sebastian delved in his pocket and produced a report which he handed to Finn. 'Here is my report which might help.' His eyes twinkled. He seemed to be hugely enjoying himself.

Finn took the report. 'Thanks anyway.'

They decamped to the local wine bar for much needed sustenance. They ordered food, and drinks and discussed what they had heard.

'Christ, Finn. So, it's not looking good, is it? Either Ross Maclaren had a fake done and is trying to sell his painting in New York, or the painting has been swapped whilst at Jeremy's.'

Finn sipped his pint and tried to compose his thoughts. 'Hmm. I suppose Maclaren could have created a fake just to appease Jeremy, but I don't think so. He seemed to be genuine about the painting, he was proud of it, and he sent it to Jeremy knowing full well he wouldn't sell it. Anyway, why would he need the money with his book being completed? What do you think?'

Harriet shrugged. 'I agree with you, in which case Sebastian is right and the painting could have been swapped whilst it was at Jeremy's and the original sent to New York for sale.'

Finn sipped his beer. 'And Maclaren could have sold the painting earlier if he was short of money. I have the distinct impression he wanted to hang on to it because of the family history. And why would he use secure transport if he didn't think it was genuine?'

Harriet nodded. 'So, if it was substituted whilst at Jeremy's then who are the suspects? Gerrard?' Harriet's eyes widened as she suddenly thought of something. 'What about Penny Mercer? She's a painter, she could have done the forgery and maybe Freddie did the swap as he's at the yard every day.'

Finn groaned. 'Don't remind me and to think that I placed him there.' He shook his head in disgust. He felt like a whole jumble of information was suddenly settling into place, suddenly the facts were starting to fit together. After a while he seemed to come to a conclusion. 'Right, we need a plan to flush out the forgers. I have an idea.' His eyes were bright with anticipation.

Harriet looked expectant.

'Listen, here's what we need to do. The last thing Gerrard will want is for the fake Moss to be included in his exhibition.'

'Why?'

'Because I imagine the art world is very small. If it is exhibited as the real deal, then it will call into question the real Moss in New York and that will ruin the things for the fraudsters. There's bound to be press interest in the exhibition and the Red Navajo painting will certainly attract a great deal of attention. Think about it, if there is any doubt about the authenticity of the New York painting, then no one will buy it.'

Harriet considered this. 'But I thought that Gerrard had wanted to buy the painting?'

'He also asked Jeremy if he could put it in the exhibition, but I bet he wouldn't want it now it's been swapped and the auction for the original is very soon. If we get Jeremy to say he's had a change of mind and wants to exhibit it, what's the betting that someone will try and stop the painting getting to The Stagecoach. It's just too risky otherwise. We could ask for Maclaren's permission too. If he's involved, then he won't want the painting shown either. If we get Jeremy to ask Gerrard in earshot of Penny and Freddie, we'll include all the potential suspects then we'll flush them out.'

'But we'll need Jeremy to explain to Gerrard that he's had a change of heart.' Harriet frowned. 'Will he do it?'

Finn shrugged. 'I don't see why not. I'll ask him. Gerrard is at Catterick tomorrow, so we can talk to him then. If I offer to transport the painting and give a time, then we can be waiting for them.'

Harriet frowned. 'How will they stop the painting getting there?'

That was the million dollar question. Finn considered this.

'They could say it's too late to add it to the exhibition or put the painting somewhere out of the way. We'll know who is involved by their attitude and actions. If it's Maclaren, he'll just refuse to let it be exhibited. I'll ring him now.'

Maclaren had been reluctant initially but agreed when Finn explained to him that as the painting was a surety for a debt, it remained Jeremy's property until the debt was paid. After a few more calls everything was in place. They refined their plan and set off home.

Chapter 28

It was a chilly afternoon at Catterick and there was a small but dedicated crowd braving the cold winds. It was a lovely course and just a pity that Harriet had to be on hand to man the PJA stand. She and a colleague, Frank Finnegan had set up the small stand and were handing out free pens, sweets and leaflets to everyone who showed an interest though of course, their target audience was the jockeys and staff. Harriet had designed a leaflet advising about her service as a dietician and Nat Wilson had been kind enough to recommend her. There were other leaflets advising on the other PJA services and also information on The Injured Jockeys' Fund, the work of Jack Berry house and there were collections of merchandise that The Injured Jockeys' Fund sold, alongside the Retraining of Racehorses information. They had a small collection of Christmas cards, pens, badges and tie pins available to buy too.

Frank hugged his coat to himself. 'You go and have a look around; we'll take it in turns. There's no point us both getting frozen.'

'OK, I'll fetch you a coffee and a sandwich,' she added. 'I won't be long.'

She bumped into Christian Gerrard and his wife Sian, who was wearing a huge Russian style hat and a much more soberly dressed Pandora. She looked like a different person, gone were the goth clothes and makeup and she resembled someone who worked in an office. It was interesting that she had this chameleon like quality and seemed to reinvent herself time and time again; not unusual for youngsters Harriet supposed, remembering her own experiments with hip hop and then grunge styles.

'We're just on our way for a drink, we're meeting Finn and Jeremy before the next race. You must join us,' Christian said, steering her towards the bar. 'Our horse has an injury, so has been withdrawn, but we really wanted to support Freddie.'

'OK. I'm just working on the PJA stall. I have left a colleague there, so I haven't got long.'

'Do come,' added Sian. 'Even if it's just for a short while.'

'Yes do,' added Pandora, smiling. Harriet agreed, thinking she'd make it up to Frank later.

'You look so different,' Harriet commented to Pandora, who was wearing a smart suit and a long coat, in grey, but her black hair was now mousy, and the winged eye makeup and piercings had been removed. Even her fingernails were painted a pale pink, such a contrast to her previously black talons. She looked natural and very lovely.

Christian laughed. 'She has to look more presentable for work, that's what that's in aid of.'

Pandora rolled her eyes. She still had the teenager attitude, though.

Sian beamed. 'I think Pandora looks lovely without all that Goth warpaint.'

'She does,' Harriet agreed. 'Where do you work?'

Pandora grimaced. 'I just do a bit of work for Penny, you know, Freddie's mum, and I might start at The Stagecoach Hotel too.'

Harriet didn't have time to ask more but was glad that she seemed happier and more content that when she'd first met her.

They met up with Finn, Jeremy and Penny at the bar. Jeremy was ordering drinks with Christian.

'I'm very nervous about Freddie racing,' added Penny.

'I'm sure he'll be fine.' Harriet felt the need to reassure Penny and remembered how nervous jockeys' partners were and presumably that also included mothers.

Jeremy cleared his throat and said in a loud voice. 'I've been thinking about exhibiting the Moss painting at your do. I mean, Maclaren left it with me, so I'm sure he won't mind, so I'm happy to have it displayed.'

Christian's eyes gleamed. 'Absolutely splendid, Jeremy.'

Finn met Harriet's gaze. 'I'll pop it round to you on Thursday, Christian, save you the bother of transporting it, Jeremy. I'm seeing Freddie anyway,' added Finn, right on cue.

'That would be marvellous,' Jeremy replied. 'What time?'

'Oh, say 2ish.'

Harriet noticed that Gerrard seemed completely unperturbed by the painting being included in the exhibition, in fact he seemed positively delighted. Maybe they were wrong about him? Or perhaps he was just a very good actor.

Pandora looked troubled. 'What about the catalogue, though, Dad? It's already been printed.'

'Oh, it'll be no problem. We can easily do an addendum and append it.'

Pandora smiled. 'OK, if you're sure.'

Harriet sipped her wine and glanced at her watch. She hadn't got long, and she didn't want to leave Frank all alone.

'Do you help your father with the gallery business too?' she asked Pandora.

'Yes. From time to time. I'm learning a lot about the business.'

'Are you exhibiting any work too? Your paintings are so original.'

Pandora blushed. 'That's so kind. I do have a few in there, so I hope to generate some interest.'

Harriet finished her drink. She noticed a very beautiful fine boned woman, she assumed to be Theresa Byrne, Niall's sister had arrived looking very elegant in a purple wrap dress and a warm grey coat and scarf. She certainly had the look of Niall about her but seemed a little lost as she scanned the crowd.

Harriet dashed over to introduce herself. 'Hi, you must be Theresa, Niall's sister. I'm Harriet Lucas, a friend of Finn's.'

Theresa smiled with real warmth. 'I'm so pleased to meet you, Harriet. I must admit to feeling a bit nervous now Niall's riding.' She certainly looked anxious. Finn came over and gave her a kiss.

'Ah, I see you've met Harriet. Let me introduce you to Penny. It's her son's first race today. In fact, he's riding in the first race,' he explained. 'Would you like something to eat with us, Harriet?'

She gave them an apologetic smile. 'Sorry, I'd better dash. I'm helping run the PJA stall,' she explained to Theresa, 'so I'd better get back.'

Theresa smiled. 'Hopefully, I'll see you later.' Harriet had to admit that she was stunning. Her skin had this luminous quality, and her bone structure was perfect. No wonder Finn was so smitten.

She remembered Frank's coffee and sandwich and arrived back at the stall just as the first race had started. 'Off you go,' she said, once he'd devoured his food.

Frank smiled and hurried off to watch the first race. Harriet listened and heard that Freddie had come in fifth out of ten, on KissMeQuick, so she reckoned he'd be pleased with that. She handed out some leaflets and wondered again about Gerrard. He certainly didn't act as though he was remotely unhappy about Jeremy's painting being included in the exhibition. Perhaps he didn't want to arouse suspicion and would just shove the painting somewhere where it would be hidden from public view. That must be it, she decided. He had control of the whole place, so it would be easy to shunt a painting out of the way.

As she was explaining the work of The Injured Jockeys' Fund to an earnest woman who was keen to give a donation, she bumped into Topper McGrew.

'Can I get you anything, if you're tied up here?' he asked once he realised she was managing the stall.

'No, I'm fine. How are you?'

'Well, I was hoping to run into Finn, actually. I've some photos I need him to see.' Topper looked rather anxious.

'Right. He's here but all over the place at the moment. I'll tell him or you can just email them. Sorry, I can't just remember his email. You could send them to his mobile by What's App.'

Topper smiled. 'Now that really is beyond me. How about I send them to you, and you can forward them?'

'Right, no problem.' She gave him her email address, wondering what was so important.

'Freddie did well in his first race, did you catch it?'

Topper nodded in a non committal way. 'Yes, I saw him. I suppose his mother, Penny, is here?'

'Yes. She is. Will you be going to the exhibition next week? You know the one at The Stagecoach?'

Topper nodded. 'Yes. I love equine art. I have a painting that could be by Moss, actually.'

'Really, how interesting.' It was not surprising. Topper came from a monied rural background, so it was no surprise that he would have a valuable Moss painting too.

'Mind you, my boys, are what you call boisterous and nearly wrecked the damned thing.'

209

He went on to explain to her about them playing with Nerf guns and painting the bullets blue so they could count which one got the most on target and one of the bullets had hit the picture frame.

'The strange thing was, I removed the blue paint on the frame with paint stripper. Thought I'd made a mark on the frame, but it can't have been as bad as I thought because when I looked a day or two later, it was not visible at all. I must thank my cleaner actually. She managed to clean the paint from the walls.'

Privately Harriet thought that Topper was rather an easy going father, he spoiled his children if truth be told. Still, she remembered that he'd got divorced and maybe didn't get to see his children that much, so that was probably why. She asked a few polite questions about Giles and Tim. Topper beamed when he spoke about them which was really charming. It was clear that he absolutely doted on them.

'Anyway, stories to write, horses to follow,' he added. 'I'll bring you a little surprise back.' Five minutes later he popped back with a gin and tonic.

Despite her protests, she was pleased and touched.

'That's so lovely.'

'Just remember to send those photos to Finn, will you?'

'Of course, I will.' She wondered what was so important that he had mentioned the photos twice.

Frank came back later, and she was able to join Theresa, Seamus Ryan and Finn.

Seamus was really pleased to see her. 'Pop round when you've a minute. It's all a bit strange with Lottie leaving, after everything that happened.' He frowned. 'It might just cheer Rosie up too.' Harriet promised to do so, thinking that it must be so hard after Clare's death. Rosie had been close to her and would naturally be devastated.

Finn went off to brief Niall with Seamus as Theresa and Harriet looked on anxiously. Even Pandora seemed tense and came and joined them. Pandora seemed to be getting on well with Theresa, but then she was highly socially skilled, probably used to dealing with youngsters in the job. She recalled that Finn had said she was a teacher. Theresa had a Celtic charm that was quite infectious. She could see why Finn had fallen for her. She had a way of bringing people out of their shell.

210

Niall had lucked out and had the ride on Cardinal Sin. He managed a second place which Harriet thought was excellent, but Finn seemed annoyed about it. He then had another ride on Heavensent and managed a third, so it wasn't a bad day. Later, Niall donned his olive green coat and came and spoke to Finn and Seamus as they dissected his race together. Harriet went back to the stall and helped Frank pack up then joined Finn for the drive back home. They discussed what they had found out.

'Well, we could be wrong about Christian Gerrard. He wasn't fazed at all about the Moss painting being exhibited.'

Finn agreed. Harriet told him about running into Topper and about the photos he wanted him to see.

'Send them on and I'll look at them. Did he say what was so important about them?'

'No, but he seemed anxious for you to see them, that's all. You weren't too chuffed about Niall's ride then?'

Finn shook his head. 'He should have won with the weight advantage, he rode a bit sloppily actually. He seemed a bit preoccupied and missed a gap. At least Freddie did well, so that's something.'

Privately, Harriet wondered if Finn wasn't being a bit hard on Niall. Still, she supposed he had high expectations of him and knew his capabilities as a rider which was more than she did.

'Did Theresa enjoy herself? She's lovely.'

Finn grinned. 'Yes, which was why I couldn't say what I really thought about Niall. Still, we all have bad rides.'

Harriet wondered about this. Finn was usually such a forthright person; it was so unlike him to let personal issues affect him. It just showed how keen he was on Theresa, she supposed.

'So, the plan is to take the painting to Gerrard's and lay in wait, is that it?'

'I've been thinking about that. It might be an idea for you to take the painting the day beforehand, so that it's safe. What do you think?'

'Well, I can manage that. Did Penny and Freddie hear what Jeremy said?'

'Oh, yes, Jeremy played his part very well.' He rubbed his hands together. 'The net is closing in; I can feel it.'

211

Harriet nodded in agreement. She just couldn't help but feel that they were missing something obvious, but like a dream, it faded away when she tried to focus on it. Finn was being very vague too, which made her worry about exactly what he had planned.

'So, what do you think will happen? Will the painting get pushed out of the way, do you think?'

'I expect so. We'll soon know if it's not there when we visit, won't we?'

Finn headed back home, his head full of the plan he and Harriet had laid tomorrow to flush out the forgers. Before he even got out of the car, his phone beeped heralding a text. It was from Nat.

Can't ride due to a fall. Bloody doctors think I have concussion! Thought I'd come up to see the exhibition. Gerrard is putting me up at his new place. Fancy a meal there at 7pm?

Finn grinned. It was great to hear from his old mate and his mood lifted. Nat was always such a positive, can do person, he always cheered him up. He quickly fired off a text to Nat accepting and to Harriet to invite her, adding that if he was late, they should contact the police. He was keen to say that this was just a precaution on his part. He made his way down the pathway towards the entrance to his flat. He was so deep in thought, he didn't notice them, two people hovering by the door. It was about 10 o'clock and the evening was cold and the skies clear, which suggested a frost. At first, he thought the men were just waiting to be let in, but it was quite unusual for callers to arrive this late on a weekday. He pulled up his collar, his head full of the plans for tomorrow, trying to outwit the forgers. He was about to pull out his fob from his pocket when he heard a voice from the shadows.

'Hey, have you got the time, mate?'

Finn spun round. 'Yes?'

He dimly recalled a man dressed in dark clothing with a beanie hat pulled well over his face loom towards him. Then he felt a sharp pain in his head before he felt himself fall into oblivion.

Chapter 29

Taverner felt that progress was slow. He reviewed the evidence with DS Wildblood, hoping that his down to earth sergeant might be able to help him. The Superintendent, Lewis Wilson, drifted in and out, more to get some sound bites, than anything else it seemed, and disappeared off again once he saw them hard at work.

Taverner addressed his Sergeant. 'So, we're closing in on Jamie Doyle, but speaking to the guards in Ireland, it seems like if he was a drug dealer, it's pretty much low level and he's not a major player, and not someone they would think would be capable of murder. He knows Joel Fox, worked for them, but there is no evidence of any particular contact lately.'

'So, the trail's gone cold, guv,' agreed Wildblood. 'Forensics have looked at the false fingernail and it doesn't have Clare's DNA on it, so it could belong to a potential murderer, presumably a woman.'

Taverner felt deflated. 'Yes, but how many women commit murder? Practically none.'

Wildblood nodded. It was certainly true. 'But they do, occasionally.'

'And the dash cam footage from opposite the Ryans' drive just shows the odd dog walker, coming past the entrance to the Ryans and back again. At about 9.45 in the evening, it showed Clare driving into the yard and that was that.'

Wildblood shivered at the thought of Clare going off to check on the horses, something she had done countless times before, and not coming back alive.

Taverner sighed. He bit into the bacon sandwich which Anna had helpfully provided for him for breakfast from their local café.

'And there's no one else who had a motive to murder Clare, is there? We must be missing something.'

Wildblood shrugged. 'We have no other suspects, do we?'

Taverner shook his head and repeated what Clare's boyfriend had told Finn McCarthy about Jamie Doyle.

'So, the DNA from the fingernail in being cross checked with all female employers at the Ryans?' he asked.

'Yes, that's right.'

Taverner studied a map of Walton carefully. 'Of course, they could have come to the yard by a different route, on foot, for example.' His finger pointed at a footpath that went past the end of Ryans' land. 'Look, they could have gone down this way and then across that piece of land and then into that field and into the yard.'

Wildblood nodded. 'I suppose they could.'

Taverner drained his cup of Earl Grey tea and finished his bacon bun. 'Right come on then, let's go and look.'

Anna frowned. 'Isn't that a bit hands on for a DCI? You'd never catch Sykes doing that.'

Taverner shook his head. 'Indulge me, besides, Sykes isn't here and if you want any help for your inspector's exams, you'd better humour me.' He sighed. 'Besides, I could do with the fresh air.'

Wildblood grinned. She was hoping to qualify as an Inspector but didn't want to leave the team to take up any promotion for now, so had mixed feelings about it.

'Right, y'are.'

The road did have a public footpath which led to the edge of the Ryans' land but in order to get to the yard they had to cross a wet field, over a stile and then bear left and over a post and rail timber fence into the Ryans' fields. They walked along the footpath which was a little wet underfoot. It was a coolish winter morning and Taverner reckoned they had about half an hour before the heavens opened, judging from the darkening skies. Wildblood hugged her coat to her and was glad she was wearing sensible boots. She struggled to keep up with her much taller colleague, who strode out ahead.

'Yer know how to spoil a girl,' Wildblood grumbled as she skipped over a puddle. Taverner walked on but not before scrutinising the pathway. It was a pleasant enough walk, and he would have enjoyed it were it not for the task of searching the pathway and undergrowth for anything that may have been discarded by the murderer. When they came to the fence stile

214

which led to a muddy piece of ground leading to the Ryans' field, Anna peered at the puddles and made her excuses.

'I'll stay here and let you do the honours, guv.'

Taverner nodded, deep in thought and climbed over the stile and beyond into the muddy field. Wildblood turned around, drew her scarf around her neck and looked at the fields. On a nice day it would be a picturesque spot, but not today. To make matters worse, the wind bit at her exposed flesh. She waited for what felt like an age. Taverner was about to climb over the fence into the Ryans' field when he suddenly bent down. He fished in his pocket for something and then caught up with Anna, grinning from ear to ear. He was holding an evidence bag with a small item in it.

'Look, a cigarette butt that was left just before the Ryans' field. If it matches the DNA on the false fingernail and we exclude stable staff then we could be in business.'

Wildblood peered at the stub. 'There are faint smears of lippy on it too. Happen you're right and it is a woman!'

They drove back to the station in a much better mood. Taverner gave the bag to Patel who dashed off to Forensics with it. He logged onto his computer and saw that there was an email with attachments from DI Johnson who was heading up the case against Niall Byrne. Gabriel was keen to find out if the police had searched the car for drugs, though he suspected that Jamie Doyle could have thrown them out of the car window or used some excuse to leave the vehicle to deposit the drugs somewhere, before picking them up later. These were typical behaviours of drug dealers. He opened the attachments and read on with interest. What he read shocked him, so much so, he reread the sentence several times. The car had been searched, but there was no evidence of drugs whatsoever, but what was in the car boot amazed him. He stared at the paragraph for some time, just to make sure he had read it correctly. In the boot was a painting of racehorses, wrapped up in a horse rug. He read that when questioned, Byrne had said he was taking the painting to the tip for a relative.

He wandered back into the team office. 'I want details of all art thefts in the area, however obscure.'

Haworth did a double take. 'Art thefts? Won't that have gone to the Art and Antiques Squad? I did a spell in there, as you know. Helped put away that forger, Archie Todd, who fooled all those experts, all from his workshop in his shed.'

'Right, let's get going on those inquiries and get the forensic testing done as soon as possible.' Taverner wanted to stop Haworth going on about his old cases, it was all very fascinating, but they didn't have the time to listen to him today. He motioned his head towards Anna. 'We need to go and have a chat with DI Johnson.'

'OK.' Wildblood had heard of him and knew which department he worked in. 'About a traffic offence?'

The team had all fallen silent as they waited for the answer.

'No, about a painting.'

Chapter 30

Finn felt like his head had been split open, it was fuzzy and sore when he moved, he gingerly opened his eyes and it was completely dark apart from a line of light which edged round a door, the floor was strewn with straw and there was the unmistakable, soothing scent of horses. As his senses recovered, he realised that he was in a stable, his arms were attached to a chain which was linked to the tying up ring in the back wall. His wrists were bound and attached to the chain by a plastic tie wrap which dug into his skin. His arms felt numb from being permanently raised overhead, and it was turning colder by the minute. He peered at the chain that bound him but could hardly see anything. He moved his arms upwards, and he heard the metallic jangle of the chain which thankfully was long enough for him to remain in a sitting position. He managed to stand up, somewhat unsteadily and tried to feel what the tie ring was attached to and how secure it was. Damn. It was set in a brick wall and when he pulled at it, there was absolutely no give. None whatsoever. Christ! And the tie wrap dug into his flesh. It was of a solid plastic construction that would not give way easily.

He tried shouting and screaming and listened intently to the sound of his own voice echoing out into nothingness and then silence. Where the hell was he? He remembered texting Nat back and arranging to meet him and Harriet later at The Stagecoach Hotel. Christ, the painting! This was all about the bloody painting. He'd planned his campaign minutely in order to flush the forgers out, but it hadn't even entered his head that they would strike the evening before he was due to pick up the picture. He had underestimated them and that had been a serious mistake. He had thought the culprit would sideline the painting in a subtle manner, maybe apprehend him as he set off with the art or he expected Gerrard to apologise that they hadn't been able to arrange for an addendum after all, or for him to omit the painting to the website, as a way of hiding its presence. But they had taken more extreme action a day earlier than he thought they would. At least he had asked Harriet to remove the painting from Jeremy's and it was

217

languishing at her parents' house. Her father, being an ex-policeman, had good security and friends to call upon if there were any attempted break ins. He also would ask few questions, Finn knew, as he was aware of their role working undercover for the racing authorities.

He thought about the forgers. He had some idea who they might be. He shuddered when he thought of what the enemy was capable of and what they might do to him to ensure that he didn't ruin their plans. Rage coursed through him. Fuck them! He had to get out. He had no idea where he was or what time it was. He used his mouth to yank back his sleeve to see his wristwatch. Just past three in the morning. His head throbbed, his whole body ached, but sheer rage coursed through his veins. If he could escape, then he could still enact his plan for tomorrow and he would really need to be alert and prepared. He had made the fatal mistake of not taking his enemy as seriously as he should have, and he would not do that again. Huge sums of money were at stake, and this alone was sometimes enough to push desperate people to desperate acts, and he berated himself for not considering this. All he had to do was get out of here and then he would still be able to thwart them.

He began by tugging at the tie ring hard several times, then by lying down and pushing against the wall with his feet, to try and force the ring out of the wall. He continued for the count of 30, then tried manoeuvring his legs round and tugging from a different angle, first one side then another. The chain remained rigid and unmoveable. Christ, how large were those bloody screws? He felt the cold creep into his legs and used his legs to scrape together the straw into one place if the worse happened and he had to stay overnight. He thought back to what he remembered about the weather forecast and tried to forget that they had predicted a cold snap with sub zero temperatures tonight. Well, you're not bloody staying here, he told himself, so get a move on. He listened to the silence around him. The stables were unused as he couldn't hear the sound of horses, but the earthy smell still lingered. The dark was complete and the quiet absolute, apart from the distant rumbling of traffic on a road some distance away and wild animals, like foxes. He heard the swoop of an owl and the rustle of creatures in the undergrowth all around him.

He turned his attention to the chain and the tie ring and began his tugging, varied the angle repeatedly and pulled again. There was still no bloody give. He tried to think about the painting, who could have faked it and swapped it. Prior to talking to Jeremy telling Gerrard he'd changed his mind about exhibiting the painting, he been certain it was him who was behind the forgery. He had the know-how, the position and he knew lots of artists who he employed as art restorers, but now he was not so sure. He had analysed the reaction of Gerrard first hand. The man's reaction was completely normal, there was not so much as a twitch or a frown. In fact, he had seemed genuinely pleased about Jeremy's change of heart. Something didn't ring true, he was either a very good actor or he had no problem with the painting being exhibited, but maybe that was because he had a plan to make sure it never arrived for the exhibition. Who else was involved? Penny Mercer? She was an accomplished artist, he knew, who had undertaken many pet portraits. Maybe she and Freddie were hoping to restore the family fortunes by forgery? There was an explanation that he hardly dared to think about, so he shut it out of his mind for now. He felt a murderous rage at the thought that he'd been played, by Freddie, his mother and the whole bloody lot of them. He wrenched at the tie ring again and began the ritual of shifting from side to side to pull it from a different angle. He felt a draught from the inside wall and knew that this was a stable block with a lower inner wall. If he could just pull the chain from its fittings, he might have a chance of scaling the wall, because the draught suggested that the adjoining stable door might be open. His heart jolted, as hope leapt like a stag.

Finn was exhausted and rested before trying his tugging method all over again. Christ, it was hard work. He felt himself drifting off in the cold and covered himself in straw during the rest periods as he tried to conserve energy and keep himself warm, but it was getting harder and harder to focus. He rested for the count of 40 and made himself pull at the chain with his feet on the wall pushing back. He moved round and tried another angle and pulled with his arm and pushed with his legs for all he was worth. At last, he felt some give and one last pull and he fell to the floor as the chain came out. He ducked and managed to avoid the tie ring recoiling into his face. Euphoria coursed through him. He breathed deeply before staggering to his feet and dragged himself to the stable door. He pushed at the top stable door which was solid. He felt along the door edges where faint light flickered through and wondered how on earth he was going to get out of this. He could try to navigate the wall between the stables but it would have to be mostly by touch and he was worried about falling. He sat down in the straw, which was mercifully clean and tried to think. He felt in his jacket pocket, dragging the chain along with him. They'd taken his phone, of course, but in his other pocket his penknife, the one he always carried for cutting the string on bales, and for cleaning out horses' hooves and the like, was still there. He felt a flush of energy and elation. He studied the edge of the stable door and pushed at it to see where the outline darkened where the bolt was. Maybe, just maybe, he could wedge the edge of the penknife into the door and somehow lever the door open and force the bolt back. It wasn't going to be easy but with renewed enthusiasm, he set about feeling for the edge of the blade of his pen knife, pulled it out and set to work. It was hard with his wrists still bound together and awkward to position his hands but possible. He positioned his feet further apart so that the effort of forcing the penknife didn't cause him to topple over. He identified where the bolt was and tried to manoeuvre it by pushing it with the knife, trying to fix the point to one end of the bolt and force it backwards.

Eventually, he became tired and despondent. It was hopeless and he gave up and felt around the stable, thinking that he might have to scale the wall after all. He was feeling the cold bricks which were covered with rubber at the bottom, when he trod on something, a long wooden pole. He felt for the end of it and almost cheered when he discovered it was a familiar item, a pitchfork. He bent over to pick it up and set to work on the door again, placing the tines in the slight gap of the top door and levered the handle backwards as hard as he could. The length of the fork should amplify the force, he reasoned. He pulled the pitchfork back and door gave just a little and so he redoubled his efforts. Eventually, after several more attempts, he heard something snap, and the top door swung open. He leaned out and released the bolt of the lower door and stepped out. He peered into the dark skies, as he crept around the yard. This stable block didn't appear to be used but he advanced as carefully and quietly as he could, he saw that there was a much larger yard up ahead where several horses were stabled. He saw the cold mist of their breath and listened to the rhythmic chewing as they tackled their hay nets. He had no idea where he was. Was it the Mercer's place? He hadn't actually been there, so he couldn't tell.

First, he needed to get rid of the tie wrap to release his hands. The dawn was breaking and that allowed him to explore his surroundings. In the stable next door, he found an old scythe. He ran his fingers along the mercifully still sharp blade and manoeuvred his wrists so that he could cut the plastic. After careful positioning, so that he didn't cut himself, the tie wrap suddenly snapped open, and he felt utter relief that his hands were now free. He flexed them, buttoned up his jacket, shook his legs to get rid of the stiffness and slipped out onto the pathway that led to a large farmhouse.

Finn crept as noiselessly as he could down the path, his eyes trained on the farmhouse for any sign of life, there was only a large outside light. He managed to run for cover behind the conifers that lined the driveway. He continued and came to a narrow road. He tried to acclimatise himself, but he didn't recognise where he was at all. There were a few houses around, all in darkness. He glanced at his watch, it was nearly 4.30 am and the world would shortly be waking up. He tramped along the road, unsure where on earth he was going, but determined to continue with his plan. He needed to get to his flat first. He decided he would flag down a car if one ever appeared. As he strode on for several minutes, he heard the distant rumble of a car as it approached, and the headlights appeared. It was now or never. Finn moved towards the centre of the road with his hands raised, as he heard the screech of brakes.

Chapter 31

Harriet felt restless and had struggled to sleep as she knew that things were coming to a head. She felt wired and had decided to get up early and go for a jog. The morning was chilly and the skies grey and forbidding as she ran. Her route around the town was quiet and the streets empty. The movement soothed her, as she thought about the case. There was something nagging away at her consciousness that was important, but she couldn't quite work out what it was. She thought about Niall Byrne and everything that had happened to the passengers in the car he was driving on the night he was arrested for drink driving. One was dead, another seriously injured and of the other two, Jamie had left Walton, closely followed by Lottie. Surely, that wasn't a coincidence? Then she thought about the Red Navajo painting. She'd been astonished when the Maclaren painting was judged to be a fake. Yet she trusted her uncle implicitly, so what on earth had happened? She sifted through the facts carefully to the backdrop of her feet thundering upon the pavements and the sound of her beating heart. She had believed Maclaren's version of events, so that meant that the painting must have been substituted whilst at Jeremy's. Who could and would have done such a thing?

Then it came to her, the facts seemed to settle finally in her brain in a way that made sense at last. She remembered what Topper McGrew had said about his painting which he believed to be by Gideon Moss. His children had been shooting Nerf guns, the foam pellets coated in blue paint, when one accidentally stuck to the painting. He'd later noticed this and removed the blue paint from the frame and left a lighter smudge and then when he looked again another day, it had miraculously vanished. It was around the time that he had employed a new cleaner. Suddenly she knew! Cleaners could come and go into properties unseen, their overalls and cleaning carts rendering them almost invisible. Supposing he had used Penny Mercer's cleaners? A plausible explanation now seemed obvious. They would have noticed the Moss painting, Penny had then painted a substitute and the cleaner, maybe even Penny herself, had swapped the original for the forgery! Was Freddie involved too? She thought he must be, in fact he could have swapped the painting at Jeremy's. Excited, she tried to ring Finn when she got in but there was no reply, so she left a message. It was only past 7 am, so he might be in the shower or riding, she reasoned. She just hoped he would reply soon, because she was bursting to tell him her theory. The more she thought about it, the more she was convinced she was right.

The young man, Jack, had stared at Finn suspiciously. He probably did look awful with an injury to his temple, with straw and dirt on his clothing. Then Finn noticed some riding boots in the backseat and Jack squinted at him as if trying to place where he knew him from.

'Hey, you're not Finn McCarthy are you?'

Finn grinned. 'Yep, listen I was mugged, and I really need to get back to my place in York. If you could take me, I'd be eternally grateful.'

Jack agreed readily enough. Thank the Lord, thought Finn, many drivers would have taken one look at him and continued on their way, and he couldn't blame them. Jack drove carefully, giving him sidelong glances every so often. His eyes took in his appearance and the bruising and abrasions on his wrists but said very little.

'I remember watching you ride as a kid.' Finn nodded thinking that the lad was probably just old enough to have seen him in his heyday. 'So, what happened? You really ought to go to the police, you know.'

Finn nodded. 'I know. I just need to pick up something from home and then I will. Thanks so much for picking me up. It was just a random attack. Anyway, where are you off to so early?'

Jack yawned and grinned. 'Oh, I stayed over at my girlfriend's and couldn't sleep. I work at Broadhursts, do you know them?'

Finn did. It was a small racing yard just outside York, so hopefully the lad could drop him off without too much trouble. 'Yes, is your guvnor Stuart Broadhurst, with the good chaser, Something Borrowed?' Despite feeling like crap, Finn found that he still wanted to talk about horses. He found it reassuring and calming.

Jack grinned. 'Yes, I look after him actually. He's the only good horse we have though, the others are donkeys. I've only been there a few months.' He glanced shyly at Finn. 'I know you're a jockey coach, so do you mind me asking, how do you get to be a conditional?'

Finn went on to explain the process. He really didn't mind, it was the least he could do and it took his mind off his aching limbs and the pain in his head. He explained that he would need to be apprenticed to a trainer, where he was likely to get rides and had a weight allowance on a sliding scale until he had 75 winners, which he had to achieve by the time he was 26.

'Thinking of it, are you?'

Jack shrugged. 'The place I'm at is too small, but I can move, I suppose. I'm only 17, I've just passed me driving test, so I'm gonna see if I can get a job in Walton.'

Finn nodded, deciding that he liked Jack Briggs. He drove with precision and had an air of confidence about him. He wondered if he rode with the same care.

'Good idea. I can recommend Jeremy Trentham, Seamus Ryan and Vince Hunt as trainers. If you can get yourself into a larger yard and can ride, then you've a good chance to make a conditional.' He ran his eyes over Jack. 'You'll be the right size for National Hunt, I daresay. Can you ride?'

Jack grinned. 'I rode as a kid, did pony club then my parents got divorced and the horse and trailer had to go. So, it all stopped, but I was on the teams, so yeah, I can.'

The dawn was breaking, and it became distinctly lighter and noisier as they approached York. Finn was feeling calmer and immensely relieved. The surroundings became much more familiar as they arrived on the outskirts of York. Jack pulled into the car park near Finn's flat. Finn held out his hand and Jack shook it enthusiastically. He decided the lad needed more than just his thanks.

'Listen, I'm really grateful for the lift.' Fair's fair, he thought. One good turn deserves another. 'If it will help, give me your number and I'll see if there are any vacancies for stable staff in Walton. And if you want, I'll put you through your paces and help with your riding.' Finn felt about for his phone before realising that they had taken it. 'Never mind, I'll call into Broadhursts in a week or so.'

Jack grinned. 'You'd do that for me?'

'Of course.'

Jack nodded. 'Well, I hope the cops catch the buggers that mugged you. See you then.' He gave Finn a cheery wave.

Finn smiled. He hoped they did too, with a little bit of help from him.

Back home, Finn cleaned himself up, bathed his injuries and tried to rest a little. It was hard even though he was incredibly tired, but his brain was buzzing. He found his spare phone and tried to rest as it charged. He knew that he was coming to the end game, he had a good idea who his enemies were, and he had to think like they did. He ran through his plan in his head several times over, took a painkiller, drank some coffee and ate a bacon sandwich. Then he fished out his spare set of car keys, scooped up his phone, a torch, wrapped up three of his own paintings in blankets, dug out his trusty penknife, some rope, and set off to Trentham's. He was sorely tempted to contact Harriet and Nat but decided that this time he had to go it alone. Nat had been shot in a former case and Harriet had suffered too, so it was down to him. He knew that the forgers would expect him to be tied up for the rest of the day and when they discovered that he had gone, they would try to intercept him moving the painting this afternoon, except of course it had already been moved by Harriet.

He arrived at Jeremy's at about mid morning.

'Christ, what happened to you?' asked Jeremy, frowning when he noticed the blooming bruise to the left hand side of Finn's head and taking in his pinched look and the marks to his wrists.

'Oh, just had a bit of a run in with someone, that's all,' he replied non-commitally. 'Is the trailer around the back?'

Jeremy bit his lip. 'Yes. Listen, whatever you have planned, do you want me to come along?'

'No, it's all in hand,' Finn reassured him.

Jeremy frowned. 'Well, just don't wreck the trailer. My daughter still needs it to take her eventer around. He's a spooky traveller so we had the central partition taken out and bought a single bar for the front, is that OK?'

'Of course.' It was absolutely fine for his purposes. Finn wasn't going to use it for horse transport anyway, but he wasn't going to tell Jeremy that.

Madeleine, Jeremy's teenaged daughter from his first marriage, was now an accomplished eventer who split her time between her parents but kept her horse at her father's, though it was Laura who usually took her to events. Finn hitched up his Audi to the smart Ifor Williams 505 trailer in maroon and silver. He had used several Ifor Wiliams trailers and knew them to be well designed and perfect for what was intended. He gathered the paintings he'd put in his boot, covered them in rugs and positioned them in rear of the horse trailer towards the back. He closed the back upper doors, secured all the clips on the jockey door and the ramps and then he was ready.

It was a clear winter's day and as he drove out on the road towards Walton, the sun was threatening to venture from behind a cloud. The Trenthams lived a couple of miles outside of Walton and there was only one road that led to the town, a narrow one, little more than a track. It was isolated with fields and trees on both sides. He found a spot opposite a large oak tree to the left, which was flanked by a five foot fence, pulled into a passing place and then set about stage two of his plan. He found a match in his pocket and leant down by the off side rear tyre of his Audi, unscrewed the valve cap and pressed the match into the valve. The air hissed as the tyre flattened. It was not important, he had a pump in his boot which he could use to inflate it if needs be, but for now he needed there to be a legitimate reason for leaving his car and the trailer unattended. He checked that the paintings were where they should be, locked his car and scrambled over the fence near the oak and waited.

He grew colder as the afternoon drew on and there was still no sign of the forgers. There were a few cars passing but when he looked, some slowed down to inspect his car and the trailer, presumably horsey folks just wondering if a horse was inside and whether or not he needed assistance. On seeing that both were empty, they drove on, presumably less concerned. Finn mentally rehearsed his plan, walked up and down behind the large oak to keep warm and wondered if he would have to think again. Maybe they weren't coming and had not yet discovered that he had escaped from the stable, yet he was sure they would check, if only to make sure that he hadn't died from a head injury. He forced himself to be patient and went through all the clues as to the forger's identity. Gerrard was a possibility, or Freddie and Penny working together with Henry Teasdale to restore the family fortunes by criminal enterprises. His mind flitted to others but moved away just as quickly. He glanced at his watch as the light started to fade, and the

226

temperature dropped. The hours passed by as he sat alone with his thoughts. He was due to meet Harriet and Nat later and really needed to get home. Just as he was thinking about calling the whole thing off, he heard the distant rumble of a vehicle as it slowed and parked up. He manoeuvred himself into position and silently climbed the fence, still under the cover of the oak tree as he watched the proceedings in the dim light.

There were two of them, dressed in dark clothes wearing hoodies with the hoods pulled up. He saw the taller of the two dip down to investigate his flat tyre and then try the car door. They communicated with nods of the head and the shorter man scanned the area looking to see if anyone was waiting for them. Then they came to the trailer and the taller figure opened the jockey door and turned on the torch from his phone and scanned the inside of the trailer. He obviously spotted the paintings carefully wrapped in blankets and muttered to the other man. They made a decision, and both climbed into the trailer via the jockey door to investigate further. Finn knew then that he had only seconds to act.

His sinews tensed, as he ran down from his hiding place to the trailer. His footsteps must have alerted the men and one of them came to the jockey door and landed a punch at Finn's head, shouting abuse as he did so. Finn punched him back and then barged the jockey door shut with his shoulder and bolted the door with the clips. There was no way out for them. He spotted a phone glinting on the road and picked it up. It was a basic phone, presumably one that they used to keep in touch with their big boss. What did they call them on the crime programmes? Burner phones, that was it. He pocketed it, drowning out the howls of surprise and expletives that came from the rocking trailer, happy in the knowledge that they would not be able to break free from their sturdy prison. He picked up his spare phone and began to dial as he started to feel dizzy and horribly sick from the punch to his head. Damn, there was no signal. He waved the phone about, tried to text a message before the phone slipped from his grasp, as his head throbbed. He felt himself falling as he blacked out and collapsed besides the trailer.

Harriet was looking forward to the evening with Finn and Nat. She knew that things were coming to a head with the case, and it would be great to be in the company of those she could trust. She had completed her task, which was to pick up the Maclaren painting from Jeremy's and take it to her home where her father had already been briefed as to the concerns and hadn't asked for further details. He'd vowed to guard the painting with his life. A table was booked for 7pm at The Stagecoach Hotel, so she would hope to be there by half six at least. It was no surprise that Christian Gerrard had offered to put Nat up. He was an 'A' lister in the horse world and his presence would really help promote the hotel and exhibition and give the place much needed publicity and column inches, more especially if Gerrard could persuade the couple to get married in his wedding barn. She'd had a busy week, her head hurt from the inquiries she was making with Finn, and she would welcome the chance to discuss things with them both. She'd left Finn several messages, but he hadn't yet responded. Her enthusiasm about her theory had dimmed as anxiety gnawed away at her about Finn's radio silence. What the hell was going on?

When she arrived, she found Nat sipping water and poring over the menu, but no Finn. Nat kissed her and smiled brightly. He was wearing a well cut suit and smelled of expensive cologne. Harriet who had come straight from work and was wearing a green jump suit and warm coat, wished she'd taken more care with her appearance.

'Where's Finn?' Nat asked. 'I thought he'd be here by now.'

Harriet shrugged. 'I thought he was coming with you. Have you heard from him?'

'Not since yesterday. How about you?'

'The same.' Harriet frowned and tried to calm her nerves. She had expected Finn to call her back, he was usually good at that sort of thing and checked his phone regularly. Still, he was always busy and maybe something had happened, some emergency or other. No doubt, he'd walk through the doors any time now and tell them all about it.

Nat smiled. 'I didn't expect to come back either, but I had a fall yesterday and the doc signed me off because of this.' He turned his head where he had the beginnings of a substantial bruise around his right cheekbone and into his hairline. 'Bloody fall busted my helmet. There's no real damage, but as a precaution I can't ride for a day or two as I might have concussion.' He shrugged. 'It's an occupational hazard, as you know.'

They ordered drinks and starters and chatted about inconsequential things until the topics dried up.

'I've just got a bad feeling,' added Harriet. She felt the need to confide in someone. 'You see Finn was going to try and flush out the forgers, and now he's not here, I don't know what to think.'

Nat frowned. 'Forgers? You mean the forgers of the Red Navajo painting?'

Harriet went on to explain about Sebastian's pronouncement and how she believed the Maclaren painting had been substituted with the fake whilst it was at the Trenthams.

'Finn thought if Jeremy asked for the painting to be exhibited and gave details of when he was going to transport it to here, then the forgers would try and stop him getting there with the painting. He figured that they wouldn't want it to be reported in the press what with the auction of the New York painting coming up next week.'

Nat raised an eyebrow. 'I suppose it makes sense. So, who's in the frame?' He grinned at his own joke. 'I mean who are the suspects?'

Harriet explained. 'Supposing the gang use cleaners to identify valuable paintings, complete the fakes and then swap them? Penny Mercer runs a cleaning company and is an accomplished painter, so it's possible Penny and Freddie are in it together.' She went on to explain about Topper McGrew's painting and the mystery of the damage to the frame that had simply vanished. 'But supposing that was because the painting was substituted. His is a Gideon Moss too.'

Nat's eyes widened. 'Christ, you could be right!'

Just then Harriet's phone beeped as a message came through. It was from an unknown number. The message didn't make any sense.

Meet me

She showed Nat her phone. 'What the hell is going on? Is this from Finn? Why isn't he using his usual phone?'

Nat's eyes narrowed. 'Christ Harriet, he must be in trouble. What was he planning to do?'

Harriet explained what Finn had told her.

'Hmm. We might need to tread carefully as it may be a trap. Come on, we need to find him.' He pursed his lips. 'Hey, Harriet, are you still going out with the detective? Because if you are, now it would be a good time to ring him. If Finn has rounded up the criminals, or we're being led into a trap, then we're going to need reinforcements.'

Chapter 32

Nat had opted to drive them in his brand new Mercedes, which Harriet was pleased about as she had not yet replaced her beaten up Polo. She remembered that he was possibly suffering from concussion, but decided that this couldn't be the case, not judging by his driving. Nat seemed his usual self, as he zoomed off into the night at breakneck speed.

'So, if I drive as if I'm going to Trenthams, we're likely to find him on the way if he has been intercepted by the forgers?'

'Yes, and hopefully the police will be there as well.' She had explained the situation in a garbled call to Taverner and he was on his way. He'd asked for the phone number the call had come from so it could be tracked. Harriet bit her lip. 'Why did Finn plan all this on his own and not involve me?' It was a question that had bugged her ever since she received his message.

Nat turned to her. 'Or me for that matter. I think we both know why. Finn doesn't want you putting yourself at risk and after what happened to me after being shot in the other case, I suppose he thinks he can shoulder the risks himself.'

Harriet shook her head. 'But supposing something happens to him, I'd never forgive myself. I hope he's alright!'

Nat smiled. 'Listen, he's as tough as old boots and not a man to rush into things.' He turned and winked at her. 'He'll be fine, I'm sure of it.'

Harriet couldn't help but think that he was just saying this for her benefit, as she noticed the tension in Nat's jaw and the speed he drove at. She clutched the seat as they rounded a bend.

They made their way out of Walton and on to the narrow road that led to Jeremy's yard. It was early evening, and the skies were clear as the stars illuminated their way. They drove on, Harriet going through all sorts of scenarios. She knew that Finn intended to drive to Jeremy's and pretend to pick up the painting then she was to meet him at The Stagecoach Hotel where she thought they would see what the lie of the land was, look around the place and make contact with Gerrard. Clearly things had taken a different turn and she couldn't help but feel a little bit hurt that Finn had decided to go it alone.

'You OK?' asked Nat.

Harriet realised that her body was rigid with tension. 'Okish or I will be when we find out what is going on and if he's alright.' Another thought came to her, Finn was clearly interrupted in sending the message which led her mind to all sorts of horrible possibilities.

They rounded the corner of the single track road. The moon was a brilliant orb in the sky illuminating the patchwork of hedgerows and trees that lined the route. Nat braked sharply as an animal darted over the road, a grey dog sized creature, possibly a badger. She shivered, her eyes straining to see what was ahead. Suddenly she saw something.

'Look, there. Isn't that Finn's car and a trailer?'

Nat pulled over in front of the car, the headlights showing Finn slumped on the floor. He opened his eyes as they approached. His face was bloodied and he looked like he'd taken a real beating.

'What the hell is going on?' asked Harriet as she rushed to meet him.

Finn gave them both a wry grin. 'I'll explain later. They are in there.' He pointed at the silver trailer.

Harriet was about to ask more when just then the whole lane was flooded with light as police cars arrived at the scene, sirens blaring and car doors crashing as officers swarmed into place.

Taverner walked towards them. 'Is everyone OK?' He scanned the group, taking in the bruising to Finn's temple and head which was blooming nicely. His eyes rested on Harriet. 'Are you alright?'

Harriet nodded.

'So, where are these criminals then?'

Finn staggered to his feet and walked round to the trailer. 'In there.'

Taverner was appraised of the situation and gesticulated to the officers to move everyone away from the jockey door, except for uniformed police who were ready and waiting with handcuffs to arrest the pair. Harriet waited with trepidation for Taverner to open the jockey door and for the criminals to be revealed. She glanced at Finn who looked ashen and preoccupied too.

'Police, you are surrounded. Come out with your hands up and leave any weapons on the floor. I repeat. You are surrounded,' Taverner shouted.

He prised open the clips to the jockey door and two figures emerged, blinking at the light from the vehicles. The first figure was small and Taverner pulled back the dark hood to reveal a snarling woman. Pandora Gerrard. She muttered expletives as she was handcuffed. The other figure was taller and leaner, and the person's face was obscured by a hood too. The figure leapt out, and made a run for it, dodging past the waiting officers and past Nat who swore and gave chase across the fields. Nat gained on the figure and rugby tackled him to the ground whilst officers followed. Eventually, the man was dragged to the waiting cars. Nat pulled down the hood to reveal a slim, darked haired young man. Niall Byrne.

Harriet gasped. 'Bloody hell, you two! Is there not a Mr Big in the operation?'

'We'll find out, shall we?' Finn pulled out the burner phone which one of them had dropped when they searched the trailer. He pressed the keys of the last number dialled and pressed speaker phone. The call was answered quickly.

'Oh, Niall. Thank God. What's going on? I've been trying to ring yer.'

Theresa. Taverner took the phone and muttered to a couple of uniformed officers who sped off to arrest her. Harriet took in Finn's shuttered, tortured expression and touched his arm.

Nat dusted down his beautifully cut suit and grinned. 'It's Armani, you know, but it'll be fine.' He clapped his hands together. 'Well, all's well that ends well. I don't know about anyone else, but I could do with a stiff drink.'

Epilogue

Jeremy Trentham threw a party on New Year's Eve, to celebrate Admiral Jervis's return to his yard. Ross was in attendance and was celebrating his finished book which had been published to great acclaim. His publishers were thrilled at his latest offering and were predicting even greater sales than any of his previous books, and there were already rumours about TV companies sniffing around.

Finn, Harriet and Gabriel were amongst the guests and also included Rosie and Seamus Ryan, Tom Kennedy, who was still in recovery but making excellent progress, as well as Nat Wilson, Livvy Jordan, several conditionals, including Freddie Mercer and Lottie Henderson, who had been persuaded to return to the Ryans, Penny Mercer, Tony Murphy, Tom Kennedy and Topper McGrew. Harriet's uncle, Sebastian, had also joined them and was enjoying his role as an advisor to the police about other art frauds which had been committed by the forgers. The Ryans were also accompanied by their newest conditional, Jack Briggs. Finn had been as good as his word and had seen the lad ride and recommended him to the Ryans. They had a vacancy with Niall Byrne languishing in prison. Finn felt that Jack had great potential when he had seen him ride and was quick to point this out to the Ryans.

Laura, Jeremy's wife, had provided a splendid buffet and was filling and refilling people's glasses. Jeremy beamed.

'I'm so delighted to welcome you all here, we have plenty of reasons to celebrate; not only have I got the best prospect in my yard for next season, Admiral back, but I've also repaired my relationship with Ross and his family. The real Red Navajo painting has been returned and the criminals rounded up. And I couldn't have done it without Finn and Hattie. Let's raise a glass to them both for their crime fighting!' There were enthusiastic cheers. 'And let's not forget our brilliant local police, headed up by DCI Gabriel Taverner!'

There were several more cheers. Taverner looked pleased to be included in the plaudits.

Jeremy beamed at the assembled group. 'Now. Do please tuck into the food and mingle. We are going to have a fabulous season with Admiral, I can feel it in my bones!'

Nat had already ridden him in various races, he had won handsomely in each and the plan was to step up the class, aiming ultimately for the Cheltenham Gold Cup. Nat's season was going from strength to strength, and he was already many winners ahead of his nearest rivals and likely to be champion jockey again this year.

Harriet saw Topper McGrew, ever the opportunist, talking to Ross Maclaren and asking if he could send him his own manuscript for an appraisal. She hid a smile. That was Topper all over. He had also expressed an interest in featuring Ross and Red Navajo's history in one of his articles. Freddie and Penny were talking to Lottie Henderson and the Ryans were chatting to Tony Murphy about Niall and Clare.

'We were just taken in by the lad, I suppose. And to think of what happened to Clare,' explained Rosie. 'Mary, mother of God, I can't believe they'd be capable of doing such a thing.'

Tony was listening patiently. 'I know, it must be so hard to accept, but on the bright side Lottie has come back and I understand you'll be using Tom once he's fully recovered and, of course, you have a new conditional now.'

Tom smiled. He was still using a walking stick, but the physio was going very well, he'd had some dietary advice from Harriet which would enable him to rebuild his muscle and he hoped to return to racing in a month or so.

Seamus beamed at the young man. 'We certainly will, it's what Clare would have wanted.'

The Stagecoach Hotel and Spa was up for sale. Christian Gerrard and his wife were apparently too humiliated by Pandora's actions to face anyone. Of course, the art exhibition had been cancelled and the original Moss painting returned to Jeremy from New York after some negotiations with the FBI. All the other paintings were in the process of being recovered including Topper McGrew's. Christian was reported to be considering investing abroad and was in the process of selling his horses including Kinder

Scout, to Ross Maclaren who had already been given a huge advance for his next five books and had decided to expand his string of horses. Things were looking up.

'So, how did you know the Moss painting had been stolen?' asked Ross. Harriet explained about Nat seeing an identical painting in the catalogue of a New York gallery. 'We took the liberty of taking the painting to my uncle who advised us it was a fake, a good one but a fake, nonetheless. We didn't tell you as we wanted to find out who the forgers were and get your original painting back.'

Livvy explained about her role. 'I was doing a photoshoot in New York and Nat asked me to pretend to be interested in the painting and I took a friend along, Will Molyneux, who verified the painting as being original.'

It was a lot for Ross to take in. 'So how did you know it had been swapped at Jeremy's? I mean, I could have had a fake made, for all you knew.'

Jeremy harrumphed. 'Oh, we knew you'd never do that!' Harriet raised her eyebrows at this, and Jeremy looked a little shamefaced because, of course, that was exactly what they had thought.

'I found out that Niall had a stolen painting in the boot of his car when he was stopped for drink driving, that's why he drove away,' added Gabriel. 'And when Topper McGrew told Harriet about the Moss painting of his which had damage to the frame that had mysteriously disappeared a few days later, it all made sense. You see, Topper's original painting had been replaced too. Pandora, who was working for Penny's cleaning company, had seen the painting, realised it was a Moss, studied it, reproduced a good fake and swapped them.'

Topper smiled. 'Thankfully, I have my original painting back now. The one common denominator between Jeremy and me, was the fact that we used the same cleaners supplied by Spick and Span. That was how they did it. Of course, suspicion fell on Penny and Freddie, but they were entirely innocent.'

Penny looked downhearted. 'Pandora Gerrard had filled in for some shifts. Her father thought she was rather spoilt and made her do some down to earth work. He thought it would help her but instead she saw an opportunity, she was so desperate to get away from her father and make it on her own. She never forgave him for divorcing her mother and she blamed him for her mother's subsequent breakdown, you see.'

'So how did Niall and Pandora meet?' asked Tony Murphy.

'Pandora was taught by Theresa Byrne and became friendly with Theresa and then met Niall. The threesome cooked up the plan between them,' added Finn. He remembered stumbling into Theresa's studio and finding the paintings and collections of old frames, they had used, all passed off as students' work. Finn had gone to the school and found she no longer worked there. He felt he'd let everyone down because it was obvious then that she had been lying. He had failed to confront the facts because of his relationship with Theresa and he felt angry with himself for being taken in by her.

'So, Pandora spotted the paintings, did the fakes, swapped them whilst cleaning and Niall moved the paintings and arranged their sale all masterminded by Theresa, Niall's sister?' asked Penny.

'Yes, that seems to be how it worked,' replied Gabriel.' I was suspicious when I found out that Niall's drink driving case had not yet gone to court. The police were struggling to get witness statements from the people in the vehicle Niall was driving because Niall was intimidating them to prevent them disclosing the real reason why he drove off from the police in the drink driving incident.'

Finn took this in. He had always thought that Niall's actions were extreme but again he'd allowed himself to be persuaded that it was nothing more than youthful high jinks. He made a mental note to not ignore his gut instincts in future.

Topper cleared his throat. 'So, what about the photos I sent Harriet which showed a young horseman and woman visiting someone at Lindholme prison?' He looked at Penny and Freddie somewhat apologetically. 'I had thought that you were visiting your father in prison, but I can see now I was mistaken.' Freddie bowed his head as if to accept his apology.

Gabriel nodded. 'Ah, yes. Harriet passed the photos on to me and I can confirm that they were pictures of Niall Byrne and Pandora Gerrard. They were visiting Archie Todd, an infamous forger currently languishing in HMP Lindholme. He had committed some daring forgeries and even now there are disputes about a Michelangelo painting that is currently in pride of place in an art gallery in Rome, which he claims to have painted from his workshop in the North. It seems they were seeking advice from him about future fakes, and he was to have a cut of their profits.'

Sebastian nodded. 'Archie Todd is well known in artists' circles. Completely self taught, he is an amazing talent. He could have been a highly successful artist in his own right, but sadly followed a different path. The painting you referred to was authenticated by art experts all over the world, so they do not want to lose face. The lure of easy money was Archie's downfall, and it seems Theresa's too. The painting of Red Navajo is estimated to be worth upwards of five million, it was the skill of the painting and the subject, a rare painting of one of the most prolific and successful thoroughbred sires in the early twentieth century, or so I'm told, which makes it so valuable.'

Ross looked rather shell shocked by the valuation. The world of art forgery was indeed a lot more complex and lucrative than any of them could ever have imagined.

'I don't understand why Niall told people about the painting in the first place,' commented Topper. 'I mean it was foolish to say the least.'

Tom came in here. 'I was a bit drunk on the evening and so was everyone. Niall had been boasting about the fact he was going to come into some money and Clare and Lottie saw the painting and were suspicious. I think he was drunk and naive and trying to impress us all. Then when he sobered up, he was intent on silencing us. They murdered Clare, made threats to Lottie and Jamie, and then Niall tried to wipe me out in that race because he assumed Clare had told me everything. He couldn't risk the real reason for the car chase coming out, I suppose.'

There was a silence as everyone took in the havoc that three greedy and wicked people had wrecked on the community, killing a stable lass, almost paralysing Tom and terrifying Lottie and Jamie to prevent them speaking to the police.

Finn was quiet but looked thoughtful. He had been like that a lot lately.

'So, who followed Clare and shut the stable door?' asked Seamus. 'Who actually did the deed and as good as murdered Clare?'

'It was Pandora Gerrard. We have DNA matches to a false fingernail and a cigarette butt found at the scene,' added Taverner. He studied Finn.

238

'We also found a closer DNA match between Theresa and Niall Byrne, they are actually mother and son, not sister and brother.'

Finn nodded. He had already received a letter from Theresa from prison apologising for involving him in their scam and promising that the feelings she had for him were genuine. She has explained that her motives for her crimes were driven by a need to protect Niall, her son. He had thrown it into the bin. Not that it made him feel any better, it still hurt like hell some months on. He had been taken for a fool by them both and he would never forgive them for that. Harriet had been trying to jolly Finn out of his morose mood since he had found out about Theresa's involvement, without much success.

Harriet tried again. 'Look, you weren't to know. You're not to blame for anything that happened, you're really not.'

It was a well-worn topic between the pair of them. With Gabriel and Harriet's relationship progressing well, she worried about her old friend, especially now she was seeing less of him. Finn still blamed himself and was haunted by Theresa's beauty and the promise of a relationship which was completely based on lies. He also realised that if he had quizzed Theresa more about the school she was supposed to work at, then the crime would have been solved much more quickly. Sadly, he couldn't have prevented Clare from being murdered though, a fact Harriet liked to remind him of on bad days.

'I just feel like I've been taken for a ride, not only by Niall, who I always supported, but also Theresa. I'm afraid, I can't forgive them.'

Nat patted his arm. 'But you can forgive yourself for being taken in by them. We've all been wrong about people, all of us. You shouldn't be so hard on yourself.'

Finn laughed. 'Maybe. I supported Niall because he was a bit of a hot head and an underdog and reminded me a bit of you and me in the old days. Where would either of us be if people hadn't given us a chance back then?'

Nat laughed. 'Nowhere, I agree. But you win some, you lose some, that's my philosophy. Listen, you've been taken for a ride but that does not mean that in time, you shouldn't get back on the horse again, does it?' He clapped Finn on the back. 'Onwards and upwards!'

Finn nodded. He was stretching the racing analogy somewhat, but Nat was right, of course, he was. It would just take a bit of time, that was all.

Livvy hugged Finn. 'Any woman would be lucky to have you.' She took in Finn's expression. 'I know, I know, I went off with Nat, so I should probably shut up, but you mustn't sell yourself short.'

Topper pulled out his phone. 'I know what I wanted to tell you, I did some research for my column and to cut a long story short, it was about thoroughbred DNA. Did you know that some researchers believe that a horse's colour and pigmentation in terms of markings is strongly linked to their speed? In other words, horses who resemble their sire, grandsires and great grandsires in appearance, colour and markings, are much more likely to inherit their speed gene. So, with that in mind, I came across a yearling colt that looks rather like Red Navajo. He's up for sale at Doncaster shortly and guess what, he does have Red Navajo in his genetic background, going way back.'

He showed them a photo of a chestnut horse with almost identical markings to Red Navajo which they passed around. He even had the same almost entirely white foreleg. Ross beamed.

'Wow. When is the sale?'

There were no prizes for guessing what some of Ross's literary earnings were going to be spent on. The lure of owning a Red Navajo lookalike who would hopefully inherit his speed, was very tempting.

Tony Murphy stepped up and raised his glass. 'And just to let you know, Finn is going to be promoted, so here's to Finn.'

Everyone raised their glasses. Finn would be given additional responsibilities, but much of these would involve working more for the BHA Integrity Services. His role and Harriet's within the BHA remained secret, with good reason, which is why Tony hadn't been specific about the details of his new job.

Jeremy cleared his throat. 'We all have much to look forward to, let's drink to next year and future successes!'

They all raised their glasses as the champagne flowed. Finn was pleased to be promoted too. The role also included greater undercover work for the racing authorities, of course. Where there was money, there would also be dishonest people, trying to bend and break the rules to their advantage. He was assured that he could still call upon Harriet, whose role as a dietician was paid for partly by the BHA, as the pair had proved more than a match for criminals. Of course, their work for Jeremy did not involve the BHA, but their success had certainly prompted the authority to promote him. Onwards and upwards as Nat had said. He sighed. He had much to be grateful for, he was surrounded by friends, immersed in a job he loved that involved protecting the sport he lived for. And of course, he'd be working with Harriet again. He caught her eye and smiled. So, one way or another he was suddenly going to be a lot busier, which was just the way he liked it.

Author's note

The horse Red Navajo, is based on a much more modern, similarly marked thoroughbred, Top Notch Tonto. The gelding had a successful flat career. He was trained by Brian Ellison, and won six races in total, including a listed race at York in 2015. He garnered a great following, not just for his unusual looks but also for his sweet temperament.

The information about art fraud and techniques to combat them, is based on my research and any mistakes are my own.

Thanks to the many people who helped this book come to fruition, not least my friends and family who have always supported me.

About Charlie De Luca

Charlie De Luca was brought up on a stud farm, where his father held a permit to train National Hunt horses, hence his lifelong passion for racing was borne. He reckons he visited most of the racecourses in England by the time he was ten. He has always loved horses but grew too tall to be a jockey. Charlie lives in rural Lincolnshire with his family and a variety of animals, including some ex-racehorses.

Charlie has written several racing thrillers which include: **Rank Outsiders, The Gift Horse, Twelve in the Sixth, Making Allowances, Hoodwinked and Fall From Grace.** He has also written a detective novel**, Dark Minster,** set in the city of York and featuring DI Gabriel Taverner and DS Anna Wildblood. A new detective novel is due out in early 2023.

You can connect with Charlie via twitter; @charliedeluca8

Email: charliedelucaauthor@outlook.com

Charlie is more than happy to connect with readers, so please feel free to contact him directly using the button on the website.

www.charliedeluca.co.uk

If you enjoyed this book, then please leave a review. It only needs to be a line or two, but it makes such a difference to authors.

Printed in Great Britain
by Amazon